LINDSAY McKENNA

is proud to have served her country in the U.S. Navy as an aerographer's mate third class—also known as a weather forecaster. She was a pioneer in the military romance sub-genre and loves to combine heart-pounding action with soulful and poignant romance. True to her military roots, she is the originator of the long-running and reader-favorite Morgan's Mercenaries series. She does extensive hands-on research, including flying in aircraft such as a P3-B Orion sub-hunter and a B-52 bomber. She was the first romance writer to sign her books in the Pentagon bookstore. Today, she has created a new military romantic suspense series, Shadow Warriors, which features romantic and action-packed tales about U.S. Navy SEALs. Visit her online at: www.lindsaymckenna.com
https://twitter.com/lindsaymckenna

MERLINE LOVELACE

A career air force officer, Merline Lovelace served at bases all over the world, including tours in Taiwan, Vietnam and at the Pentagon. When she hung up her uniform for the last time, she decided to combine her love of adventure with a flair for storytelling, basing many of her tales on her experiences in the service.

Since then, she's produced more than eighty action-packed novels, many of which have made *USA TODAY* and Waldenbooks bestseller lists. Over eleven million copies of her works are in print in thirty countries. Be sure to check her website at www.merlinelovelace.com for contests, news and information on future releases.

COURSE
OF ACTION

Lindsay McKenna
and
Merline Lovelace

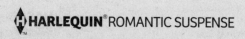
HARLEQUIN®ROMANTIC SUSPENSE

ISBN-13: 978-0-373-27845-9

COURSE OF ACTION

Copyright © 2013 by Harlequin Books S.A.

The publisher acknowledges the copyright holders of the individual works as follows:

OUT OF HARM'S WAY
Copyright © 2013 by Lindsay McKenna

ANY TIME, ANY PLACE
Copyright © 2013 by Merline Lovelace

Recycling programs for this product may not exist in your area.

Printed in U.S.A.

www.Harlequin.com

Contents

Dear Reader,

I hope you're all having a marvelous start to the holiday season! This month, you'll want to get that pulse racing with these four unforgettable romances from Harlequin Romantic Suspense.

We are thrilled to have these two military-themed gems from bestselling authors Lindsay McKenna and Merline Lovelace, entitled *Course of Action* (#1775). A Navy SEAL rescues a damsel, who turns out to be his dream come true, while another couple, masquerading as husband and wife on a dangerous mission, find their own happily ever after. Colleen Thompson contributes a fabulous story, *The Colton Heir* (#1776), to our popular miniseries The Coltons of Wyoming with a harrowing tale of unveiled secrets and the past posing a perilous threat. Plus, a long-lost Colton finally makes his appearance.

Don't miss C.J. Miller's *Protecting His Princess* (#1777), which features an Arabian royal who breaks with tradition to have the life that she wants. Will she find love with the distrusting—and disturbingly handsome—FBI agent who's keeping her safe? Let's welcome new author Lara Lacombe, who debuts with *Deadly Contact* (#1778). Here, a beautiful scientist and an FBI agent must work together to stop a bioterrorist attack on Washington, D.C. Will true love win out over danger?

As always, we deliver on our promise of breathtaking romance. Have a wonderful November and happy reading!

Sincerely,

Patience Bloom

Senior Editor

OUT OF HARM'S WAY

—

Lindsay McKenna

To the U.S. Navy SEALs, who give their lives so that we may enjoy the freedom we have in the United States of America. And equal gratefulness and thanks to the SEAL families who sacrifice heavily on the home front.

Chapter 1

Madison Duncan couldn't still her excitement. She wanted to see the Afghan horses near the house where she was staying. She slipped away from the U.S. agricultural mission in the Shinwari leader's home.

Earlier, when she and the six men on her mission had been driven in with their Marine Corps escort, she'd spotted a corral of Afghan horses out behind the three-story mud-and-rock house. She was the horse breeding expert on the humanitarian mission to help the Shinwari tribe improve their horses. And now, Madison simply couldn't wait any longer to take a look at the animals.

Taking a side door, she quietly slipped outside. It was dusk, the sky a cobalt dome above the valley ringed by the high Hindu Kush mountains. Already, she could see stars so close that it took her breath away.

They were ten miles from the Pakistan border, and the Marine captain, whose duty it was to keep this group of U.S. civilians safe, had told her they were in the badlands. The area was heavy with Taliban and Al-Qaeda activity and skirmishes. The captain warned her no one was safe without military escort, even inside the five-foot mud wall that surrounded Lar Sholten, a large village of two hundred people.

She could barely see through the semidarkness of the June evening, the dust fine and rising around her knee-high black leather riding boots as she headed toward a corral of rock and mud. Inside were about ten Afghan horses.

Her heart quickened with anticipation as she pulled her denim jacket a little tighter around her. At six thousand feet, the night air turned cold, and she wished she'd brought more than summer clothes. At least her jeans helped shield her from the dropping temperature. She just needed a good, bulky winter sweater.

Some of the horses nickered as she walked up to the wooden gate. Smiling, Madison put her hand over the chest-high wall, calling to them. "Hey," she cooed softly. "Come on over…" These were small horses, maybe fourteen hands tall, sturdy with thick necks. Their heads still bore some resemblance to their Arabian ancestors with small muzzles and short, fine ears. A gray horse with a thick, scruffy black mane walked over. Madison had been told that the Afghans always rode geldings. Tribal leaders were the only ones who could ride a stallion. The mares were kept solely for breeding purposes.

She smiled and saw how large the brown eyes were on the gray gelding. Scratching his ears, which he

loved, she tried to look at the animal's overall conformation.

The Shinwari tribe had signed papers with the U.S.,
asking them for help. Her father, John Duncan, owned
a Trakehner stud farm in College Station, Texas, and
had been invited to go along. He'd broken his ankle and
couldn't make it, and Madison pleaded successfully to
be allowed to go in his stead. She'd been raised with
the Prussian warm-blooded horses that had a global
reputation for refining and improving any other breed
of horse.

At last, she was here with these beautiful animals.
She focused on the gray horse and stood on tiptoes to
look over at his legs. He had a short back and fine-
looking head, all reminiscent of earlier Arabian breeding. Afghanistan, at least in the eastern portion, was
nothing but rocky mountains and desert, and the Arabian influence on these horses was telling.

She moved to the wood-slatted gate and knelt down,
running her hand down the animal's front leg. He had
a short, thick cannon bone, which was good for moun-
tainous areas. Surprised at how nice his front legs were,
her mind automatically went to the next step. Her job
was to assess the horses and determine what breed
could improve them. The leader of the village had said
he wanted a taller horse because not all Afghans were
short, although she'd seen many who were.

It was getting too dark to see, but Madison stood
there, her arms wrapped around her body, listening to
the soft snort of the horses inside the corral. Soon, she'd
need to return since she was alone and it was dark. The
U.S. mission was staying at the home of Timor Kahn,

the Shinwari chieftain. There, the Marine detachment would guard them twenty-four hours a day.

She looked up. The stars were now huge and hung so close that she thought she might reach out and touch them. Madison heard the wind gusting down off the mighty Hindu Kush. The valley was long and wide with a river running through it. Everything seemed so peaceful. She noticed some of the horses lift their heads, ears forward, hearing something she could not.

Madison thought it might be one of the Marine guards who had discovered her missing and come looking for her. She'd probably get chewed out. The Marines were jumpy and wary. Yet, as she absorbed the night sky and the snort of horses, the place seemed so placid.

Suddenly, her world erupted. A strong male hand clapped over her mouth. Madison was jerked backward off her feet. Her nostrils flared and a scream lodged in her throat. She was slammed to the ground. Her head struck the dirt with force, almost knocking her unconscious. She heard a hiss and an order in a foreign language. Struggling, she felt a rag shoved into her mouth and then tightened around her head so she couldn't scream. Terror flooded her as she tried to kick out at her unseen attackers.

Oh, God! Her mind shorted out as she felt her arms jerked behind her back and rough ropes being looped around her wrists. The bindings bit savagely into her skin and she cried out, the sound dying behind her gag. Breathing hard, she barely saw faces. Men's faces. They wore turbans. Their eyes were filled with hatred. She was jerked roughly to her feet.

Madison tried to struggle. Someone threw a black

wool hood over her head, and she tried to yank free. The hands of the men propelled her swiftly forward. She tried to fight, until one of her attackers slapped her. Hard. Her knees almost buckled from the blow. Madison was half dragged and half carried away from the house.

Nose bleeding, her cheek smarting and throbbing, Madison was put up on a horse. She heard the mutterings of men around her. What was going on? What was happening to her? A rope was looped around her left ankle and then passed beneath the belly of her horse. Her right ankle was also tied.

Raw terror compelled her to try to cry out. She fought the bonds holding her hands behind her back. Her legs were tied such that she couldn't lift them to kick the horse she was on. She was trapped.

In moments, she heard a flurry of action around her, and then her horse lurched forward into a gallop. She nearly fell off, but yanked herself forward, gripping the fleeing horse with her long thighs. She'd been captured!

As they rode hard, the pounding of hooves thundered in her ears. She heard a whip strike the rump of her horse. The animal grunted and leaped forward, galloping faster. Tears jammed into her eyes. Oh, God, she shouldn't have left the house! She should have listened to the Marines! What was going to happen to her? How could she get loose?

"Raven Actual, this is Raven Main. Over."

Frowning, Petty Officer, 2nd Class Travis Cooper answered his radio. He was in his hide, his .300 Win-Mag sniper rifle on a bipod searching for an HVT, high value target, that was to come across the border. It was his job as a SEAL to take the target out.

"Raven Actual," he answered, wondering what was going down. He didn't get a call unless something went seriously wrong. He was in his hide five hundred feet above the desert floor on the rocky slope of scree, waiting for his HVT. Above, the stars glimmered and danced in the night sky.

"Be apprised an American woman, Madison Duncan, has been kidnapped by the Taliban. We've got a drone watching the group's progress toward the border."

Surprised, Travis scowled. An American woman? Out here? His mind spun with a hundred questions. "Roger, Raven Main." So how was he involved in this?

"She has been kidnapped from the Shinwari village of Lar Sholten, ten miles west of your position."

He sat back from his position of looking through his Nightforce scope. "Roger that, Raven Main." And just exactly what did Lieutenant Brad Scofield, his LT and head of Delta Platoon back at Camp Bravo, want him to do about it?

"Raven Actual, you are the closest to where it appears the Taliban is headed. They're pushing though the night to make the border, so they must have night vision capability."

"Roger that." Travis knew the U.S. military couldn't throw lead at the kidnappers. The bullets or bomb could kill the American woman, too. He was beginning to see the handwriting on the wall. He'd been in his sniper hide for two weeks, watching and patiently waiting for this HVT to leave Pakistan and sneak across the border into Afghanistan. And it was his job to identify him and take him out.

"Raven Actual, we need you to interdict this group of five horsemen and take them out. It's imperative Ms. Duncan be kept alive and rescued. Over."

Grimacing, Travis said in his West Texas drawl, "Roger that, Raven Main. You got an ETA when they're gonna come by my area?" Hell, that group of Taliban could split off or ride elsewhere other than where he was. However, Travis's hide was probably one of the most perfectly placed for watching the traffic across the border.

"Raven Actual, Master Chief Braden will be in touch with you as this goes down."

"Raven Main, what about dropping a couple of SEALs to apprehend them?"

"Negative, Raven Actual. The minute they hear a helicopter coming toward them, they're going to scatter and hide in those caves. Right now, we have drone eyes on them and they are moving toward the border."

Well, hell's bells. Travis scrubbed his face. "Roger, Raven Main. Do you have an ID on this kidnapped American?"

"Roger, am transmitting to your laptop right now."

This was not what Travis wanted. He couldn't give away his hide position. He'd been out in the mountains for weeks, hunting and waiting. "Hold, Raven Main," he muttered, leaving his sniper rifle where it sat and moving into his hide. He grabbed his laptop, opened it up and then connected it via satellite phone. It was the only way to receive or transmit pictures and other intel. The screen was in low light mode so it couldn't be seen by the enemy, who were always in the caves around his hidden position.

The color photograph, a passport photo, of Madison Duncan opened up. His heart jumped for a moment. She was young. He quickly scanned the passport and other provided information. Blond hair, blue eyes, twenty-six years old and from College Station, Texas. Hell, she was a Texas gal. That made this more important to him because he was from Texas. And it didn't hurt a thing that she was damned good-looking. And single, according to the intel. Madison's shoulder-length blond hair had been streaked several shades and colors by the sun. Her face was oval with a broad brow, high cheekbones and a beautiful mouth. Yeah, that mouth could get him into a lot of trouble, and he smiled to himself.

"Raven Main, you got anything else on the package?" Like, what the hell was she doing out here in the badlands?

"Roger, Raven Actual. She's part of a U.S. agricultural mission to help the Shinwari tribe. Her father owns a Trakehner stud farm and she's over here to look at Afghan horses and suggest better breeding methods to the tribe."

Trakehners? Travis had heard about the breed but his familiarity was with the quarter horses on his father's ranch. "Roger that. How did she get kidnapped?"

"According to the U.S. Marine Captain who was in charge of protecting this group, she slipped out of the house at dusk. They found evidence of a struggle at the horse corral."

So, the Texas gal disregarded the Marine's orders to stay with the group and remain guarded. Travis shook his head. Sounded like a Texas gal to him, all right. Strong minded, stubborn and, as a result, kidnapped. "Roger that. You said five horsemen?"

"Roger. All carrying AKs. They've got her bound and hooded. She's riding in the center of the group and can't possibly escape on her own."

No, Travis imagined, she sure as hell couldn't. He felt sorry for her, but he also felt anger. If the woman had trusted her Marine contingent she wouldn't be in this fix.

"Any idea of what they're going to do with her?"

"No. Our best guess is they're going to move her into Pakistan and, most likely, demand a ransom."

Travis sighed and quirked his mouth. "Either that or sell her as a sex slave."

"That, too," Lieutenant Scofield said.

Which was why she had to be rescued, Travis thought.

"Any idea who's got her?"

"Roger. Hill tribe members, from what we can ascertain."

Great, the hill tribe with Khogani leading it was constantly making war against the Shinwari. Both claimed the Khyber Pass area. And that was the only route between Afghanistan and Pakistan.

"Roger that." Travis sighed. "That means I'm probably going to give away my hide, LT."

"Yes, it does."

"*If* I can spring her loose from those bastards, I'm on my own. There's Taliban crawling all over this area. You won't be able to get a Night Stalker helo down here to pick us up. I'm going to have to gun and run with her until I can get out of this immediate area."

"Understood."

"Keep me updated on their progress and location." To Travis, this was looking like a FUBAR of the finest kind. There were thousands of Taliban and Al-Qaeda crisscrossing this border area. It was a hotbed of activity and one couldn't just drop a helo into it because the enemy would see it, fire on it and, most likely, destroy it. No, *if* he could rescue this damned bull-headed Texas brat, it meant being on the run for days, possibly, before an extrication mission could be called to get them out of this area.

"Roger that, Raven Actual. Out."

Travis put the sat phone down on his rucksack, scowling into the total darkness. There were thousands of caves all around this area. The Taliban used them regularly to hide from drone eyes and from the deadly Apache helicopters that stalked them.

He pulled the cover off his watch and saw that it was midnight. Rubbing his bearded jaw, he thought about the possibilities. He had to act fast. Once again, he examined the live video feed of the Taliban fleeing with the kidnapped woman. They were moving at a steady trot and it was clear to him someone had night vision goggles or they wouldn't be able to ride through the darkness.

His thoughts turned to his buddies from back home. He and five others from Rush Springs, Texas, had been on the football team that captured the state championship. They called themselves the Sidewinders, striking like a rattler and beating more powerful teams. All six of them had a sidewinder tattooed around their right biceps. And during those four years, they were like football gods to their small Texas town in the panhandle.

Shortly after graduation, they all went into the military. And it didn't surprise Travis that all six of them went into black ops. He grinned a little, thinking about Duke Carmichael, one of the Sidewinders. If he'd gotten this plate of hot potatoes, his good friend, who was a combat controller in the Air Force, would probably die laughing. Of course, Duke had been a real favorite among the girls at the high school, and he had a hell of a reputation for bedding as many as he could. Given that a woman was involved in this op, Duke would leap at the chance to rescue her.

Only problem was, he'd seen Duke at Bagram when he was finishing up an assignment with another SEAL team. Duke had been shot in the thigh and was headed for Germany on a C-5 to get patched up. His friend would be out of commission for a while, but knowing Duke, who was not one to sit around, he'd find a way to stir up trouble.

Travis missed the other Sidewinders. They did stay in touch, occasionally crossing one another's paths in the black ops world. When they did, a cold beer at a bar was the standard celebration, filling in the blanks of what was going on in their lives. The last he'd heard from Duke was that he was bored out of his skull while healing up stateside.

Travis put the happy thoughts away and began to gather all his equipment and store it in the sixty-five-pound ruck he'd wear on his back. Normally, he was a very patient person, which was part of the sniper personality, but he wasn't going to leave this hide until he was *sure* that group of riders would pass his way. He'd worked too hard, for nearly a week, finding this spot and creating a place where he'd not be detected.

If the group continued to come in his direction,

he was most likely going to have to leave his hide, move lower on the slope and hope like hell he'd intersect them. If that group rode a mile away from him, he wouldn't be able to stop them. And she'd be plunged into a void more terrifying than any nightmare. Damned stubborn woman.

He'd grown up on a West Texas ranch and knew all about Texas fillies who were unlike most other women. This Madison gal was a horsewoman. And she obviously didn't follow orders, traipsing off on her own. That was good and bad news. If he got a shot at the Taliban riders, he'd have to hope she'd keep her head about her. He had to take the enemy down in swift succession. What he didn't need was some wimpy woman who couldn't think coolly in a crisis. All the Texas women he'd known growing up were solid and not given to hysteria when the chips were down.

Travis scowled. At twenty-seven, he'd been married and divorced. Thank God, no kids came out of it. And his job as a SEAL had definitely put his marriage in the hurt locker. Marrying Isabella Winborne had been a lifelong dream for Travis. They'd grown up in Rush Springs and had been high school sweethearts. Travis had stupidly made the mistake of promising Isabella he'd marry her. He'd joined the SEALs at eighteen, and he'd waited until twenty-one to make good on that promise.

Isabella came from a very rich Texas family and her parents didn't want her marrying him because he came from a middle-class Texas ranching family. But like any Texas woman, Isabella was headstrong and fought her family. Snorting softly, Travis remembered their divorce when he was twenty-four. It was messy.

There'd been a lot of hard feelings in Rush Springs. His parents had had to deal with the fallout. Travis had been overseas and missed it. Until he'd gone home.

Yeah, he knew about strong-willed Texas women, for damn sure. Pulling out his Sig Sauer 9 mm pistol, he put a bullet in the chamber. His mind lingered on that bad patch in his life. He'd loved Isabella, but his life as a SEAL had interfered and the marriage had dissolved over time like a ticking time bomb. Isabella wasn't prepared for the months he'd be away. There was a ninety-percent divorce rate among the SEALs and she'd been a casualty of it, and so had he. Travis swore that, from that moment on, he was *not* going to fall in love again. At least, not while in the SEALs.

Now it appeared he'd gotten entangled with another headstrong Texas woman: Madison Duncan. He felt bad for her because he knew this particular enemy hated American women on a par with American men. She would not be treated well and that ate at him. Rape came to mind and he tried to ignore the possibility. They could beat her to death, as well. He hoped she had strong Texas genes because she would need them to survive this. *If* she survived it at all.

Travis could imagine that SEAL HQ at Bagram was going nuts at this point since Madison's rescue had fallen on their shoulders. Yeah, they were black ops, but he wondered about the political fallout on this escapade. If the SEALs didn't get this done right, their name would be tarnished in the American press and the world. Not something that the admiral running the SEALs wanted, Travis was sure. And everything was landing on his shoulders. With the lack of intel, he had to rely on her being from Texas and assume she'd be tough enough to deal with the situation.

His mind skipped like a rock over a pond's surface. He knew the cave system in this area like the back of his own hand. He'd spent three deployments here along the border. That was the good news. There were some caves and systems he knew intimately. The Taliban favored certain caves, but he'd done his homework over the years, finding others where he could hide and not be discovered. Those caves were around and they'd most likely take advantage of them. *If* he could rescue her. *If* she lived. *If* she wasn't injured. *If* she was ambulatory. Pushing his fingers through his longish black hair, his eyes narrowing, Travis knew he needed some luck. Would he get it?

Madison didn't know how long she'd been on the trotting horse. Blinded by the hood, her arms and shoulders now numb, she tried to remain on board the animal. There was never any talking among her kidnappers. They just relentlessly pushed their horses. She could smell the sweat on her own horse. It was stumbling regularly, which meant it was tired and needed to rest. She had tried to push the rag out of her mouth, but couldn't. Dying of thirst, her face swollen and her nose still leaking blood every now and again, she felt bruised everywhere.

Anguished, Madison knew she'd screwed up royally. She should have listened to the Marine captain. Why, oh why, did she let her curiosity get the best of her? She'd been so excited about seeing Afghan horses. She worried about her mother and father. By now, they probably knew she'd been captured. God, she was causing them so much worry and grief. Wanting to be a good representative of the United States, Madison had jumped into this with both feet. Her father felt she could do it. Her mother, Tess, a large-animal vet, had doubts. She worried about Madison being in a country at war.

Misery overwhelmed her. She had no idea what was going to happen to her. Her father always called her a "risk taker." Yeah, she was, but this time, she'd gone too far.

The horses slowed. Finally, they stopped. Relief flooded her body. Her legs were raw and she could feel her ankles were numb where they'd tied her. The rope was beneath the belly of the horse, and if she fell off, she'd be killed by the horse's back hooves striking her body and head.

She heard men's voices speaking in a language she thought was Pashto. Someone untied one ankle. She was yanked roughly off the horse. Madison was allowed to fall to the ground. Her legs collapsed beneath her. Her head struck the ground, dazing her. She was yanked upright, the hood torn off. Blinking, her hair a tangled and unruly mess around her face, she realized it was still night. A man leaned over and untied her mouth. She spat out the rag.

Her arms were numb. She'd felt blood earlier, warm and leaking down her long fingers. Now she felt nothing. Her shoulders ached and burned as she watched her captors lead the horses over to a small pool of water at the bottom of a large, rocky canyon. The quarter moon gave her just enough light to see what was going on.

One man, his eyes black and glittering, came over

and untied her hands. He stood with his rifle and threw a bottle of water into her lap.

Madison reached out for the water. Her fingers were numb. Fire shot through her shoulders as she moved toward that precious bottle of water. Closing her eyes, she gritted her teeth and then forced her unfeeling fingers around the bottle. It took a minute to unscrew the lid but when the water flowed into her mouth, Madison groaned. She gulped down the water, feeling lightheaded and weak. When she finished it, the man threw her another bottle. She drank three of them before she was sated. Her stomach growled. The last time she'd eaten was at noon. She looked up at the soldier. Cringing inwardly, she noticed the raw hatred in his eyes as he glared down at her.

Madison looked past him and saw all six horses drinking deeply at the pool. Their bodies gleamed with sweat. They'd been pushed hard. As she scanned the area, Madison thought they were in a canyon from what she could make out in the deep shadows. Could she escape? Oh, God, if only she could! Everywhere she looked, it was desolate and desert. Craning her neck, she looked at the group of men standing, their heads together, talking quietly. What were they going to do with her? Where were they taking her?

Her hands began to wake up. She could feel blood coming back into them, the pain almost unbearable. Pushing the hair off her face, she felt close to tears. What had she done? How was she going to get out of this? As she looked up at the soldier guarding her, Madison felt the crushing answer. She wasn't getting out of this alive. She didn't know the area. She had no water and no food. These men knew this land because they lived here. Once again, she could only feel dread for what would happen to her. Her one stupid, childish and selfish mistake had landed her here. Tears burned in her eyes and she shut them. Madison didn't want them to see her cry and she sucked it up, burying it deep within her.

"Get up!"

Madison snapped her head up. Another man in dark clothing stood, his hands on his hips, glaring at her. "Y-you speak English?" she rasped, her voice hoarse.

"Get up!" He gestured sharply to her.

Madison stood on wobbling legs. She saw the expression in the leader's face, behind the black beard hanging halfway down his narrow chest. He turned and said something to the soldier. They both looked at her.

Suddenly, Madison felt like raw meat for sale, and it scared the bejesus out of her. Were they going to rape her? Oh, God…

"Move!" the man barked, gesturing for her to walk to where the horses stood.

Instantly, Madison moved. Relief shot through her. They weren't going to rape her. No…no, not that. Dazed, weak from not eating, she was pushed toward the horse she'd been on before. In minutes, her hands were bound behind her once more. Groaning, the pain hot and burning across her shoulders, she was forced back onto the horse. They dragged the rope beneath the horse's belly and again her ankles were bound. They placed the hood back over her head. The men mounted and the soldier who had guarded her tied the reins of her horse to the back of his saddle. They kicked the animals, moving out at a fast trot.

Madison found it tough to ride in this position. She

compressed her lips, looking around but seeing nothing. From earlier, she knew they were moving out of the canyon and back on to the desert floor. Up ahead, huge mountains rose to her right. Where were they taking her? Her mind cartwheeled with terror. Wasn't anyone going to try to rescue her? Did the Marines even know she was gone? When she didn't show up at dinner, surely they'd realized something was wrong.

Tears began to leak down her drawn cheeks. Madison was alone. No one knew where she was or what had happened to her. With one stupid decision, her life, as she knew it, was over.

Chapter 2

Travis hissed a curse as he saw six riders coming right around the slope of a mountain. It was barely dawn, grayness tinging the mountain peaks above him. He used the Nightforce scope on his sniper rifle and counted five Taliban riders guarding someone in the center. That had to be Madison Duncan, but he couldn't positively identify her with a black hood over her head. His eyes narrowed as he watched the horses moving at a swift trot. They were only three miles from the border. He spoke into his radio transmitter.

"Raven Main, Raven Actual. I have the package in my sights."

"Roger. You are authorized to take action."

Dammit, this was not going to be easy. Travis moved his scope, checking out the ground between him and the enemy. The Taliban were smart in remaining near the slopes. There was one piece of flat and open land where he could take his shots. Already, he had two more mags of three bullets each beside his left hand. He had to take out five men.

His lips lifted away from his teeth as the group turned in his direction. The woman's horse had its reins tied to the back of a Taliban soldier's saddle. That was not good. The possibility of the horse bolting, frightened and wild-eyed, as he started taking his shots, was very real. And with Madison Duncan helpless, there was no way she could jump off even if she wanted to. He saw the rope beneath the horse's belly, saw her ankles tied to each end of it. *Sonofabitch*. Travis quickly painted a verbal picture for his master chief.

His heart slowed down because he willed it. Snipers could control their bodies like no one else could. His finger brushed the two-pound trigger on the Win Mag he had shoved against his right shoulder and pressed tight to his cheek. This didn't look good for the American woman. There was a good possibility that when he shot the rider and he fell off, the horse would leap and run away.

His only recourse was to put a bullet in the head of the fleeing horse to drop it. And when it collapsed, Madison's horse would more than likely plough into it. The belly rope around her ankles would stop her from being hurled over its head. Madison had no way to safely dismount and would very likely be crushed beneath that thousand-pound horse she rode. These were problems Travis had not expected. No one had. It put her at real risk.

His mind moved at the speed of light. There was little wind this time of morning, which was a plus.

The light was getting brighter, and he could now see the group clearly through his sights. Which one to take out first, second, third? He tried to guess what the soldiers would do once they saw one of their friends lifted out of the saddle and punched six feet backward, dead before he hit the ground. The bullets were supersonic, moving faster than the speed of sound. The boom of the Win Mag would follow. That gave Travis time to pump more bullets into the targets before he had to drop the empty mag and slap another one into his rifle. By then, all bets were off. It would come down to the element of surprise and him shooting fast enough so that none of the soldiers could shoot Madison Duncan, once they knew they were under attack. And shoot her they would.

His other concern was that his Win Mag did not have a muzzle suppressor. If one of the soldiers saw the flash of his rifle being fired, they would target him. Travis had no problem with that, but he worried more that the soldiers would scatter to minimize the chances of the rest of them being killed.

This wasn't going to be easy at all. He'd hoped they'd tie her hands in front of her. Hoped they wouldn't have put a bag over her head. For a moment, he wondered how much pain she was in, knowing she'd been captured ten hours earlier. She was probably frightened out of her skull. If she got injured, there was no medevac flying in to take her out. It was simply too dangerous for a helo and its four-person crew to come anywhere near this area right now. So it all fell on Travis's shoulders.

He watched the group move straight toward him.

They would be across the half mile of open, flat ground shortly. It would be there that he'd take them down.

Travis was under cover five hundred feet above them, well hidden in the scree, lying prone on his belly. He kept his ruck beside him. His heartbeat slowed even more. His first target would be the rider who had Madison Duncan's horse in tow. Watching the Taliban spread out more, he smiled a little. These would be one-thousand-yard shots, easy enough to accomplish with the Win Mag. Travis set the dials on the rifle and settled in. There was a point where a person's breath stopped. It was called the still point, a magical half second lull between the inhale and the exhale. And that was the point where a sniper would shoot.

His finger brushed the trigger. The boom of the rifle jerked and rippled all the way through his body. He didn't even wait to see if the bullet hit his target, moving to the second and third horsemen. By the time he released the spent mag and slapped in the next one, Travis was settled and situated. He was minimally aware of men flying off their horses. He couldn't hear anything at this distance, but he saw one horse rear up and then turn to gallop off. Quickly, he sighted on the other two soldiers who were now looking around, fear etched in their faces.

Too late, you bastards. You're going straight to hell.... And he took the fourth and fifth shots.

Travis leaped to his feet, leaving his rifle behind, jerking the 9 mm Sig Sauer pistol out of his drop holster and hurtled down the scree. Below, five men lay unmoving. The horses, thank God, startled and upset, had moved together, circling one another, wild-eyed. He hit the flat plain and ran hard toward the milling group of anxious horses. He kept his eyes on Madison Duncan who was sitting very still on her horse. She was doing the right thing, Travis thought, pulling up his Sig as he approached the carnage.

His gaze moved swiftly to each of the soldiers. None of them moved. He crooned softly to the horses, walking slowly toward them. The animals milled, snorting, their ears moving back and forth in fear. Okay, the soldiers were all dead. He holstered his pistol and approached to within six feet of the first horse.

"Ma'am?" he called, "I'm Travis Cooper, U.S. Navy. I'm here to rescue you. If you can just sit very still until I can get my hands on the reins of the horse, that would be helpful. Don't talk. Don't move. Just slowly nod your head once if you understand me."

Madison quivered violently, unable to see anything. The soldiers had put the hood back on her head but they hadn't gagged her. Sweat had covered her as she'd heard men screaming, then nothing. The horses had become frightened. When she'd first heard the loud, booming sound, she knew it was a rifle, but she couldn't see anything! The man's Texas drawl brought down her fear just a notch. Her shoulders were still numb. She slowly moved her head forward as he'd requested.

The horse she rode snorted. She could feel the animal tense. Oh, God. Who was this man? Definitely American. Her mouth was dry and she wanted to see him.

Madison sat quietly. She heard his voice again, a soft sing-song as he came closer. Her horse snorted and moved sideways.

"Easy, easy, son," Travis crooned, not meeting the

horse's eyes, knowing that would threaten him. He approached the horse from the side and slowly eased his hand toward the animal's sweaty, glistening neck. The horses had been ridden hard and ruthlessly. Their nostrils were wide open, showing red up inside the passages. Travis placed his hand on the horse's reins, relief shooting through him.

"Ma'am? I've got the lead horse's reins. Now, you just keep sitting quietly, and I'm going to work my way back toward your horse. The reins of your horse are tied on the back of this horse's saddle. Just slowly nod your head if you understand me."

Travis moved furtively, constantly crooning to her horse whose eyes were rolling. The animal was skittish, and the last thing Travis needed was for it to bolt. The horse's nostrils flared, picking up his scent. Travis didn't smell like the other riders. The horse suddenly planted its front feet, getting ready to bolt.

"Whoa, big guy," he called to the horse. "No need to bolt, son, just stand down, stand down." He eased the knot out of the reins. More relief rushed through Travis as he gripped the reins in his left hand.

"Okay," he told her, "I've got your horse's reins. I'm going to come up beside you and cut off that belly rope."

He heard her gasp a little. Travis could see her shaking in the saddle. Feeling sorry for the woman, he pulled his KA-BAR from its sheath and quickly sliced the thick rope. Her legs were now free. He slid the knife back into the sheath.

"We're almost home free, gal," he told her softly. "I've got the horse's reins in my one hand. I'm going to come up on your left side and slide my arm around your waist. When I do that, I want you to relax, trust me and I'm going to pull you off this horse. Got it?" He looked upward, watched her nod. Heard her erratic breathing.

As he slid his arm around her waist, Travis felt her relax. "Okay, here we go," he said and then lifted her away from the saddle. She was probably five foot seven and weighed around a hundred and thirty pounds.

Madison groaned and clenched her teeth as he hauled her off the horse. Pain and burning shot through her shoulders. He was strong and tall, that much she could tell. And then she picked up his scent, a combination of sweat and his own unique maleness. Her feet touched the ground and she gave a soft cry as her legs gave way.

Travis gently guided her to sit on the earth. He released the horse and focused on the woman. Taking off the hood, he saw her blond hair was mussed and her blue eyes were filled with pain. Quickly, he moved behind her, unknotting the bonds and releasing her wrists.

"You're safe," he rasped, carefully pulling the ropes free. He scowled. Her wrists looked like hamburger; her fingers were covered in dried blood. Rage flowed through him over what they'd done to her. He knelt in front of her.

"Madison Duncan?" he asked, holding her terrified blue gaze.

"Y-yes…." She tried to move her arms, grimacing as she did so.

"Travis Cooper, ma'am." He kept a hand on her shoulder. "Where are you hurt?"

Madison struggled to speak. "I'm…thirsty…."

He pulled a bottle of water out of a cammie pocket,

opened it and handed it to her. "Here you go. Drink your fill." Well, it wasn't going to happen. Huge tears formed in her eyes as she tried to move her hands.

"I—I can't," she managed. "M-my arms are numb. I can't feel anything."

Travis slid his arm around her shoulders. "It's all right," he said soothingly. And he placed the lip of the bottle against her mouth. Damn, but she was twenty times better looking than the grainy color passport photo he'd seen of her on his laptop. Her hair was long and slightly wavy, halfway down her back, with streaks of darker blond, cream and more gold colors.

She drank, the water spilling out the corners of her mouth, dribbling down on the dirty tank top she wore.

"Slow down, gal. There's more where that came from." He held her eyes, giving her a slight smile meant to help her relax.

Travis kept his hearing keyed. The five booms from a Win Mag would be instantly recognized and any Taliban in the area would know it was an American sniper. The dawn was barely upon them. The sky was indigo and a few stars still blinked above. She finished off the bottle of water.

"Good," he told her, throwing it away. "Now, talk to me. Where are you hurt?" He prayed like hell she hadn't been raped. The slope of her left cheek was swollen and there was dried blood around her nostrils and chin. Plenty of blood had spilled on her tank top as well, and Travis knew she'd been hit at least once.

Madison tried to move her hands. Her fingers wouldn't work. They felt cold and numb. "M-my shoulders and arms hurt."

"That's from being tied in that position for so long,"

he told her, running his hand across her shoulders. He could feel Madison trembling. And to her credit, she was trying to keep it together. Yeah, she was a Texas gal, through and through.

"They hit me," she whispered, trying to look up at him through her hair. Lifting her hand, she tried unsuccessfully to push the hair out of her eyes. She saw his bearded face, his dark green eyes narrowed intently upon her. He was dressed in cammies, a boonie hat on his head. His mouth was thinned. Travis Cooper. He'd rescued her. She was safe, alive.

"Anything else?" he asked, trying to steel himself. Her eyes grew cloudy and she quivered in his arms.

"N-no.... Why did they do this?" She searched his hard, weathered face.

"Kidnapping is profitable," he said. Damn, but she was beautiful. Her eyes reminded him of the dawn sky, a deep cobalt blue. Her pupils were large and black, a thin black crescent curved around the outside of her iris, emphasizing them even more. He gently pushed some of her hair away from her face to hold her gaze. "Look, I need to get you back on a horse. We need to hightail it out of here. I've got a cave in mind where we can hide and get out from under the Taliban's gunsights." He looked down at her. She reminded him of a disheveled, broken doll. "Can you do that?"

"Y-yes, I can."

"Good," he grunted, unwinding and standing. "Stay here. I need to get my ruck and my rifle. I'll be right back."

The horses had huddled around them. Travis took off at a fast trot across the flat land toward the scree slope. He knew horses were herd animals. They were used to humans and hopefully would remain with Madison while he picked up his gear. As he ran, he called back to Camp Bravo, giving them information on the package and her present medical condition.

"You've got forty Taliban on horseback three miles north of you, heading your direction."

Yeah, well, Travis had expected the Win Mag would wake up every Taliban in the area. "Roger that." He filled the master chief in on his escape plan and gave him their GPS position. Travis located his ruck, strapped his Win Mag to the outside of it and pulled the ruck over his shoulders, then swiftly turned and headed down the scree.

In the distance he could see Madison was sitting, her head bowed, her arms hanging uselessly at her sides. God, he felt sorry for her and lengthened his stride, urgency pushing him. Three miles could be covered damn quick by men on horseback.

Madison looked up, watching the Navy man jogging toward her. He was tall, probably at least six feet. And lean, like a starved wolf. It was his oval face, those wide-set green eyes of his and that black beard that made him look hard. He'd just saved her life. Emotions welled up in her. She watched as he slowed to a walk, picked up the reins of one horse and then walked over to the dead soldiers.

What was he doing? She frowned, watching him quickly take off vests, cloaks and trousers from two of them. In no time, he had the clothing strapped on to the back of the saddle. Turning, he walked over to her.

"How are you doing?" he asked, kneeling down, searching her dirty, sweaty face.

"O-okay...." Her heart took off when he gave her a

lazy smile. His entire face changed and he almost became handsome.

"Now, you wouldn't lie to me, would you, darlin'?" He could tell she was rallying beneath his softly spoken endearment. Her mouth…her mouth was meant to be kissed. Full lips, with the corners of her mouth curving naturally upward. Groaning to himself, Travis knew he couldn't go there.

"I'm okay," she managed. "I know I look a sight, but—"

"You look beautiful," he assured her huskily. "I'm going to help you stand. We need to get going."

He lifted her up by her waist as if she weighed nothing. Madison was surprised because he was lean, not heavily muscled or bulky. When she got to her feet, she grabbed for his upper arms. And then she grunted with pain, her hands falling lifelessly to her sides. To lift her hands above her breasts brought nothing but red-hot pain and burning. She bit back a cry.

"It's okay," he rasped, slipping her beneath his arm, holding her close so she had something to lean on. "I'm putting you on this horse. Ready?"

No, she wasn't ready. Her arms were as useless as if they were stuffed with sawdust, her fingers unable to curve or hold on to anything. Madison felt the tension, knew they were still in danger. "Yes…" she whispered.

He nodded, the look in his eyes giving her strength. Her legs did work and she was able to lift one up and over the saddle. Once she was on the horse, he held the reins up to her.

"I—I can't hold on to them," she whispered, distraught. "I'm sorry…."

"No problem," Travis murmured, patting her thigh. "Just sit tight for a moment."

Madison watched him walk over to another horse, throw the reins over its head and mount up. This man knew his horses and certainly knew how to ride. He rode back and brought the reins over her horse's head to hold in his long, large-knuckled fingers.

"You ride?" Travis asked. He knew she did, but didn't know if she could hold on right now, given what she'd already been through.

"I'll hang on," Madison promised grimly, forcing her dead fingers into the horse's thick mane. He gave her a grin for the first time, a boyish look coming to his features. It filled her with hope.

"Good enough," Travis murmured, turning the horse around. "We're going to be moving fast. Got some bad guys coming our way. If you're having trouble hanging on, yell. I'll stop and we'll figure out another plan of action." He pinned her with his gaze. Travis could tell she was in shock, her blue eyes cloudy, her features stressed and confused.

"Let's go," she managed, her voice hoarse. "I'll hang on."

Texas steel. Travis nodded. He saw the determination in her eyes, in the set of that luscious mouth, now thinned with purpose. He clapped his heels to his horse. The animal grunted and leaped forward into a canter. The wind whipped by them as Travis followed a slope that gently curved to the west. His horse was tired and he didn't want to push too hard. Looking over his shoulder, he confirmed that Madison was riding all right. That was a relief. He didn't want to have to carry her on his horse. That would slow them down way too much.

* * *

Madison thanked God for her steel thighs gripping the horse's barrel as they galloped in and around mountain slopes. Her hands were nerveless. Her shoulders ached like fire. But from the waist down, she was just fine, moving in sync with her cantering horse. The wind felt good against her face, drying the sweat, the air pure and sweet without that horrible hood over her head.

She watched Travis ride, his body in rhythm with the movement of the horse. Who was he? Navy in the desert? It didn't make sense. She had so many questions to ask him. Every once in a while, he'd look over his broad shoulder, checking on her to make sure she was all right. Madison felt his protection even though it wasn't anything she could see with her eyes. And it made her feel safe when she knew they weren't.

Within an hour, they halted at the entrance to a cave. Madison noticed a series of caves down the length of the mountain. Travis dismounted. Gripping the horse's mane, Madison forced herself to get off under her own steam. Her knees weren't strong, but she could stay upright. Travis gave her a glance and she was glad to regain a bit of independence.

"What can I do?" she asked, holding the reins he handed to her.

"Nothing," he said. He removed the clothes from the rear of his saddle and put everything near the cave entrance. "Stand over there," he said, pointing to where the clothes were stacked.

Confused, Madison did as he instructed. She watched him lead the horses out beyond the cave entrance and drape the reins over their necks. Her mouth dropped open as he slapped them on the rumps and they went charging off at a gallop.

"What are you doing?" she cried out.

Travis turned. Picking up the clothes, he put them into her arms. "Carry these," he ordered brusquely. "Go into the cave and stand over there." He pointed.

Breathing hard, she glared at him. "You just got rid of our transportation! How could you?"

The man scowled, his mouth compressed as he pulled his huge knife from the sheath on his left thigh and chopped a large branch from a nearby bush.

"Stop yelling," he told her. "Voices carry." Her eyes widened and she did as she was told but not before giving him a mutinous look. Quickly, Travis used the brushy end of the limb and covered their tracks. Backing into the cave, he kept sweeping them away.

"See that tunnel back there?" He hitched his chin in that direction.

"Yes." Madison was furious with him. Who the hell did he think he was? He'd just sent off two good horses that could have gotten them to safety! What was he thinking?

"Go over there and wait for me."

Madison stood on the white, smooth tunnel surface. The tunnel forked to the right and left. The sun was just rimming the Hindu Kush peaks, rays slanting brightly into the cave where Travis was brushing out their footprints. Once he got to her side, he slid his hand beneath her elbow.

"Your arms feeling okay?"

"Yes, I can feel them a little."

"Can you carry those clothes?"

She felt the piercing gaze of his and looked away, still angry with him. "Yes."

Travis grunted and pulled out a penlight and handed it to her. "Can you hold this?"

Madison wasn't sure. Blood was coming back into her fingers and she felt nothing but throbbing pain in them. Their fingers touched momentarily and she clumsily took the small light. "I think so."

"Get going up that tunnel." He pointed to the fork he wanted her to take. "We've got to go about half a mile on a gentle climb upward. I'll catch up."

She gulped and nodded. Why had he chased the horses away? Why? She moved on shaky knees, watching her step on the worn surface. The tunnel darkened until all she saw was the light ahead of her. Everything echoed eerily as she stumbled once, the sound reverberating endlessly.

Where was Travis? Suddenly, Madison felt terrified again. *Alone.* He was nowhere around. Halting, she almost turned around and went back down the tunnel, but she remembered the hard look in his eyes, the guttural order to start walking. She had to trust him. But why the hell had he let their horses run away? That was crazy!

Madison sensed more than heard someone approaching her. She turned. A gasp tore out of her as she saw Travis right behind her. Heart pounding, she froze.

"You scared me!"

"Sorry," he murmured, giving her a sheepish look. "I walk silent."

Gulping, Madison shook.

"Tell you what," Travis said softly, taking the penlight from her. "You grab hold of my belt here." He pointed to his left hip. "And I'll take us the rest of the way up."

Sliding her fingers around his web belt, she nodded. Madison was more than willing to let him lead. He knew where he was. He started off slowly, cutting his stride in half for her. She was grateful, since her knees were still wonky and her energy was fading. Madison didn't know what time it was, only that she hadn't eaten for a long time.

Travis moved up to the right, taking another tunnel. And then the tunnel got very steep and he branched off into another one. He could feel Madison clinging to his belt, heard her breathing in rasps and he slowed even more. They were near eight thousand feet and the air was more rarefied. Texas was flat as a pancake and at sea level. He imagined her lungs felt as if they were on fire right now from the altitude difference. Still, he was pleased she was a fighter and she kept putting one foot in front of the other.

Madison felt woozy. When Travis suddenly halted, she ran into him. And then, she felt her world coming apart, black dots dancing in front of her eyes. "T-Travis," she whispered, clinging to his belt, "I don't feel so good." That's the last thing Madison remembered saying, the words echoing as if she were very far, far away from them.

Chapter 3

The prick of a needle in her left arm woke Madison up. Blinking groggily, she realized she was lying down on a cave floor. Her eyes focused on the man kneeling over her, putting an IV into her arm.

"Wh—" she croaked.

Travis taped the IV down on the inside of left arm. "You're dehydrated," he explained softly. "Just lie still. We're safe in this cave for now."

Sunlight was shining brightly from somewhere. Her mind wasn't functioning. A cave and it was sunny? Madison felt his closeness, that powerful sense of protection emanating from him toward her. His brow was sweaty, his eyes narrowed and mouth pursed. She could smell the sweat on his cammies. Madison stared up into his darkly sunburned face. His black hair was scraggly, not in a military short haircut. Brow wrinkling, she managed, "Who *are* you?"

His mouth curved a little. "I'm a Navy SEAL, darlin'. Black ops. You heard of us?" He rested his arm on his knee, absorbing her. She was filthy, but then she'd been kidnapped, given too little water and no food, most likely. Travis saw her dark blue eyes wander a bit and then focus on him. Damn, even now, she could turn any man's head. He reached out, pushing some of that unruly blond hair of hers away from her cheek.

"SEALs? Really? But...I thought you were at sea, not in a desert."

He smiled a little and pushed the boonie hat off his brow. "We operate on land, sea and air. I'm land bound for now," he joked. Looking up, he listened for any sounds echoing down the tunnel to indicate nearby Taliban. Travis heard nothing. He focused on the liter IV of Ringer's lactate that was feeding her electrolytes in order to quickly get her back into a stable condition.

"I—I must have fainted," Madison muttered, looking around. The cave was huge. She heard water dripping somewhere. The sunlight pierced only so much of the cave, the rest of it was shadowed or grayish-looking to her.

"How long has it been since you ate?" Travis asked.

Already, Madison was feeling better. Less muddled. More focused. "Umm, noon yesterday? I don't even know what day or time it is."

He looked at the watch on his wrist. "0800." And then he saw her puzzled look. "Eight a.m. You were kidnapped at around eight p.m. yesterday evening. You've pretty much been in the saddle and tied up for about eleven of those twelve hours."

He wanted to touch her again but hauled back on his desire. This woman was scared, she'd been beaten and was clearly in shock. She was his responsibility. It was his duty to protect her and see that she made it out of this mess alive and in one piece. "Did you eat at all during that time?"

"No," she whispered. Looking up, Madison saw a huge IV bag hanging off the cave wall. "Are you a doctor, too?" She knew nothing about SEALs, about black ops. Her world orbited around horses.

Travis took the boonie hat off and ran his fingers through his damp, sweaty hair. "I'm a sniper and a combat corpsman." He grinned a little. "I kill and I heal, depending on who it is."

Madison didn't find that funny at all. "You killed those five men."

"I had to, or you and I wouldn't be sitting here discussing it right now." Travis saw her face turn florid. Yeah, killing got to everyone. He didn't enjoy it, but sometimes, it had to be done. He put two fingers on the inside of her left wrist. Her pulse was slowing down. Getting fluids into her was working. Her skin was soft and velvety. God, he'd been out in the badlands too long when he could feel himself responding to just touching a woman's wrist. He released her. "How are you feeling now?"

"Hungry?"

"That's a good sign."

"My parents...do they know I'm okay?"

He nodded. "I called my master chief that I'd rescued you. He'll make sure your parents know you've been recovered. I'm sure they'll notify your husband, too." He didn't add that they weren't out of the woods by a long shot. But he didn't want her upset; her eyes still conveyed shock. She'd been through hell and Travis didn't need to stress her out any more.

Closing her eyes for a moment, suddenly emotional, Madison whispered unsteadily, "I'm not married." Had been, once, but what had she known at eighteen? Not much. At twenty-six Madison was focused on her father's breeding farm operation. Her two-year marriage had shown her she didn't have a clue as to how to choose a decent man. She was far better at evaluating horseflesh than she was at evaluating men.

Madison looked up at Travis. "I was so stupid... so stupid.... They told me to never go outside without a Marine guard." She wiped the tears away. If she was expecting censure, she didn't see it in the SEAL's dark, shadowed eyes. Just having Travis near made her feel safer.

"Look, most civilians don't understand how dangerous it is out here. Don't be too hard on yourself." Travis reached out and smoothed some of her blond hair off her brow. He sure liked touching her.

For whatever reason, Madison pulled him. Hard. But she was too deep in shock and survival mode to do much else right now, although Travis could see the fear ratchet down just a little more every time he did touch her. He tried to tell himself he was just being a compassionate corpsman. Yeah, right. All he wanted to do was stare at her.

"It was a stupid mistake. I put a lot of people at risk doing what I did. All I wanted to do was go out and look at the Afghan horses in the corral. They were only a hundred feet away from the house." Madison bit her lip, her voice dropping with despair. "I didn't think it would harm anything. They were so close and I was dying to get a look at them, at their conformation...."

"Horse crazy," he murmured, smiling a little. "My folks have a cattle ranch in West Texas and I grew up with quarter horses. I understand your excitement." Travis could see the anguish in her eyes. "Don't be hard on yourself. No one's pointing the finger of blame at you."

She sniffed and shored herself up. Every time Travis reached out with those long, large-knuckled fingers of his and grazed her hair, her scalp prickled with heat and pleasure. The look in his green eyes threw her off. She almost thought he wanted to... *No.*

She wasn't emotionally stable right now. It would be easy to misread his face, his intentions. And yet, she felt such coiled power around him. He appeared casual and relaxed, but her senses, as muddled as they were, told her differently. It was as if he were a big, bristling guard dog watching over her. She was grateful beyond words.

What would it be like to kiss this man? Oh, she was really on emotionally rocky ground, for sure.

"Do you feel like getting something in your stomach?"

Nodding, Madison tried to sit up. To her chagrin, she found herself incredibly weak, as if her body had melted down on her and wouldn't cooperate. "I hate feeling so powerless," she muttered, pushing herself upright.

"Dehydration will do it," Travis murmured. "Here, let me help you." He slid his arm around her shoulders and propped her up against the cave wall. She was usually grateful for her strength. Someone who worked around horses became pretty physically fit.

Travis settled her against the wall as if she were a lightweight. And he was so close, his face inches from hers for those fleeting seconds. She felt his moist breath across her brow and cheek. So incredibly masculine, his scent drove her to distraction. Yeah, he was as sweaty and dirty as she was, but she found herself inhaling his scent as if it were a cologne. And it was doing wild, unbidden things within her.

Travis sat back on his heels, his hands coming to rest on his long thighs, watching her. Madison was aware of their attraction. He could have moved those scant inches and captured that soft mouth of hers. Kissed her. And she'd seen that awareness flare in his eyes when he'd drawn close to her. Damn, why couldn't she have been less gorgeous? She watched as he hauled his ruck over and pulled out a protein bar. He handed it to her.

"Try this on for size. You're in shock and shock does funny things to people," he said. Their fingers met. Heat flared inside her. Travis added, "People get real emotional and they feel out of sorts. You probably will, too."

"Thanks," Madison whispered, her whole hand tingling. Travis had a working man's hands. They were large, powerful and she saw so many new and old scars across them. When he'd handed her the protein bar, she'd noticed the thick calluses on his palm. Inwardly, her breasts tightened and she felt heat plunge into her womb. The man could melt her with his thoughtful green gaze.

"Take it easy eating it," Travis warned her, pushing to his feet. He walked over and picked up his M-4 rifle, which was leaning against the wall. "I'm going to check things out and I'll be back in about half an hour. You rest, okay?" The sunlight was making her blond hair gleam with gold, wheat and tawny highlights. How badly Travis wanted to slide his hand through her hair, feel the weight of it, smell it and allow the strands to glide through his fingers. Disgusted with himself, he left, making his way down the dark tunnel. He knew this area well and didn't even bother turning on a penlight to show him the way.

What the hell was going on here? His mind spun with its own kind of shock. Okay, he'd been out here with his platoon for four months. There weren't any opportunities to meet a woman at Camp Bravo, for damn sure. The women at the FOB were either Apache combat pilots or medevac pilots. Being on deployment was like turning into a monk. Until Madison dropped into his life. *Hell.*

Madison was sleeping when Travis returned. He entered the cave silently and saw her with her head on her arm, curled up in the fetal position against the wall. His heart twisted in his chest. He placed his weapon against the wall, took off his boonie and shed his gear. His gaze never left hers. That long, thick blond hair framed part of her face; her lashes rested against her pale cheeks. He grimaced and kicked himself for not thinking about giving her a sleeping bag. The IV was empty so he pulled on a pair of gloves and walked over to where she slept.

Feeling the pinch in her left arm, Madison dragged her eyes open. "Umm," she managed. His fingers were on her arm, removing the IV.

"Sorry to wake you," he said huskily. "IV's done and I need to get your arm patched up."

He tried to ensure his hands were tender. She closed her eyes, as if simply absorbing him. "I must have dozed off," she said, her voice sounding wispy.

Travis dropped the IV at his side and pulled out a large Band-Aid, which he placed on the inside of her arm. "You'll sleep a lot," he told her. "Best way to get rid of shock is to sleep." He watched her eyes open and God help him, he wanted to drown in that dark blue gaze. Her lips were soft, parted, and it would be so easy to brush that full lower one with his thumb. Travis thought reconnoitering for half an hour to make sure the Taliban had followed the horses would snap him back into his focus. But it hadn't.

"I'm thirsty," Madison whispered, watching him get up. "Is there more water?"

She noticed the frown on his face, the look in his green eyes. She swore she could feel him wanting her, man to woman. It must be the shock. Pushing up into a sitting position, she dragged the mass of hair across her shoulders. She felt so dirty, the grit rubbing inside her clothing, making her feel absolutely miserable.

Travis pulled another bottle from his ruck, opened it and handed it to her.

"Thanks," she murmured.

Travis busied himself, pulling out his sleeping bag and unrolling it. He shook it out and opened it up so she'd have something to sit on besides dirt. Silently, Travis gave Madison credit. She wasn't complaining. There was determination in her face. The woman had backbone. Out here, that counted.

She'd finished off the bottle of water—now he

needed to get some food into her. Grabbing the empty bottle and some purification tablets, he walked over to the dripping water in the rear of the cave. There was a small pool of icy water, snowmelt coming off the mountain above them. He dropped the tablets into the empty bottle and filled it with water.

Madison sat on the soft, thin sleeping bag, grateful to be off the dirt. She watched, curious about everything Travis did. He seemed far away or preoccupied. When he sat down, crossing his legs and hauling his MRE into his lap and giving her hers, she screwed up the courage to ask him a question.

"Why did you let our horses go? I thought they were our way to escape."

Travis opened the spaghetti. "We're twenty-two miles from Camp Bravo, the nearest American forward operating base. There are several Taliban groups searching for us right now. I slapped the horses and made them leave because I was hoping the Taliban would follow their tracks. They'd lead them away from where we're hiding. I've checked twice since we got here, and that's what they did. They're following those two horses to God knows where—and I don't care where, so long as it's far away from us."

Madison felt like an idiot. "Oh," she whispered. Lifting her head, she met his warm green gaze. "I was really pissed."

"Yeah, I know."

"I'm sorry." She rubbed her brow, feeling the grit beneath her fingers. "I seem to be saying that a lot with you."

"You're in an alien environment. I don't expect you to know what's going down. Just trust me, though,

Madison, to get you home safely. All right?" Travis
pinned her with a hard look. Her expression grew apologetic and he felt bad. Being out as a sniper for weeks
on end, he wasn't used to diplomacy. He was usually alone in a dangerous place with only his wits, his
knowledge and hunting skills to keep him alive. "Don't
mind me," he said. "I'm a little more tired than usual."
It was as close to an apology as she was going to get.

"I've been a real pain in the ass."

She had a nice butt, no doubt about it, but Travis
couldn't go there and say anything. Right now, Madison was embarrassed and trying to find a way to make
up for her anger about the horses. She'd stopped eating
and Travis needed her to get her energy back as soon
as possible. "My master chief said your father owned
a horse farm in College Station?" Maybe getting her
mind off her mistakes and on to something positive
would help her rally.

"Yes, my father was on the Olympic cross-country
team a few decades ago. He'd always wanted to bring
Trakehners to the U.S., and he and my mom made it
happen."

"I don't know much about the breed," he said.
"Quarter horses I know."

"Texas is quarter horse central," Madison agreed.
"Trakehners are a European breed, very tall, beautiful
and intelligent. They're often bred to Arabians, Thor-
oughbreds and other warm-bloods to improve them."

"And that's why you were with that American del-
egation?"

Nodding, she began to eat once again. "Yes. My father was invited to go along but he broke his ankle and
he asked me to go instead." Chewing on her lower lip,

she scowled. "I'm sure he's sorry about it now." Madison felt terrible for disappointing her father. They had put such high hopes on this journey to Afghanistan.

"I'm sure he's relieved you're safe," Travis murmured, no doubt seeing the pain in her eyes.

Madison knew her father would be dismayed. Wanting to cry, feeling horribly vulnerable, she choked it all back down inside herself. Travis had done enough for her. He was charged with her safety. He didn't need a crybaby on his hands, to boot. "You said your parents have a cattle ranch?"

"Yeah, Rush Springs. I grew up there and was a cowboy until me and my football buddies joined the military." Travis smiled fondly. "I had six buddies on the football team, and we called ourselves the Sidewinders. Our team took the Class A football title for Texas and we were just this Podunk town out in the middle of scrub brush, desert and cactus."

"You guys must have been really good," Madison said, watching his face relax. It was a secret pleasure to watch him eat, the way his lips moved, sending heat sheeting down through her like a lightning strike. And his hands… What would they feel like, moving across her body? There was gentleness in him. He might have to kill the enemy, but his touch with her was always tender. She was shocked at her own sexual hunger for him. It was wrong, and she felt torn and guilty. He was more than likely married to a beautiful woman and had a couple of kids.

"We were a force to be reckoned with," Travis agreed amiably. "All my buddies joined different branches of the military the day after we graduated. And we all ended up in black ops." He smiled a little.

"I just saw Duke Carmichael, one of the Sidewinders, a couple of months ago. We crossed paths at Bagram. He's a black ops Air Force CCT, communications specialist. I was deploying into Afghanistan for six months and he was just leaving on another assignment. When we do cross paths, we catch up on one another's lives."

"Six months over here?"

"Yeah. SEALs are on a two-year cycle. We spend eighteen months back in the States and most of the time we're renewing our skills, taking courses in our area of expertise and learning new weapons systems. Then, the last six months is rotation over here. I'm with Seal Team 3 and we're always deployed to the Middle East. Other Seal teams take care of different parts of the globe."

"I didn't realize," Madison admitted. "How do your wife and kids handle you being gone so much?"

He raised a brow and gave her an amused look. "SEALs have a ninety percent divorce rate. I'm in that statistic because I'm a SEAL."

Her heart pounded a little. "Well, then," she stumbled, "your girlfriend? A significant other?"

Travis just shook his head and paid attention to eating his MRE. "I have a lousy track record," he muttered.

"I'm sorry," Madison said quietly, holding his gaze. "You're a hero in my eyes. That shouldn't mean you have to be so alone."

His heart squeezed unexpectedly beneath her sincere voice and expression. He could entertain having her as his woman, no problem at all. But as with all the rest of his experiences, women in his life went one way and he went the other.

"You get used to it," Travis said, avoiding her searching blue gaze. The woman could melt rocks with those eyes of hers. Hell, she was melting him and he wasn't sure what to do about it. Did Madison know her own feminine influence over him? Oh, in his high school days, because he was part of a star football team, he hadn't wanted for girls. Every cheerleader had set their sights on the Sidewinders. And Travis had enjoyed his high school years. "Why aren't you hooked up with a guy?" he asked.

Blinking over the blunt question, Madison shrugged. "I don't know. Maybe too many hours of training our horses and showing them? Running a breeding facility?" She opened her hands and added, "I love what I do, Travis. There aren't a whole lot of single guys my age that are in the horse business. Most horse farms and breeding facilities are family run."

"What do you like to do for fun?" He had images of her jumping into a river and skinny-dipping. Madison might seem shy, but he'd seen her strength under fire. He liked her way too much. She was appealing to him. Somehow, this blond-haired beauty was turning his world upside down and making him think differently about settling down.

Shrugging, Madison said, "You'll laugh at me."

"No, I won't."

The sparkle of life came to her eyes for the first time and it damn near stole his breath. Her cheeks flushed and her eyes were so alive. An ache, a really crippling ache, grabbed hold of his lower body. Would Madison look at *him* like that as he made love to her? His mind and his body rocked on that heated, dangerous question. "Tell me."

"I have two passions in my life," she said, feeling his genuine interest, feeling warmed by that intense look that made her yearn to kiss him. "I love my horses but my hobby is sort of boring by a lot of people's standards. My mom, who is a large-animal vet, taught me quilting when I was a teen. I love making quilts for the elderly. I belong to a local women's quilting club and we get together once a week to work on our latest quilt to help those who have so little."

"Are you a throwback to another era and age?" Travis wondered aloud. "My grandmother quilted. My mother never picked it up, too busy raising us kids on a cattle ranch."

"Maybe the word *old-fashioned* fits me, then?" Madison felt shy and broke away from his burning gaze. God, she felt like the man had X-ray vision and could undress her with his eyes. She didn't feel threatened, but rather, desired. Very desired. Was something going on between them, something invisible? Whatever it was, she felt shaky, needy and hungry. Granted, Travis Cooper was a man's man. There was no strutting. No bragging. He was quiet. Confident. She'd not met many men like him. And it drew her powerfully.

Old-fashioned.

Yeah, Madison certainly was. Travis smiled a little to himself as he finished off his meal. Madison seemed uncomfortable about admitting it to him. The Texas girls he grew up with were strong-willed and knew what they wanted. And they didn't apologize for chasing him or his other friends to get their attention. He watched her nervously move her fingers clasped in her lap. "So, you were born in Texas?"

"Yes."

"Horses consumed your life from when you were a little girl onward?"

"How did you know?" Madison was shaken by his insight into her.

"Just a guess," Travis murmured, giving her a slight smile, trying to put her at ease. At least she'd eaten her meal and that was a positive start. Putting his MRE away, he said, "I've got a towel, washcloth and soap in my ruck." He hooked a thumb over his shoulder toward the pool. "That's glacial water and it's damned cold, but you could strip out of those ruined clothes of yours, get washed and cleaned up. I've got some shampoo somewhere that I can scare up so you can wash your hair." He saw her sudden response, hope coming to her eyes.

"Really? Oh, I'd give anything to get clean." Madison wrinkled her nose, opening her hands, the fine silt and grit on them.

"I thought so," Travis said, unwinding and walking to his ruck. Rummaging around, he found the items and set them on the sleeping bag near her leg. He added a clean T-shirt and a set of his trousers for her to wear because her clothes were torn and ruined. "I'm going to go check out our environs. Be back in about an hour, maybe a little less. Will that give you the time you need?"

Madison nodded. "Yes, thank you." And tears suddenly sprang to her eyes. "I don't mean to cry," she whispered, trying to push them off her cheeks.

"Hey," Travis growled, kneeling down next to her. He cupped her face, lifting her chin just enough to look deeply into her marred gaze. "Never apologize for tears, darlin'. You've been through a lot." And dammit, he was going to kiss her if he didn't stop right now.

Dropping his hands, he gave her an apologetic look and stood up. He had to leave or they were both in trouble. Walking over to his M-4, he picked it up and threw the boonie hat onto his head. "I'll see you later."

Shaken, Madison could still feel the warm, callused hands cupping her jaw. His mouth had been inches from hers. Her breath had snagged, her pulse skyrocketed as he surprised her with his unexpected attention. Closing her eyes, she pressed her palms to them, feeling shaken, a quiver rocking through her womb. She released a huge sigh, then scrubbed her eyes and slowly stood up. Her skin burned with pleasure where his hands had slid across her jaw, holding her, looking so deeply into her eyes. She didn't know what to do. Her world had turned upside down last night. Madison was still cartwheeling emotionally, unsure of herself.

Getting the towel, wash cloth and soap, she walked slowly over toward the pool that now glinted with sunlight. Her heart was pounding. And it wasn't out of fear. She *wanted* Travis to kiss her. And then what?

Chapter 4

Travis moved silently into the cave an hour later. He saw Madison standing in the sunshine, looking up through the hole in the cave roof at the blue sky above. His body went on red alert. His T-shirt did nothing but emphasize her breasts and slender body. The trousers were far too large on her, bulky, and she'd rolled them up as best she could around her ankles. But that T-shirt... He took a deep breath, grappling with his desires.

"Hey," he called, letting her know he'd come back. Madison started and jerked in a breath. "God, you scared me!" She placed her hand against her wildly pounding heart. Travis gave her a look of apology as he placed his rifle against the wall. He was sweating, his skin glistening, that hard look on his face. Only his eyes softened as he shed his gear and stripped down to his T-shirt and cammies. The man had a body that simply took her breath away.

"Sorry," he said, meaning it. He walked over to her and frowned. "I thought you were going to wash your hair."

Madison made a face. "I didn't want to sound like a whiner," she admitted self-consciously. "My shoulders… I can't lift my arms above my chest to wash my hair. It's too painful."

Frowning, Travis reached out, his large hands covering her shoulders, feeling around the joints. "They're screwed up because your hands were tied behind your back for eleven hours straight." She flinched a little when he took her arm and slowly started to raise it. Lowering it, Travis shook his head. "You might have torn rotator cuffs." If that was so, she would be unable to lift her arms very high at all. It would take a good four to six weeks until she could lift her hand over her head once again.

"That's not good if they're torn," she muttered, wildly aware of his body, how close he was to her, the care burning in his eyes. Even as he examined her shoulder joints, it sent streams of pleasure through her.

"There's nothing I can do except give you Motrin for the pain," he told her, reluctantly releasing her. Travis stepped back because if he didn't, he was going to kiss that mouth of hers. "Want to live dangerously?" he asked, grinning down at her as he placed his hands on his hips.

Puzzled, Madison stared up into his face. All that game face had melted away. The man who stood in front of her right now was pulverizingly sexy. Sensuality dripped off him. "Aren't we doing that already?"

He chuckled. "I'm used to it. This is an ordinary day for me out here in the badlands." He lifted his hand and gently caressed the tangled strands. "Let me wash your hair for you."

Stunned, Madison blinked. "You?"

Travis shrugged. "Why not? I can position the bag and the ruck over there by the pool and get you to lie down. All you have to do is hang your head over my ruck and I can wash your hair." Travis felt the heat flowing to his lower body. What would it be like to touch that mass of golden hair? He'd literally been itching to thrust his hands through it, to feel it. Madison looked thoughtful.

"I'd love to get my hair washed," she admitted, hesitant. "Are you sure you wouldn't mind doing it?" Just the idea of the intimacy of the act sent her pulse racing. She saw amusement in his eyes, that mouth of his relaxed, corners hitched upward. Being touched, really touched by Travis, sent crazy signals all through her body.

"Naw, piece of cake. I used to wash our quarter horses all the time, scrub them down, clean them up."

Madison laughed softly and shook her head. "I'm hardly a horse, but I get the drift. I'll do almost anything to get that horrible grit out of my hair. It's driving me up a wall."

She was driving him up a wall, but it wasn't her fault. Travis nodded. "Okay, so let me get the bag and ruck over there."

"Do you have a comb? A brush?"

"No brush. But I do have a comb in my ruck."

"Shoot," she muttered. "Even if you did, I can't lift my hands high enough to comb my hair out."

"I'll do it for you."

Madison watched him walk to the bag, pick it up and shake it out. Travis was not only going to wash her hair, but comb it? That sent a streak of heat down her body. She wavered, wishing she could stop wanting him. Travis had done nothing to indicate he wanted her. Except for that look in his eyes. That intense stare, that hunger she swore she felt coming from him, embracing her.

Closing her eyes, Madison wasn't sure if she was going to cry or scream. For the hour he'd been gone, her emotions were flying around and she'd barely held on to them. *Shock.* God, she never realized what shock did to a person until now.

Still, Madison wanted her hair washed no matter what her feelings were doing. As Travis got everything in place, she forced herself to walk over to the pool. He was kneeling next to the ruck, his hands on his long, hard thighs.

"You don't have to do this," she said, giving him an unsure look.

"I *want* to do it." Travis patted the ruck. "Come on, lie down. Head here and I'll hold you."

Madison chewed on her lower lip and finally eased down to her hands and knees on the sleeping bag. "You're sure going above and beyond the call of duty on this one, Travis."

He gave her a bemused look and watched as she lay on her back. "SEALs are used to doing just about anything to survive in the badlands. We think outside the box. I never thought I'd put washing and combing a woman's hair on my list of things I could do."

When she put her head over the ruck, Travis curved

his hand beneath her long, slender neck, cupping the back of her head. At first she was stiff.

"Relax," he urged, picking up an aluminum cup he kept in his ruck.

Madison eyed him worriedly and then dutifully closed her eyes. His gaze moved across her body. Her full breasts definitely gave his T-shirt new meaning. Her nipples pushed against the fabric. Madison was a curvy woman, not a stick-like model. He preferred his women with some meat on their bones, the softness of their curves, molding them beneath his hands.

Shutting off his desire, he absorbed the luxury of guiding her hair into the water, watching the flaxen colors become even darker. Her hair was so long, the strands so thick. He slid his fingers to the nape of her neck, easing the strands outward into the water. God, it was a delicious sensation feeling those smooth, thick strands moving like molten gold across the water, sliding through his fingers like wet silk. He felt himself harden and forced himself to focus. He dipped the cup in the water.

"This is going to be ice cold," he warned her.

"Oh, I already know that." Madison laughed, sliding her hands across her belly and linking her fingers. "I didn't care. It just felt so good to be clean."

Yeah, he knew that one. "Okay, give me your trust," he coaxed. Travis felt her relax more and finally, she allowed him to hold her head and neck fully. *Trust.* He wanted to tell her she shouldn't trust him. Thank God she couldn't read his mind. She'd never have relaxed in his hand at all. As he ladled the water across her head, her breath hitched for a moment.

"Told you it was cold," he said wryly, wetting her

hair. As he looked at the strands beneath the sunlight lancing across the cave, he admired the different colors.

Madison grimaced. "It is, but I'm so grateful you'd do this for me." And she was. His long fingers easily held her neck and her head. The water was stinging and took away from the pleasure she felt with his fingers upon her flesh.

"This will be a story you'll tell your kids someday," he joked, getting her hair completely wet. After setting the cup aside, he took the bottle of shampoo and drizzled it across her head.

"I wish I didn't have a story to tell at all," she admitted, frowning, feeling the stroke of his fingers begin to wreak another kind of magic. Oh! His massaging fingers made her purr. And then, to her consternation, her nipples hardened. *Oh, no.* There was nothing Madison could do about it, the slivers of heat radiated from her head to her breasts and then dove farther down. The man's touch was scorching. Unsettling. Never had Madison felt this way, her body responding hotly to his firm touch.

"I can't blame you for that. You went through hell," Travis said, sad for her, but not missing the hint of attraction between them. Her hair was oozing with bubbles, his fingers sliding across her scalp and he watched as she utterly relaxed, lips parting, enjoying his caress. Once he'd thoroughly cleaned her hair, he began to massage her scalp. His erection was killing him. He ached to shift, to relieve the pain. *Damn.*

"Your hair is so thick. Like a horse's mane," Travis teased, trying to get his mind off his own anatomy. Impossible, but he was going to try.

Madison smiled a little. "Spoken like a true Texas boy."

Laughing, he nodded. "That didn't exactly come out right. You have beautiful hair, thick and silky."

"My mother has thick blond hair. I got lucky and inherited her gene." She wanted to groan with pleasure as he continued to carefully and thoroughly wash her hair. He'd probably take her groan as a sign of pain, not pleasure, so she bit down on her lower lip to keep quiet.

"You doing all right?"

"Umm, yes…it feels…wonderful."

Travis smiled. *Wonderful?* Hell, this was foreplay in his book. Her face went soft, her lips ripened. All he wanted to do was cup her chin, angle her toward his mouth and kiss her until they melted into each other. He quickly rinsed away all the soap, her hair obviously clean even in the pool of water.

"I'm going to ease you into a sitting position and get your hair wrapped up." He grabbed the towel.

Madison sat up as he wound the towel around her long, wet hair. She smiled to herself. His care made her heart open wide with ribbons of happiness. His slight awkwardness was touching to her.

Travis pushed the ruck out of the way, and with one hand on the towel, he got Madison to turn around. "I'm going to lean up against the cave wall and you're going to sit between my legs. I'll dry your hair enough to run a comb through it."

"Okay," she said, her voice a little breathless. She felt him sit down and saw his long, hard legs appear on either side of her. She sensed his heat, smelled him and his hands moving with luxurious slowness to dry her hair. Thick, wet strands fell around her face and shoulders. Madison smiled softly. Travis was all thumbs, but who cared? The fact he'd do this for her made her want him even more.

After placing the damp towel around her shoulders, Travis pulled the comb out of his cammie pocket. Madison sat straight, legs crossed, her hands in her lap. Easing his fingers through that dark blond mass, Travis urged it across her proud shoulders until all of it hung like molten gold between her shoulder blades. He went to work to tame it.

"Start at the ends," Madison told him, "and work your way up."

Travis nodded. "I can take apart my M-4 blindfolded and put it back together again but when I see the tangles and snarls in your hair I don't have a clue." He laughed.

"You're doing fine," she whispered, closing her eyes. Her scalp prickled and tingled with sparks of heat when his fingers accidentally grazed her. It felt so good. So…intimate. So hot. Madison could feel dampness collecting between her thighs and groaned to herself. She wanted to lift her hand and skim it down his hard, long thigh, wanting to feel his muscles leap, feel his response. Did he feel it, too?

Travis forced himself to focus on just her hair. God knew, he wanted to do so much more. And all too soon, her hair lay wet and gleaming, slightly curled, halfway down her back. In a selfish move, he slid his hands beneath the heavy curls and lifted them to his face, inhaling their fragrance. The fire within him expanded exponentially, making him clench his teeth for a moment until he wrestled himself back under control. Gently allowing her hair to lie against her back, he struggled and took in a deep, ragged breath.

"Could you braid it?"

Travis froze for a moment, caught up in the blaze within his body. "Braid?" he managed, his voice gruff sounding.

"I always plait my hair into one long braid. That way it's out of my way." Madison twisted a look over her shoulder. The expression in his eyes was raw, hungry. And just as swiftly, that burning look was gone. Her lips parted and Madison felt suddenly shaky, understanding more was going on than she realized.

"Yeah, I can braid it. Sort of like braiding a horse's tail," he said.

Oh, hell. He'd blown it! Madison's expression told him everything. Travis wrestled inwardly with himself. His desire clashed with his sense of what was right and wrong. And he was acting more like a teenager than a grown, mature man. Worse, she'd caught him at it. So much for SEAL stealth, right? Furious with himself, Travis softened his voice. "Well, maybe not a horse's tail, but you know what I mean?"

Madison wisely turned around. "I know what you mean," she whispered. Unsure, she sat primly, shoulders thrown back, spine straight, hands in her lap. Her heart yearned for him even more now. Madison felt him divide her hair into three thick plaits, confidently weaving her hair into that braid she'd asked for.

"Do you have sisters?"

Travis frowned. "No. Can you tell?" he asked wryly, looking up and seeing her profile and her lips curving.

"No, not really."

"How about you? Sisters? Brothers?" His fingers felt on fire, wanting desperately to maintain contact with her. Travis frowned, knowing he wasn't controlling himself as much as he wished he could. Somehow, Madison had crawled into his heart, his body and innocently staked a claim on him.

"No, only child."

"What will you do once we get you out of here?"

"Go back to the ranch. Tell my parents how sorry I am I screwed this up for them."

Travis always carried string in one of his pockets. He let the braid sit against her back, dug out the string, cut off a piece of it with his KA-BAR and then tied it around the end of her braid to hold it in place. "I think they're going to be far happier to see you home than be angry about it," he told her. "There. Your braid is done."

Madison turned around between his long legs and sat back on her heels. She pushed her damp palms against the cammies she wore. "Thank you. You have no idea how good it makes me feel."

He wanted to feel, all right. Her. Every square inch of her flesh. Explore her. Feel her react to him. Listen to happy sounds caught in her throat as he pleasured her. Travis met and held her sincere and grateful blue gaze.

Madison looked like the girl next door, some shorter curls soft and dried at her temples, giving her a mussed appearance. She needed no makeup. *Nothing.* Her cheeks were flushed pink and that mouth of hers damn near did him in. Forcing himself to get up, Travis said, "Glad to be of help."

Just then, his sat phone beeped, and he leaned over his ruck and picked it up. "I'll be back," he told her, hurrying out of the cave. The rocks prevented a solid link between him and his master chief. There was a tunnel that led outside the nearby cave and he took it. Moving outside, he clicked it on as he saw the sun setting in the west.

"We've got Night Stalkers scheduled to pick you two up at 2000," his master chief told him. He gave Travis the coordinates of where it was going to land.

"Taliban activity must have reduced?" Travis demanded, looking up toward the snow-covered peak far above where he stood.

"Yes. What's her latest medical condition? Is she ambulatory?"

Travis gave him the info. There was no way to hoist her into a helo hovering above the ground. It was going to have to land, which made it even more dangerous for everyone. Taliban could lurk around, and not even a drone could find them unless it had thermal imaging capability.

"We've got drone eyes on the landing zone. Just get her there and we'll get you two to Bagram."

"We'll be there. Out." Travis was tangled with relief and sadness. It was good Madison would be airlifted out, flown to Bagram where she'd get a C-5 flight out to Germany. From there, she could book a commercial flight home. And she'd be gone. Out of his life. Forever.

Turning, Travis sat down on an outcropping watching the sun setting behind the Hindu Kush. The sky was a darker blue, a few clouds turning a bright gold color near the peaks. The same color as Madison's rich, thick hair. Even now, he could remember the sleekness of the strands, the beauty and strength he'd held between his fingers. Rubbing his face savagely, he couldn't figure out what was the matter with him. Six months of enforced abstinence could make anyone a little nuts. So what was different? He sat there chewing through the possibilities like a dog with a bone.

Finally, Travis stared flatly at the rock in front of him, his mouth thinning. It was *her*. It was Madison. Damned if there wasn't some kind of living, breathing, heated connection between them. Was it about sex? Hell, yes. Was it more? Muttering a curse under his breath, Travis stood up, pacing. He was losing his mind over this woman and he hadn't even kissed her!

What to do about it? He stared darkly at the tunnel that led back to the cave. *Do the right thing.* Find out if she felt the same. *Or not.* Travis realized he was about to make an utter fool out of himself. To make it worse, Madison was reeling with shock. She could be drawn to him for all the wrong reasons. Wiping his mouth, Travis gripped the sat phone a little harder and walked back into that tunnel. He had to know one way or another.

Madison was sitting on the sleeping bag, wrestling with one of her rolled-up pants legs, her brow scrunched as she tried to bend the thick material. She lifted her head when she sensed rather than heard Travis come back into the cave. Her heart took a little bounce of fear. He looked disturbed about something. His black brows were down, his eyes narrowed.

"Is everything okay?" she asked, sitting up, leaning against the wall.

Travis placed the sat phone in his ruck. "I don't know, Madison." And he saw her pale. Dammit! "No, everything's fine. We're going to hitch a helo ride tonight at nine o'clock. We'll be taking you back to Bagram air base." He forced his face to relax because he

saw the terror banked deep in her eyes. He came and
sat down, facing her. He placed his arm across her legs
and studied her in the building silence.

"That's good, isn't it?" she asked, feeling the intensity around him. Was it worry? Sadness? Her fingers
curled into her palms because it affected her deeply.
She had strong intuition, had developed it around raising horses and training them. There was torment in his
narrowed green eyes. Something was wrong.

"Yes," he said, trying to relax. "You're almost
home."

She twisted her fingers in her lap. "Thanks to you."
And she reached out because she needed to make a
physical connection with Travis, her fingers touching his arm. His flesh was sunburned, hairy and the
muscles leaped beneath her fingertips. "I wouldn't be
here right now if it wasn't for you, Travis. I owe you so
much. I can't even begin to think of how to thank you."

He picked up her hand, wrapping his fingers around
hers. "Listen," he told her, his voice deep and firm.
"You owe me nothing, Madison. I was just doing my
job. If another SEAL sniper had been closer to the
action, he would have been handed the assignment,
instead. And you would have been in equally good
hands."

She savored the dry strength of his fingers, the
roughness of them as he gently held her hand. Her
heart began skipping beats, her throat growing dry because the look in his eyes was hungry—for her. "You'll
always be my hero," she whispered. "No matter what
you say."

Travis took her hand and placed it on her thigh. Lifting his hand away, he forced out the words that had to

be spoken. "Madison, I need to know if there's something going on between us. I feel it. Sometimes I think I see it in your eyes, your expression, but I'm not sure."

He took a deep breath, feeling as though he had just jumped off a cliff and was headed straight down to his death. "I like you. A helluva lot. I didn't mean to feel like this…it just happened." His mouth flattened and he avoided her gaze. What a coward he was. Travis forced himself to meet her eyes, see the warmth in them. It was enough of a positive sign to get the rest of this out of his craw.

"I know we haven't known each other long. But… what I was thinking…hoping…was once I get rotated back to the States in two months. I'd like to come and see you." His heart was thudding in his chest. His mouth felt dry. Travis had never wanted anything as badly as he wanted Madison and he was afraid of her answer.

"I feel it, too," Madison admitted haltingly. Opening her hands, she whispered, "It was just there, Travis. Between you and me. At first, I didn't know what to think. You said I'd feel rocky emotionally because of the shock." She shook her head and gave him a rueful look. "I don't think what I feel is shock, but what do I know? I've never almost been killed and then rescued at the last minute."

Travis sat very still, his heart wide open, hope sizzling through him. "I wasn't in shock," he said, "and what I was feeling for you had nothing to do with the rescue." It still could from her end and Travis knew it. Searching her face, he could see Madison's sincerity and honesty. He could feel her wrestling, maybe grappling with his admission. Madison had a lot of internal strength. He'd seen it.

Tears burned in her eyes and she gave him a self-conscious look. Her lower lip trembled. "Ever since you rescued me, Travis, all I've wanted is to ask you to hold me, but I was too afraid to do it."

Ah, hell, he was screwed. Without a word, Travis moved next to her, slid his arm gently around her injured shoulders and brought Madison against him. The moment she pressed herself against his chest, her brow resting against his jaw, her hand sliding around his rib cage, a seismic quake rolled through his body. She smelled so damn good to him, sweet with a little spiciness in her damp hair. Her breasts pressed against his chest, her hips nestled next to his. And he surrendered.

"It's going to be all right, darlin'," he rasped against her ear, blond tendrils tickling his nose. Closing his eyes, Travis inhaled her scent as if it was food for his soul. She felt so damn good in his arms, soft, curved, warm and alive. Always aware of her shoulder injuries, Travis held her loosely as she snuggled deeper into his arms, her cheek coming to rest on his shoulder.

He pressed his lips to her drying hair, felt the strength of it beneath his mouth. Felt the warmth of her tears on his T-shirt. Skimming her long, curved back, he whispered sweet, soft words to her, wanting to take care of her. Travis slid his hand across her head, the gesture nonsexual, of one human cherishing another.

He chastised himself silently because he hadn't noticed her need to be held. Blame it on being mission focused, not human focused. SEALs weren't exactly trained to be social workers. Madison made him very aware of being human in every possible way. It was their blazing chemistry that fed the flames of his desire to love her, take her and fuse them into oneness. More than anything, a fierce protectiveness rose in him for her.

Madison's tears finally ceased. She wiped her eyes shakily with her fingers and pulled out of his loose embrace. Feeling sheepish, she gazed up at Travis. His eyes were so green, so filled with life that her breath caught in her throat. She fought for breath.

"Unless you tell me otherwise," Travis told her in a guttural tone, "I'm going to kiss you, Madison."

Her breath released softly and she nodded, taking the lead, leaning forward, lifting her mouth toward his. Nothing, nothing in her life had ever seemed so right as in that moment when his mouth tentatively touched hers. Her hand came to rest against his chest. She could feel the solid thud of his heart beneath her palm. The moment halted and swam heatedly between them at the first brush of his mouth against hers. It was light, almost grazing, eliciting fire within her. And the second time his mouth met hers, it was a little more solid, less tentative, inviting her to respond. As his roughened fingers slid up her jawline, her flesh turned to fire. He angled her mouth just so, and the third time his lips met hers, they curved hotly against them. There was nothing tentative about his kiss this time.

A soft moan caught in her throat as he took her deep, his lips cajoling, asking her to participate fully, not to be shy, but to be bold. Madison lost her mind in the best of ways, melting into the inferno of his kiss that told her so much more than his words ever would. As his tongue lavished one corner of her mouth and then the other, a quiver arced through her.

Madison wanted more, so much more, straining against Travis, wanting to be a part of him, no longer separate from him. He slid his hands upward, trapping her face, moving his tongue slowly into her mouth, sliding against her tongue. Her moan became stronger, and if it hadn't been for the burning pain beginning in her shoulders, Madison would never have wanted the kiss to end. His hands elicited tiny sparks of pleasure along her jaw, his mouth wreaking havoc through her womb and breasts. This man knew how to kiss, knew how to take a woman to her knees and then melt her into him.

"God," he uttered against her lips. "I don't want this to ever end…." Travis's lower body turned to steel, hot steel. He wanted Madison in every possible way but it was the wrong time and place. Afraid that shock was driving her, he didn't want to take her. Instead, he had to have faith that whatever had sprung to life between them was about a helluva lot more than life-and-death sex.

Easing away, Travis opened his eyes, drowning in her turbulent blue gaze. The hunger for him was there. Fierce. Demanding. Her fingers dug into his shoulders, silently pleading with him to finish what he'd started. Travis couldn't. He just couldn't.

"This is going to have to do," he said regretfully, kissing her lightly, wanting more, not daring to go there. "Do you understand, Madison? If I take you now…"

"You're afraid it's about me almost dying? A knee-jerk reaction?"

Travis closed his eyes, rested his brow against hers, holding her face between his hands. "I am. I want more than that, Madison. I want *you*. And I want you when

you've settled down, when this kidnapping is past."
Travis pulled away, searching her moist eyes, looking
down at her wet, glistening lips. "I want to come to you
when you're no longer in shock. When you're whole
again, Madison. I want you to see *me.*"

Gulping, she pulled out of his hands, feeling the
heat of his body, tasting him on her lips. "I…I understand." At least, she was trying to. The pressure,
the ache deep in her body was nearly overwhelming
to her. Madison studied him in the growing, scalding
silence. Yes, whatever they had was still there. Alive.
Vibrant. Filled with promise. "Okay," she choked out.
"I get it. I really do."

"I'll find you," Travis promised huskily, holding her
gaze, probing deep into her eyes, wanting her so damn
badly he could turn the world upside down. "When I
get back to Coronado, I've got sixty days of leave. I'll
come find you." He frowned, his voice dropping, becoming gritty. "That's the only way this is fair to both
of us, Madison. A clean start. No high stakes. No life-
and-death stuff to mess with our heads or skew our
feelings." He slid his thumb across her cheek, pushing
away the tear. "You deserve that and so do I."

Compressing her lips, wanting to kiss him again,
Madison managed a soft, "Yes." And then she wondered if she'd ever see Travis again. The sincere look
in his intense green eyes said she would. "I—I just
don't want to lose you.…"

Chapter 5

Madison wasn't prepared for the dog and pony show she walked into at Bagram air base. A female Navy lieutenant, a public relations specialist, met her as soon as she stepped into the helicopter operations building. Lieutenant Amanda Carter, in her late twenties, gave Madison a quick smile that didn't reach her eyes. Madison was quickly shuttled into a small side room and she was glad Travis was still at her side. He didn't have a happy look on his face as he stood back and let the officer talk with her.

"We've got reporters from around the world wanting to speak with you," the officer told her. "And it's important that you do not discuss who rescued you, or give any names or any details about your rescue."

Madison nodded, casting a swift glance at Travis, who stood by the door, his M-4 across his body, his arm resting casually on it. "I don't want to speak to anyone," she whispered. "I just want to go home." Her heart was pounding in her chest and she felt vulnerable, wanting to escape. She needed Travis for so many reasons, and now Madison felt him being torn away from her.

"I'm sorry, but you're going to have to give a statement. That's why I'm here to help you, Madison. We need to sit down and put something together that you can read from. And you can't take any of their questions even though they'll want more feedback from you."

Madison felt confused. "I'm tired," she told the woman. "I'm really not feeling up to this."

"Ma'am?" Travis said, getting the Navy officer's attention.

"Yes, Petty Officer?"

"She needs to go to the hospital to be examined first." He enunciated it clearly so Carter understood that she couldn't throw Madison to the news wolves who wanted to shred her soul. His eyes hardened and he held the officer's growing scowl. "Do what's best for the survivor here," he told her in a growl, his protectiveness coming to the forefront. "She can talk to the news people later. *If* she wants to."

Carter frowned. "You're dismissed, Petty Officer."

Madison tensed. "Are you leaving?" she asked him, feeling panicked.

"Please give us a moment, ma'am." Travis held Carter's dark gaze.

Carter looked hard at him. She was an officer. He was enlisted. He was supposed to follow her order. But one look in the SEAL's eyes and, no doubt, she knew she'd lost the battle. "All right," she snapped, harried. "Make it fast!" And she huffed out of the room.

Travis made sure the door was locked after the officer left. As he turned, he noticed how pale Madison looked.

"Hey," he murmured, losing his hardness. "It's going to be okay." He put the M-4 barrel down on his left shoulder and reached out, grazing her cheek. "You're in charge here, darlin'. You don't have to do anything you don't want to do."

Her eyes changed, grew less anxious as he stroked her cheek with his thumb. God knew, he wanted to do so much more. If he could, he'd protect Madison, get her to the hospital E.R. for an examination and then hustle her off to someplace quiet, away from the snooping reporters. But Travis couldn't.

"I—I didn't expect this," Madison whispered, reaching out, resting her hand on his forearm. And her heart was tearing open because she knew he was leaving. She didn't want Travis to go. Her emotions were wild. The pressure from the Navy officer made it worse.

"Hey," he rasped, sliding his arm around her, bringing her gently against him, "when that Navy officer comes back in, stand your ground. Tell her to take you to the hospital. And tell her you're not going to speak to any reporters." He gazed down at her upturned face. Tears were in her eyes and he could feel her vulnerability. Travis kept his anger hidden. He needed to help Madison up and over this stressful time. And stress it was. All she wanted was to go home. To feel safe. To be with her parents and have some sort of continuity to her life once again. Leaning down, he kissed her wrinkled brow. "Got it?"

Madison leaned into him, pressing her face against his chest. "Yes, I got it." Her skin tingled where he'd placed a chaste kiss on her brow. Looking up, she melted beneath his warm green gaze, that half smile hooking one corner of his mouth. A mouth she'd kissed. A mouth she wanted to kiss again. "You promise to come see me when you get stateside?"

"I will." His grin widened and he cupped her cheek. "You look like you don't believe me."

His hand was rough and cherishing against her cheek. She pressed her cheek into his palm, closing her eyes for a moment, not wanting to tell him good-bye. "I'm afraid I'll never see you again, Travis." Her voice was unsteady as she lifted her head. The power, the sense of protection, his demeanor all spoke of a confident warrior who wasn't afraid of anything. Or anyone. Not even an officer.

"SEALs are good for any promise they make," he assured her. He had to leave or he'd kiss her sense-less. And Travis knew that Navy officer was probably popping rivets right outside that door about now. "I'll show up, darlin'. You just get your big girl panties on and take charge of your life with that Navy officer. She has to obey *you*. Not the other way around. Okay?"

"I will." She wiped her eyes. "Thank you…thank you for *everything* you did. You put your life on the line for me."

He felt his heart lurch in his chest, wanting to have one more minute with her, knowing it was impossible. "You're welcome. I need to go. That Chinook is waiting for me. I'm expected back at Bravo." He leaned down and gave her a swift, hard kiss. Madison leaned up, her lips hungry, wanting him as much as he wanted her.

Another time. He had to leave. Breaking the kiss, his mouth tingling with the softness of her lips, he drilled a look into Madison's wide, moist blue eyes. "I'll see you in two months. Take care of yourself."

The August heat was rising, even at seven in the morning. Travis had just driven into the Skyline stud farm and met with the manager, Tom Baker. He'd introduced himself and asked if Madison was around. Dressed in a red polo shirt, jeans and cowboy boots, Baker seemed wary about a stranger showing up at this time of the morning. He had no appointment and the owners were out of town. Travis told him that he'd been part of the team that had rescued Madison, and that made all the difference in the world. Tom had pumped his hand, thanking him enthusiastically. Travis nodded and took the man's sincerity for what it was. SEALs liked to keep a low profile and didn't need civilian adulation, and he took the man's gratitude in stride.

Tom had taken him out of the office of the two-hundred-acre farm and pointed to a group of pipe corrals about a quarter of a mile from the office. He said Madison was working there with Odin, the Trakehner stallion. Travis thanked him and climbed into his black Chevy pickup and drove slowly down the gravel road toward a huge area where there were all kinds of corrals, a tack house and a wash station.

He parked by the tack house, a white one-story building with a wooden porch and two rockers. Closing the door quietly, he spotted Madison in the largest oval ring. He pulled his black baseball cap from the seat and settled it on his head.

There was fog lying in the cup-shaped area between

the four small, round hills surrounding the training arenas. He didn't want Madison to see him yet and walked just close enough to watch her. She was dealing with a tall stallion, a blood bay, his reddish-brown coat gleaming in the sun's rays as they crested the hill. The stallion, he guessed, was Odin, the Trakehner breeding stud. His mane and tail were black, as were all four legs from the knees down. The stallion had a large white blaze on his face.

Travis's heart began a slow pound as he angled enough to watch Madison work the stud on a longe line. He smiled a little. She was wearing canary-yellow riding breeches, a short-sleeved cotton blouse and black leather boots that almost reached her knees. She sure had long, beautiful legs.

Her gold hair was caught up in a long braid between her shoulder blades. He felt himself go hard with need of her. His gaze focused on Madison's face. Her expression was one of intensity as the stallion, who was more than a little frisky, bounced, leaped and bucked around in a large circle on the longe line in the sandy arena.

The stallion dwarfed her, which worried Travis. That was thirteen hundred pounds of animal testosterone on four legs and she weighed, what? A hundred thirty or forty pounds? He moved closer, concerned. Studs could be mean. They could turn on a person in a heartbeat. They liked to bite and get their way.

Travis crossed his arms, watching Madison handle that fiery stallion. Her voice was firm and calm, coaxing the horse to trot around in the circle. Odin continued to snort and toss his head. Travis's respect for her grew over the next fifteen minutes as she handled the seventeen-hand stud like a pro. Any concern he had for her vanished. Now he was getting to see Madison for the first time. In her world. Her environment. The look on her face one of rapture because she loved what she was doing.

Even better, he realized she had full use of her arms again, and that was good news. Unable to help himself, he stripped her with his gaze. He appreciated her curviness, knew how good she would feel between his exploring hands.

Some of his desire ebbed as he wondered if Madison would be glad to see him or not. Two months was a long time. And he hadn't contacted her at all, even though, during the time away, she was never far from his mind or his heart.

Travis watched as the stallion wound down. Madison had let him trot and canter, blowing off most of his steam so that he settled down and listened to her. The animal was magnificent, lean as a Thoroughbred, but taller, well muscled with a long, arched neck and a delicate, well-defined head. Odin's small ears constantly flicked, listening to Madison's husky voice, watching her facial expressions and body language. Yeah, it was a living dance between woman and stallion and damned if it wasn't breathtaking.

His mind moved back to those days with her in Afghanistan, the shock that had made Madison emotional and not her real self. The woman he saw out in that arena was in charge. Her confidence was impressive.

Rubbing his chin, having shaved his beard off as soon as he'd arrived stateside, he smiled a little. Yeah, this was going to get interesting now. Was the "old" Madison, the one who was in shock, who had been so drawn to him, still there? He was about to find out.

* * *

Madison was starting to pick up the slack on the longe line, getting ready to put the stallion out into his pasture for the day when Odin jerked his head up and looked toward the gate to the arena. His nostrils flared wide and he whuffed. It was a snort of challenge toward an intruder. What was that all about? Madison turned and glanced in the direction the stallion was intently watching.

A gasp broke from her. Travis! Every cell in her body tingled with shock and then rampant excitement. He was wearing jeans, a polo shirt, the black baseball cap drawn low over his eyes. His walk was loose and casual, hands at his sides as he came down the slope toward the arena.

He'd come! He'd promised he would. Her pulse leaped. As he drew close enough for her to see, his chiseled mouth curved into a lazy grin of hello. She couldn't stop staring. Travis looked so different! The civilian clothes instead of his military gear. Even more breathtaking, he was clean-shaven, revealing just how handsome he really was.

"Hey, you," Travis called, standing at the gate, resting his arms on the pipe rail.

Madison didn't know whether to laugh, cry or run to his arms. When he pushed that cap up to reveal his face, her chest tightened with so many emotions. His green eyes blazed with warmth. Her body went hot, hungry need coursing through her.

"Travis…" she whispered, her attention on the stallion who was glaring at him like he was an unwanted suitor and intruder.

"Better watch that stud," Travis warned her, hooking

his chin toward the blood bay stallion. "I don't think he's too happy to have another male in competition with him." He smiled.

"Oh…yes," Madison muttered, swinging her full attention to Odin.

"Were you taking him out of the arena?" Travis asked, straightening.

"Yes. I'm going to take him over to his pasture. Would you open the gate?"

Nodding, Travis walked over and pulled the long, wide aluminum gate open. "Nice animal. A handful, though."

She felt shaky with excitement. Odin sensed it, lifting his tail and prancing as she shortened the lead on him. "He sure is," she agreed. Travis was standing five feet away from her, looking so damn good. The red polo shirt was like a second skin, revealing his powerful chest and broad shoulders. But it was the warmth in his eyes that made her knees go weak.

Travis closed the gate after they'd walked out of the arena. The stallion was dancing around, eyeing him, snorting. Yeah, he was competition and the horse knew it. *Maybe.* Madison appeared happy to see him, but that didn't mean much. He caught up with her and walked at her side.

"How are you doing?" he asked.

"Okay."

"Your shoulders?"

"Fine. Good as new. How about you, Travis?"

He pulled the cap a little lower to shade his eyes as they halted at another gate to a small, green pasture. "I'm good." He opened the gate for her. Standing aside, he watched Madison lead the stallion into the pasture.

With just her firm voice, she made him stand still as she unhooked the longe line. Once free, the stud leaped away, galloping down the pipe fence, whinnying to his mares, who were in another pasture.

Travis grinned. "He's full of himself. Is he always like that?"

Madison looped the longe line into her left hand and walked out of the gate. "He's being nice this morning."

"Is it because he's hot-blooded?" Travis asked as he shut and locked the gate. The sun glinted on her blond hair. He remembered holding that thick, shining mass in his hands. When she turned and faced him, his throat tightened. He wanted her so damn badly on every level. Maybe in two months she'd met another man? A hundred different rejections came to mind. He shoved his hands in his pockets and fell into step with her as they headed to the tack room.

"He's always like that," Madison said. "Male testosterone unleashed."

"You handled him well." She could handle *him* well, too.

She smiled at him. "Unlike me in the cave, when I was falling apart?" His mouth drew into a slight smile and it sent heat streaking down through her. She'd kissed that mouth of his. Wanted to kiss him again.

Shrugging, Travis opened the door to the tack room for her. "You were in shock." And he could sure as hell tell the difference between then and now. Now Madison was confident, knew her mind, wasn't at all shy or retiring. He liked that fierce warrior look in her blue eyes. She knew her power, knew herself. And damn, that made him want her twice as much as before.

Sunlight shafted through the large window into the

tack room. The wonderful odor of leather and leather soap encircled him. He watched her hang the longe line on a hook on one of the walls. She had the sweetest-looking body, tall, willowy and luscious. He leaned against the door, his arms across his chest, absorbing her into his body, into his heart.

"Yeah," Madison said with a laugh. "I was a mess back then, wasn't I?" She turned, her heart in her throat. The sunlight backlit Travis and he looked powerful, even at ease.

Travis nodded as she walked to within a foot of him. "Now you know what shock does to a person. Unless you actually see it or experience it yourself, you really don't know how it can devastate a person." He saw the reflective look in her blue eyes, gold dappling their depths. How he wanted to kiss her. Something told him to wait. He was a sniper with infinite patience, and she would be worth the wait.

"You're right," Madison said. She turned and said, "I usually go to breakfast at this time. I get all the training done in the early morning because of the heat. Would you like to tag along?"

"Yes. Let me buy you breakfast."

Travis sat opposite Madison in the red leather booth at Tex's Diner. It was filled with patrons and they'd been lucky enough to grab the booth from two departing customers. He sat there, his long legs spread out beneath the Formica table, white coffee mug between his long, spare fingers. Madison wore no makeup, and soft golden tendrils of hair curled around her temples. He smiled to himself, wanting to always remember her just like this.

Madison sipped her coffee, happiness thrumming through her. She still couldn't believe Travis was here. With her. Across the table from her. She wondered if anyone in the diner would ever guess he was a SEAL. Travis blended in, but then, he was a Texas boy and dressed pretty much like everyone else. No cowboy boots or hat, however. He'd taken off his black baseball cap earlier and set it at his elbow. When the waitress, a middle-aged woman with dyed red hair, came over to take their order, she had eyes for Travis. And who wouldn't? The man could pose for the cover of *GQ*.

"Has life settled down since I last saw you?" Travis asked.

Madison nodded and set her cup down, her slender hands moving around it. "After you left me at Bagram I had to get mean with that Navy lieutenant. She about had an aneurysm when I told her I wanted to go to the hospital and not talk to the reporters."

Grinning, Travis said, "Got those big girl panties on."

She laughed and nodded. "Sure did." Becoming serious, she leaned forward, her voice lower and said, "My God, I didn't realize how popular SEALs were until my mother and father started fielding calls from all the big news television shows. They wanted to interview me."

"Did you?" Travis wouldn't know. He wasn't anywhere near a television set.

"Heck, no. I guess I'm shy, Travis. I don't like people looking at me or wanting a piece of me."

So, there was the reticence. He sipped his coffee watching her over his cup. Madison stood out like a buttercup in a dry desert compared to the packed diner full of people. She looked so fresh and natural, and her cheeks were flushed pink. "Good for you."

"I still get calls," she muttered, frowning. "It's none of anyone's business."

"SEALs are naturally gun-shy of news organizations with good reason."

She studied him, drinking in his relaxed face. It was no longer the hard, game face she'd seen in Afghanistan. She lifted her hand and touched his right forearm. "This is new," she said, grazing a five-inch-long pink scar on the outside of his arm. "What happened?"

Her touch was electric. Instantly, his muscles contracted. "Bullet grazed me," he said, seeing real concern in her eyes. "It's nothing."

She wrinkled her nose. "It's something, Travis. It isn't that old."

"Three weeks."

Giving him a worried look, she said, "Are you in pain?"

Yeah, he was, but not there. "No." He wanted to change subjects. "Where's the nicest restaurant here at College Station?"

"Oh, that's The Republic. Very fancy. Why?"

"I'd like to take you to dinner tonight."

Madison's eyes shone with surprise. "Really?"

"It wasn't like I could exactly ask you out over in Afghanistan," he teased her dryly.

She grinned. "Point taken. Did you want to take me out then?"

"Absolutely." Travis held her glistening blue eyes that stole his heart. She was so damned authentic. "Will you?"

"Love to. What time?"

"When do you get off from working at the stud farm?"

"Around six."

"I'll pick you up at say, seven?"

"Could you make it seven-thirty?" She caught her long, thick braid and brought it over her shoulder. "After a day of working sand arenas, my hair needs to be washed."

"Want me to wash and braid it for you?" he teased, smiling. He'd never forgotten that night. Didn't ever want to.

"Not this time." She raised her arm. "I got full range of motion now."

Maybe another time. He hoped.

Madison nervously smoothed down the black jersey dress for the tenth time. She'd taken great pains with her hair, taming it, getting the curls to behave over her shoulders. Her heartbeat was high and she looked critically in the full-length mirror one more time. The black jersey clung lovingly to her figure in soft folds, the neckline just above the swell of her breasts. Her mother had given her a strand of Tahitian black pearls at her last birthday, and tonight, along with the earrings, she was going to wear them. She felt magical. Transported. The length of the dress was just above her knees and a slender gold metal belt gathered around her waist. Wearing two-inch heels was plenty for her, and she thought she looked okay.

The doorbell rang.

Her stomach clenched. Hurrying out of the bathroom, Madison grabbed her black leather purse and an angora shawl her grandmother had made for her long ago. It was black with fine, thin threads of gold woven through it. Heart in her throat, Madison gulped a breath and opened the door.

"Oh, you look nice," Madison murmured, her eyes widening. Indeed, to say that Travis cleaned up nicely was barely scratching the surface. He stood in a pair of tan chinos, a white shirt, the collar open at his throat, and a dark blue sportcoat.

Travis nodded. "Darlin', I don't have a thing on you." She looked gorgeous, that generous cloud of blond hair so thick and softly curving over her shoulders, almost touching the tops of her breasts. "That dress really shows you off," he said, his throat tightening. He felt as though he was looking at a movie starlet, not a horse trainer. And her legs. He was in such trouble, gazing down at her slender legs, those delicate ankles, firm calves, that he swallowed hard. Who knew? Her neck was elegant and he wanted to place a series of kisses along that point pulsing beneath her skin. The black pearls accentuated her throat.

"Thanks," she whispered, suddenly shy. Travis made her feel feminine. Beautiful. "I'm ready. Are you?"

Groaning to himself, Travis wanted to step into her condo, shut the door, lift her into his arms and haul her directly to the bedroom. He was more than ready. But not for what she had in mind. His mouth curved and he cupped her elbow. "Let's go."

Madison watched how the low lighting at the restaurant made Travis's angular features look dangerous. The Republic had mahogany walls with gold interspersed here and there. The blond wooden floors lightened the popular restaurant. He'd gotten a booth in

the corner so that they could look out over the patrons
and other tables. He'd ordered a house-made beer and
she had a glass of pinot grigio, her fingers around the
long-stemmed wine glass. She felt the heat from his
body sitting barely twelve inches away from her and
hungrily absorbed his nearness. Her nerves dissolved
as the evening blossomed.

"I feel like I'm in a time warp," she admitted softly,
holding his gaze. "Two months ago I was sitting on the
floor of a dirty cave with you. Now, here we are again,
clean, looking beautiful and going out to eat." She saw
him nod and consider her words.

"It will probably take you some time to not feel like
half of you is still back there and half is over here."

"Is that what it's like for you?"

"All the time."

"How do you live with it, Travis?"

His eyes grew distant at her question, and then he
took another drink of the frosty beer.

"With time, you adjust."

"How many times have you been over there?"

"Just finished my third rotation." He noticed the
pained look in her eyes. Sympathy, maybe? Madison
was so readable. And he wanted to kiss that soft mouth
of hers. Travis almost gave in to his desire but stopped.
He didn't want to sway Madison one way or another.
She was a Texas gal. If she wanted something, she'd
go after it.

"Do you ever get used to it?"

"What? Going overseas?"

"All of it. I just got a bare taste of it and some nights,
I wake up screaming." She avoided his sharp look and
took a sip of her wine.

"PTSD," he grunted. "Welcome to our world. It sucks."

"Do you have it?"

He grinned. "Most SEALs get it because of our training, Madison."

"Does it ever go away?"

"Maybe…over time. I still have nightmares from my first tour." *When I almost died.* But he didn't say anything more. The world of a SEAL was top secret. He'd taken a bullet to his left side and damn near lost a kidney. An AK-47 bullet hit him in the side where he had not slid in a ceramic plate on his Kevlar vest. Luckily, he'd pulled through. He saw her expression change. Maybe sadness. "Why do you ask?"

"I can see how badly I'm handling coming down from that trauma. I can't imagine what you guys go through for six months at a time."

"Darlin', we weren't kidnapped, either. SEALs take the fight to the enemy. We're the ones putting them in a hurt locker, not the other way around. So stop looking sad, okay?" He leaned over, pressing a kiss to that cloud of blond hair. Travis couldn't keep his hands off her. It was impossible. He caught the fragrance of jasmine-scented shampoo. He'd held that hair, felt its strength, seen the sunlight glance off the strands. She turned, her dark blue eyes soft. She wanted to kiss him. Groaning inwardly, Travis tried to tell himself to wait. But Madison, being a Texas gal, had made up her mind.

"I'm going to kiss you," she told him firmly, almost a warning. She leaned over, pressing her mouth against his. He seemed removed, maybe detached from her since they'd sat down. She wasn't sure why, but her heart told her to kiss him silly and see if it affected him at all.

His mouth melted beneath hers. As she felt his swift intake of breath, she closed her eyes, sliding her hand over his shoulder, wanting more contact with him. His response was warm, exploratory. She inhaled his scent before pulling away. Bare inches between them, her hand on his chest, she asked him softly, "Why did you come here?" Instantly, his eyes narrowed.

"I promised you I'd come and see you, Madison." Travis wasn't sure he wanted to tell her the rest of the truth, that he'd never forgotten her, that she inhabited his dreams in the best of ways, that a day didn't go by when he didn't think about her. Or want her in his bed. In his arms. He wasn't sure if he saw disappointment in her expression or not. She nibbled on that soft lower lip of hers and he ached to haul her into his arms and kiss her again.

"We need to catch up," she said, seriousness in her husky voice. He hadn't moved, his gaze locked on her. "I'm afraid you're here only because you promised." Her voice faltered. "Not because you *want* to be here."

His mouth curved ruefully. "Then let me remedy that wondering of yours." He reached out, drawing her gently into his arms. Travis wanted to give her a chance to pull away, or tell him if she didn't want to kiss him. Instead, her eyes turned an even darker shade of blue as she lifted her hands and slid them around his neck. His heart hammered with relief while he touched her lips. With feeling. She pressed herself against him and there was no question in Travis's stunned mind that she wanted him as much as he wanted her.

A moan rose in Madison's throat as she molded her

mouth firmly against his. She didn't want just a faint kiss, she wanted all of him. His mouth scorched hers, his arms anchoring her hard against him. She felt her breasts pressed against his chest, her fingers roaming of their own accord up the nape of his neck, sliding deliciously into his short black hair. His tongue moved sensually against hers, the pleasure of his mouth making her feel limp with need. His breath was warm, ragged against her cheek and his long fingers caressed her hip, pulling her against him, letting her know just how much he wanted her. Another sound caught in her throat as she strained against him.

Slowly, so slowly, Travis reluctantly eased away from her wet lips. They were breathing unevenly as he loosened his grip on her, allowing her to sit up. He saw the burning desire in Madison's blue eyes. "I guess that invisible thing we had back in Afghanistan is still with us." He smiled. She had felt so damn good in his arms.

"It never left me," Madison admitted, her voice husky with desire.

"It didn't me, either." Travis studied her in the growing silence. "I came because I *wanted* to see you, Madison. Not just a friend visiting. It's more than that, but I didn't know if you still felt the same way about me."

She reached up, touching the hard line of his jaw. "I'm glad, because I can't tell you how much I've missed you, Travis, missed your thoughts, the way you see the world." She gave him a bemused look. "You have no idea…." Because her dreams were of him nearly every night. Her worries for him. Wondering if he would show up here or not, and never wanting anything more in her life than for him to come and visit her.

Grazing her flushed cheek with his thumb, Travis leaned down and kissed her tenderly. "I was hoping you felt like I did. But I didn't know, Madison." Until this moment. Euphoria flowed like bright ribbons through him, dissolving his worry, his questions.

Madison pressed her cheek into his open palm, feeling the inherent strength of Travis, his gentleness toward her. "Tell me you're going to stay a little while." She looked up, holding his intent gaze.

"I'll stay as long as you want, darlin'." Travis wouldn't push her, wouldn't try to corral her or force her into anything. The control was in her hands, not his, where it should be. He saw a wicked expression come over her face.

"As long as I want?"

He smiled, liking the impishness in her eyes. "Yes."

She took his hand. Hers was swallowed up by his. "That's good to hear because I have a million questions I want to ask you about yourself. It's going to take a long time...."

Chapter 6

As Travis led Madison up the walk toward her condo, it was nearly midnight. She was content to lean against his body, his arm around her shoulders. The lights were low and the flowers along the walkway made it seem almost mystical to her. Her head rested against his shoulder. She'd never felt happier.

"How many questions did we get out of the way?" Travis asked her.

She laughed softly. "Fifty?"

"Do you know me any better than before?" He looked down to see her smile. He wasn't sure what Madison was going to do when they reached the door to her condo. He wanted to make love to her. That one kiss hours earlier had sent him into an aching hell of desire.

"Yes. I loved all the stories you told me about your growing-up years on your dad's ranch. I especially loved the tricks you and your brothers played on one another." His hand gently touched her shoulder. The soft angora didn't stop Madison from feeling the heat of his fingers against her upper arm. She lifted her face to his. In the shadowy light, his eyes glittered and Madison could feel him wanting her. Her mouth still tingled in memory of that kiss in the restaurant.

Travis halted at her door and turned her toward him, his hands on her shoulders. Her hair looked like spun gold in the light of the lamp above the red door. Never had he wanted to make love to a woman more. That black dress draped in all the right places, made him crave her with an intense hunger. It was her, he realized. Inside, she was part wild horse, part natural woman and her heart was as open as the wide sky over Texas. He lifted his hand and brushed her cheek, his voice low.

"What do you want to do, Madison? I can kiss you good-night at this door, if that's what you want."

She felt her entire body vibrating with anxiety and anticipation as his callused fingers softly explored her cheek, his eyes narrowed upon her, as if he were the hunter and she the quarry. It was a breathtaking sensation. "What do you want, Travis?" His mouth curved faintly.

"Darlin', this is on you. I came to see you because I want a relationship with you. I have no idea if that's what you want. If it isn't, then I'm going to kiss you good-night and I'll see you over at the stud farm tomorrow morning to share time and space with you." His voice lowered. "But if you want more with me, Madison, it's in your hands to make that call." Her darkened blue eyes softened.

Her voice came out husky with emotions. "Travis, from the moment I met you, I knew there was something special between us. It was more than physical." And then she gave him an embarrassed look and added, "Not that I didn't want you to kiss me, not that I didn't want to make love with you, because I did." Her brows fell and she slid her hand over his shirt, feeling his skin tense, the muscles leap beneath her exploration. "I can't explain it. I've tried for two months now to figure it out and I haven't." She searched his dark eyes. "Part of me is afraid, Travis. I know your job is dangerous. I realize now you'll be gone more than you'll be home. I know what it felt like to be torn away from you there at Bagram, being lonely for two months without you in my life."

He heard her fears and he'd heard them before. Anguish flared in Madison's eyes. "I didn't want to leave you there at Bagram," he managed, his voice strained. "It was the last thing I wanted to do, Madison. But I couldn't stay. I had orders to return to Bravo."

Nodding, she dragged in a breath of air. "I worry you'll be hurt." She slid her hand around his lower right arm, the material beneath her fingertips. "That bullet wound…"

He nodded. "And watching you with that stallion this morning scared the hell out of me."

She frowned and searched his shadowed face. "What?"

Travis smiled and cupped her cheek. "You were dealing with a fractious, unpredictable thirteen-hundred-pound piece of horseflesh that could have killed you on a bad day. But you don't see your job, what you love to do, that way, do you?"

"No…I don't see that."

"Be in my boots. See what I'm seeing, Madison. That was one powerful stallion. I know studs. We have a couple on my dad's ranch. They're nothing to mess with and you have to be aware around them all the time or bad things can happen fast."

"Okay," she murmured. "You're saying my job, which I love to do, is no less dangerous than yours?"

"I'm trying to draw a parallel," he told her quietly. "I'll grant bullets aren't flying and you're not out hunting the bad guys, but working around horses isn't much safer, either."

"And so," Madison said, holding his warm gaze, "you're saying that you'll worry about me as much I'll worry about you?" She wanted to reach up and touch that chiseled mouth of his with hers.

"I'm saying that life isn't assured for any of us, darlin'. We can either run from life, from living because we're scared or worried about what might happen, or we can acknowledge our fear, but follow our hearts. Does that mean it's going to be easy? No."

"Your marriage taught you that?" A flash of pain came onto his face for a moment. Madison realized she had to get beyond her own fear of losing Travis.

"It did. My wife wasn't willing to take the risks. Before I married her, I tried to explain what it meant to be a SEAL, to be gone for long periods of time. But, frankly, most people can't take that kind of on-again, off-again lifestyle." He studied her, hearing the crickets and frogs singing in the night. "Madison, I want to make love with you so damned bad I can taste it, but I'm not willing to push this. I lost a woman I loved very much because I did. I'm not willing to go that route again."

She felt his heartbreak, the pain that the relationship had caused him. Was she up to taking such a huge risk with her heart? Could she wait months without seeing Travis again? Her fingers curved gently against her palm where it rested on his chest. Lifting her chin, she said in a whisper, "I've never lived my life scared, Travis. I'm not starting now...." She broke away, dug for her key in her purse and opened the door. Taking his hand, she said, "Come in."

Travis took off his sport coat and hung it over the back of the chair in the kitchen. He watched Madison put the purse on the granite-topped island and turn to him. All he saw in her expression was yearning for him. He walked over to her, sliding his fingers through that mass of gold hair, watching her eyes turn cloudy with desire.

"Okay," he rasped, "I need to know if you're protected or not?"

She nodded. "I'm on the pill." Her whole body felt hot and shaky inside. Travis was serious, looking into her eyes, reading her, making sure this was what she wanted. "No STDs," she added.

"I'm clean, too. But I'll wear a condom if you want."

She touched his jaw. "You aren't the type to lie, Travis. Remember? I was with you in Afghanistan. I saw you in a lot of different situations and always, you were honest with me."

"Brutally so, sometimes," he said, smoothing tendrils of hair away from her eyes.

"I trust you," Madison quavered. "Because you

saved me from dying. It doesn't get any more real than that, Travis. It never will."

"Yeah," he admitted. "You're right."

"Come on." She picked up his hand and led him through the living room, down a carpeted hall to her bedroom. She felt wildly excited, scared. But Madison wanted to take this step with him. As she turned on a small lamp on her cherry dresser and faced him, she knew this was what she wanted, risk or not.

Travis gently unhooked the string of pearls from around her throat. As they fell into his hand, he placed them on the dresser, leaned down and pressed his lips to her throat. He felt her wild pulse beneath his mouth and smiled, sliding his hands to the zipper of her dress. The jersey was soft, pliant, and as he slowly pulled the zipper down to the small of her back, she trembled. It sent an ache through him; his erection was hard, pressing against his pants.

His mouth went to her ear after she'd removed the pearl earrings. He inhaled the sweet scent of her flesh, pushed aside the thick strands of her hair as he nibbled one of the lobes. Madison's breath hitched and she pressed against him, her breasts against his chest. Groaning, Travis eased the black jersey fabric aside. Her shoulders were beautiful and he kissed her slender neck and then slowly moved his lips across it, feeling her tense and sigh. Her fingers dug into his chest as he lowered his mouth to her collarbone.

Yeah, she liked this slow seduction because he wanted to taste every part of her, brand it into his body, his memory and his heart. This was a woman to be worshiped, not rushed into bed. They had all night and as he moved his tongue between her breasts, he heard her moan. She was so sensitive. So hot.

Easing away, he helped her out of the dress, appreciating the black lace bra and very lacy, but skimpy, panties. She got rid of her heels. Her long, shapely legs sent him into a new hunger. He wanted to explore those legs of hers, feel them beneath his hands, feel her respond to his touch.

Madison sighed as she took the dress and hung it over a small chair. Turning, she began to unbutton his shirt. "No fair that you're still dressed," she said, smiling up at him. His green eyes were intense, black pupils large, on her, as if he were eating her up. Her knees went weak beneath that smoldering look.

Her fingers brushed his chest and every time, Travis tensed, the sensations like hot spikes of fire diving down between his legs. As she opened his shirt, she leaned forward, placing her lips on his chest. Gritting his teeth, he welcomed her participation but she was testing his control.

"You are so beautiful," Madison whispered, taking the shirt off and smiling as it dropped to the floor. His chest was dusted with soft black hair and she saw a dark line move downward, disappearing beneath the waistband of his pants. When she ran her fingers softly through the hair, he tensed.

"No," he growled, "you're the beautiful one." He took her lips and skimmed his mouth across hers. Travis was going to kiss her more deeply but her fingers went to his belt and he froze for a moment. Smiling against her lips, he rasped, "You're one brave soul."

She grinned and opened the belt, finding the zipper,

feeling his erection straining against the material. "I handle stallions, remember?"

Travis laughed and murmured, "You're a Texas woman through and through, Madison." He groaned as she brushed her hand against his erection. She pulled his pants off his narrow hips.

"We're not wimpy," she agreed, breathless as she watched him remove his trousers. "I've been dreaming of doing this for two months."

Travis saw the twinkle in her blue eyes, saw the heat in them. "I like a strong woman and you're all of that, darlin'." He shed his boxer shorts while she removed that sexy black bra. Her breasts were heavy, perfect, and as she dropped the bra to the floor beside his clothes, he slid his fingers down beneath the elastic of her lacy panties. He eased them downward, caressing her hips, watching her eyes shutter, her lips parting with pleasure. In moments, she'd left the panties with the rest of the clothes.

Her breasts grew firm as she stood fearlessly naked before him. There was no question Travis wanted her. What she hadn't expected was for him to scoop her easily into his arms and carry her to the bed. Pleasure radiated from her hardened nipples when they tangled in the soft hair of his chest. In moments Travis had deposited her on the king-size bed. The coolness of the silk coverlet juxtaposed with the feverish heat of her skin. He lay beside her, his length against hers.

"I want the light left on," he told her, holding her drowsy, lust-filled gaze. "I want to see you, see how you look when I love you…."

"Mmm," she managed as his fingers trailed slowly, achingly, from her neck to her shoulder, and then his hand cupped her breast. Madison didn't care about the light. He made her feel beautiful, desired. She wanted Travis in her, wanted to feel him in every way, wanted to soar with him like two eagles mated for life.

Sliding her hand to his jaw, feeling the sandpapery quality of it, she pulled him down, needing his mouth on hers. At the same moment, his thumb brushed against her nipple, sending jolts of electricity down to her clenched womb. A softened cry of delight drowned beneath his hungry, searching mouth. She sank into the power of him as a man, arching against his hips, feeling the hard press of his erection against her softer belly. A hundred wild, skittering flames erupted through her and she became lost in the magic of his hands and his mouth.

Yes, this was what she'd dreamed of, what she wanted, and Madison surrendered to him in every way.

Travis eased her onto her back, his fingers tunneling through her tangled hair, holding her down so he could stare into her drowsy eyes. He smiled at her, his gaze drinking her in, his eyes glittering with a hunger that spurred her to move strongly against his hips.

"Tonight's for you," he said thickly. "A woman always comes first...." He brought her hand to his lips, kissing each finger, watching her eyes grow a deeper blue, those gold highlights appearing in their depths. Yeah, he wanted to please her, let her know just how much he cared for her and wanted to please her. Tonight, he wanted Madison so damned satiated that she wouldn't recover for hours afterward. He had a plan, he'd had two months of thinking about her, about what he was going to share with her. "Okay?" he demanded, his voice dropping to a growl as he eased her wrist above her head, holding it there with his one hand.

"Okay…" she said, her voice wispy, filled with desire. "But you can't stop me from wanting you. I'm not going to just lie here, Travis."

He grinned. "Oh, darlin', I want you to participate all you want, but just remember, you're mine and I'm going to love you thoroughly first…."

His roughened words of warning did nothing but make her feel the heat ramping swiftly through her lower body. Travis had barely touched her, and she felt the dampness already collected between her thighs. She nodded and he brought her other hand above her head. His hand was so large he could hold her captive with just one. And as his fingers traveled from her shoulder, tracing the curve of her breast, Madison uttered a sigh and closed her eyes, arching into him, wanting his hand on her taut, achy breast. The man knew how to tease her to distraction, and her breath grew uneven as she felt the moistness of her breath hover above her tightening nipple

Madison moaned and twisted against his hard, unforgiving body. He held her firmly, capturing her nipple between his lips, suckling her, moving his fingers down across her rib cage as she cried out. Never had she wanted anyone to touch her like she wanted Travis to touch her. His teeth tugged gently upon her nipple at the same time he caressed her inner thigh, feeling how wet she was. A soft cry tore from her lips, her back arching demandingly against his exploring hand as he moved to her rim, testing her.

"You are so wet," he rasped, licking her between her breasts, feeling her chest heave, her breath coming in broken, soft gasps. And she was so wild, so wanting, unable to lie still beneath him, twisting, demanding. Releasing her wrists, he settled his knees between her thighs, kneeling, watching her erratic breath, her lips swollen from his kiss, her fingers seeking him. Travis smiled and moved his hands down along her firm, curved thighs.

"Your legs are incredible," he rasped, feeling her flesh tense, watching her lush hips move as he focused on them. "Riding does incredible things to your body, darlin'." Travis met her half-closed, lust-filled eyes. Riding strengthened every pelvic muscle in a woman's body, made her butt firm, her belly taut, her legs like soft, warm steel beneath his exploring fingers. He opened her wider, trailing his fingers from her rib cage, leaning over, licking her belly, feeling her tense and moan. The anticipation made him ache.

Lying down between her legs, he began a slow series of kisses, licks, soft nips of her flesh as he lavished her right inner thigh. He heard Madison whimper, her fingers digging frantically into his thick shoulders. Yeah, she was liking it. He smiled and began to kiss the inside of her left thigh. Her fragrance filled his lungs, sending scorching fire down to his throbbing shaft.

Madison's breath jerked into her lungs as he kissed her intimately. A shudder of impatience worked through her as she felt him teasing her core. Moaning in frustration, she rubbed her hips against his exploring mouth, wanting more, much more. His roughened hands slid beneath her hips, drawing her upward, drawing her closer to his mouth. *Please, just be inside me, just...*

And his tongue explored her, seeking and finding

that tight knot of nerves. A low, guttural sound jammed in her throat. She arched powerfully against Travis, felt him grip her hips, holding her captive while he moved deeper into her, eliciting white hot reactions from her trembling body. Her orgasm built in the heat of his mouth, his breath. As he moved a finger within her, she started to come apart, a soft cry tearing out of her. Her muscles contracted violently and she felt scorching heat surrounding his fingers. His lips gave her wave after wave of intense, mind-melting pleasure.

Travis eased himself from her and placed slow, wet kisses up across her tight belly, following the damp heaving of her torso and chest. Finally, he captured one nipple with his mouth, suckling her strongly, feeling her starting to fly apart in his hands once more.

Madison opened her eyes, her breathing ragged, watching the smile in his eyes, that hunterlike intensity.

"That was wonderful." She sighed.

"We're not done, darlin'," Travis rasped, taking her mouth. He thrust slowly into her, felt her arch hard against him, a low, animal cry knotting in her throat. Yeah, he wanted to hear those sounds. It told him everything as he moved his tongue boldly against hers, opening her mouth, deepening the kiss, demanding her response.

She gripped his shoulders, wrapping her legs around his waist, pulling him more deeply within her. This woman was going to kill him with pleasure, but what a way to die.

Travis tore his mouth from hers, feeling her drink him into her wet, tight body. He didn't want to hurt her, didn't want to come so damn quickly. Teeth clenched, he moved more slowly, hearing the frustrated mewls in her throat because he kept such a languid pace. The heat built and the scalding fire of her body surrounded him.

He was tormented by her continued hip thrusts, forcing him to move, to reach so deep, to touch that magical spot that would automatically trigger her release. He felt his control shredding with her assertiveness, pushing him to his absolute limit. Thrusting, establishing a faster rhythm, he heard Madison give a cry of need, her fingers gripping the thick, hard muscles of his shoulders, silently asking. Her body demanding.

Moisture and heat built around him as he thrust, hearing her sigh, feeling her body begin to contract, tightening around him. The sweat came down his temples, the heat and dampness building as they were locked together. He heard her cries, her pleas to take her, to give to her. Oh, hell, he was in so much trouble from her bucking hips, her strength as powerful as his.

Travis took her hard, drove deep, feeling her hips meet, meld hotly with his own. And just as he felt her orgasm explode within her, his own release rolled torturously out of him. He clenched his teeth, his face pressed against her neck and shoulder, breathing raggedly, his hands gripping the covers on either side of her head. A shudder rolled through him as she cried out, frozen in the feverish deluge of the orgasm rupturing through her. The moment gripped him, her jasmine-scented hair tangled against his straining face, the sweat created by them as they moved against each other.

Resting his damp brow against Madison's, his tone was guttural. "Woman, you could make a grown man cry. You are amazing…." Travis caught her mouth, kissing her deeply. His whole body thrummed with fever and satiation. He eased his mouth from her wet, swollen lips, gazing into her barely opened eyes, soft with satisfaction. With happiness. He felt pride in being able to please her. Felt his heart open up, sending feelings through him he'd never felt before. When her mouth curved, he smiled with her. She was soft and lush beneath his hard body and he absorbed her like sunlight.

Madison gave him a weak smile, barely able to lift her hand and touch his jaw. The burning light in his eyes made her feel good. She almost said, *I love you,* but knew it was far too soon. But she did love Travis. She had from the moment she'd seen him. Her heart was bursting with love for him and she hoped it had translated through her loving him with her body, her hands and mouth.

"I'm amazing?" she murmured. "*You're* amazing, Travis." She held his warm gaze, seeing so many emotions in his face. "I've never felt like this. It's… I don't have words for it."

Travis lay on his side, drawing Madison into his arms, against his body. She snuggled into his embrace, her head against his jaw and shoulder. "We're good together, no question," he said, his voice roughened. He kissed her temple, her cheek and saw that flush across her naked body. It was a physical testament to him being able to please her and it made him feel damn good as man.

"I'm so sleepy," she whispered, sliding her arm across his torso.

"Then sleep," Travis murmured, relaxing. The last thought he had as he drifted off with Madison in his embrace was that he loved her. Would he ever be able to tell her? He had two months to find out. And he was going to show her in a hundred different ways just how much he did and how much he wanted her to be a permanent part of his life.

Chapter 7

"What are you thinking?" Travis asked Madison. They rocked gently on the porch swing as the morning sun rose over the hills. Madison had just finished putting Odin through his paces and led the frisky stallion to his paddock for the day. She wore a pink short-sleeved blouse that hid her beautiful breasts. Even now, he felt himself growing hard, wanting her. Their days were spent in hard work on the stud farm and their nights in each other's arms. Travis had never felt happier. He leaned over, kissing her mussed hair. The long gold braid lay across her shoulder.

"That tomorrow you're going to have to leave," Madison admitted miserably and looked up into his eyes. She couldn't keep the sadness out of her tone. She'd been dreading this day.

Travis moved his fingers over her shoulder as if to

calm her. Every day she wanted to tell him she loved him. Every time he loved her, she wanted the words to tear out of her mouth. Yet, he'd never whispered them to her. The way he made love to her, she couldn't believe he didn't feel something deep, something profound with her. Did he want to simply walk away? Her heart ached and she pressed her face into his shoulder, eyes shut, feeling the sting of tears behind her lids.

His other arm went around her, holding her gently, rocking them in the swing. Madison knew it could happen. That Travis would leave and never come back. He could be killed. He could have used her and walked away. Her heart sensed differently. She'd seen the struggle in his face sometimes, at odd moments when she happened to look up and catch those fleeting expressions. What *was* Travis thinking? It was so hard to pry feelings out of him. Why should she expect he was any different than any other man? She inhaled his scent deep into her lungs, nuzzling against the fabric across his chest, never wanting to let this moment go. Never wanting to let Travis go.

Travis caressed her hair. The sunlight was catching strands of it, making it look like melting gold. Her arm went around his torso and she held him tightly, as if she were losing him.

"We need to talk," he whispered against her hair, resting his chin on her head. "Do you want to do it here? Or over at the diner?"

Madison squeezed him a little closer. "No," she said, her muffled voice strained. "I'd rather talk here, Travis." She tried to prepare herself. Tried to behave like a grown-up and not a scared teenage girl losing her puppy love. It was so hard not to cry, not to break down in front of Travis. And, God knew, she'd cried often enough when he wasn't around. Tears of goodbye.

His heart clenched with pain when he heard the tremble in Madison's voice. *Damn.* Travis frowned and gave her a little squeeze. "I want to ask you one question," he rasped against her hair. "Just one…" His heart picked up in a fearful beat. What would Madison say?

Forcing herself to look up, Madison drew in a breath, her heart wide open "What?" she whispered.

Travis smoothed several tendrils from her brow, saw the pain in her blue eyes, the soft tremble of her lower lip. He was sure she thought he was going to walk out of her life. "I love you, Madison. And I want to keep you in my life. I'm not sure you love me. I think you do, but I've got to hear it from you." He gave her an anxious look, nervous and tense. "Tell me." His hand stilled on her shoulders, watching her.

"You…love me? Really?" She anxiously searched his face, the well-shaped mouth that had loved her so thoroughly. "Travis?"

"I do, darlin'. Ever since I laid eyes on you after I pulled that hood off your head. I fell for you lock, stock and barrel right there in Afghanistan."

It felt as if someone had stolen the breath from her body. Madison's eyes rounded with surprise. The first tendrils of joy thrummed through her. "Oh, Travis…"

"So, it's mutual, then?" he teased her gently, smoothing strands away from her temple.

"Mutual? Yes, it is." Madison just stared at him, tears flooding into her eyes.

"And you'd wait for me even though you know I'll be gone a lot of the time?"

She nodded. Tears drifted down her cheeks. "Y-yes,

I'd do it, Travis." She wiped them away with trembling fingers. "Something is better than nothing. And in the last two months, I've never been happier." She stared hard at him. "What about you?"

"Never happier," he admitted, hating to see her tears. He'd heard the words he needed to hear more than anything else.

Travis had gotten to know Madison on so many levels. They worked well together. It was a joy watching her train and ride those beautiful warm-blooded horses. They laughed often and rarely had arguments, although when a situation came up, they sat down like adults and hashed it out. The days and weeks had flowed like sweet, warm honey into a quiet, productive teamwork.

Her parents accepted him without judgment, were grateful for his background in horses and seemed happy that Madison was happy to have him in her life. So was he.

"Listen, I need to fess up on some things," Travis admitted, removing the tears from her cheeks with his thumbs. "I couldn't say anything until now, Madison. Until I knew you loved me as much as I love you."

"What things?" she asked, her voice hoarse with tears. His eyes changed, grew distant for a moment. And then, she felt Travis open up to her, become available once more. Over the past two months, he would sometimes detach or go away from her. She wasn't sure what it meant or what caused it. Sometimes, she thought Travis was remembering his friends who had died, the firefight where he'd nearly lost his life. In those moments, she wanted to be there for him but he wouldn't let her. Maybe it was because he was a SEAL. Or a sniper. She was never sure. And those moments didn't last long and always, when he came back, he was fully present for her, a team member again.

"My military contract is up in eighteen months." Travis saw her confused look. "It means that if I don't want to reenlist, I can walk away from being a SEAL in the Navy and become a civilian again." Her eyes widened with realization. "I'm okay with getting out if you want me to get out, Madison." His voice deepened. "I want a life with you. And I don't want to put you through it with me as a SEAL. I lost one marriage to the fact I couldn't be home hardly at all." He reached out, stroking her cheek. "I *want* to be around you. I want to share my life with you, darlin', not be half a world away fighting the bad guys. I've done my share of doing that, giving the Navy eight years of my life."

Madison sat there feeling relief flood through her. His guttural tone rifled through her, sweet and hot. His gaze was narrow on her and she felt his invisible, caressing touch. His love. "I can't see my life without you in it, Travis," she said, opening her hands. "I've grown so used to having you with me." She managed a shy smile. "We get along so well, in so many ways."

He laughed a little. "Especially in the bedroom. And the kitchen. And out riding horses on a picnic and making love on the old, tattered blanket in a grove of live oak." His mind ranged over their many creative ways to love each other. Madison was fearless, and God help him, he loved her for that. He saw her blush and look around, hoping the hired help did not overhear their private conversation.

"Well," she said archly, "more than just the bed, Travis." And then Madison relented. "You are an incredible lover." She reached out, twining her fingers between his scarred ones.

"Thank you, but I happen to love a woman who sets me on fire, burns me up and makes me feel like cinders afterward." He grinned over at her, his voice teasing. She blushed even redder, if that was possible. In some ways, Madison was old-fashioned and Travis was glad. She was loyal to those she loved. He'd seen it between her and her parents. Madison had a large, giving and sympathetic heart. Travis had felt that love showered shamelessly upon him, and was all the better for it.

He lifted her hand, brushing a kiss across her knuckles. "I want to marry you, Madison. Not now, but I figure in the next eighteen months we'll be able to continue to know one another. I'll come here every chance I get. We'll spend those days or weeks together. We'll keep plumbing each other's depths in every way. What do you think?"

"I agree," she murmured. "You'll be stateside, thank God. And you won't have to deploy to Afghanistan again. You have no idea how that lifts a weight off my heart."

"I do," he said. "Sometimes I'll be able to get a weekend off. I've got other leave coming and I'll get it on the books so you and I can share it. Does that work for you?"

She took in a long, ragged breath. "You have no idea," she murmured. "I thought you were just going to walk out of my life, Travis." She gave a pained shrug. "I was so afraid to tell you I fell in love with you. You never gave me a hint of how you felt about me."

Leaning down, he kissed her tenderly. "I was telling you every time I touched you, darlin', but I understand.

I was having problems saying it, too. I felt it was too soon, that maybe you weren't ready to hear it."

She burrowed into his arms, wrapping hers around his middle. "Isn't it funny?" she mumbled against his shoulder. "You're the bravest man I've ever known and you were *afraid* to admit you loved me?" Lifting her head, Madison shook her head, mystified as she held his smiling eyes.

"You have no idea," Travis told her wryly, "how often I called myself a coward. I could face a firefight but I couldn't face you." He kissed her nose. "I'm human."

"I love the human," she murmured. "He's an incredible man."

"And someday," Travis murmured back, "your husband. And you'll be my wife."

Madison lay in Travis's arms after making love with him. Dawn was crawling up on the horizon, the clock on the bedside table with big red numerals showing 5:00 a.m. Her hair was damp and clinging to her temples as he brought her close, kissing her brow. They were breathing raggedly, her breasts pressed against his chest. She luxuriated in the feel of his hard body, his large hand splayed out against her hips, holding her close.

"I've been spoiled," she admitted with a sigh, pulling back just enough to see his shadowy face. It was his eyes, hooded and sated looking, that made her heart widen with love for him. "And I'm going to miss you in my bed."

Travis kissed her lips and rested his brow against hers. "I'll be here in spirit." And then he grinned.

"You'll probably get tired of me pestering you every night."

"I'll welcome you with open arms, Travis." She slowly slid her fingers across the crescent-shaped scar on the left side of his abdomen. He'd almost died from the gunshot wound. Almost... Her fingers lightly grazed the puckered scar that was six years old. Travis had earned a bronze star with a V for valor during that firefight. He'd rescued his best friend who had been badly wounded, pulling him out of the line of fire, taking a bullet himself. His friend had lived, and so had he. There were other scars all over his body, a testament to the harsh conditions a SEAL lived and fought in.

She felt his callused hand close over hers.

"I didn't die," he told her.

"I know," she whispered. "But you could have."

"But I didn't." Travis eased her hand away from the scar, slowly rolled over onto his back and then sat up. He brought Madison into his arms, resting across his body, her head against his left shoulder. "Let's do something happy." He reached over to the bedside table, opened the drawer and pulled out a small green velvet box.

Curious, Madison saw him set it on the mattress next to him. He pulled her hand from his chest, picked the box up and placed it in her palm.

"Open it," he urged, leaning over and turning the lamp. Madison's brows drew down as she looked at the box.

"It's not going to bite you, darlin'," he teased, his hand moving lightly against her back.

"Is this what I think it is, Travis?"

"Most likely." He waited, watching tenderness come to her eyes as she looked up at him. She was definitely surprised.

"When did you do this?"

"I had a jeweler friend of mine in San Diego make it for you."

Gasping, Madison blinked and stared at him. "That was two months ago!" She saw him preen a little. "You knew then?"

He lost his smile and became contrite. "I was *hoping* then."

She shook her head and opened the lid. Two rings stared back at her. One was a simple gold wedding band. The engagement ring made her gasp again. "Oh, Travis…this is so beautiful." She pulled it from the box, holding it up to the light.

"The stones are blue tourmaline," he said, "the color of your eyes I love so much."

Tears came to her eyes as she lightly touched the five channel-cut blue stones set in gold. "They're beautiful, Travis." Her heart expanded until she thought she'd burst.

"The jeweler asked what you did for a living and I told him you worked with horses. He said the stones should be shaped to sit in a channel within the ring so that they lay flat and you couldn't catch them on anything." His pulse skittered with anxiety. "Do you like it, Madison?" He'd taken such a risk in ordering the rings. The tourmalines were good luck, he'd hoped, and they turned out to be much more than that.

"Can you put it on me?"

Travis nodded, "Anything the lady wants," he drawled, slipping it onto her left hand. The fit was perfect. Travis enjoyed watching her hold up her slender fingers, moving her hand one way and then the other, the light catching the clear blue stones. They were exactly the same color of her moist eyes and he slid his hand across her shoulders, drawing her against him. "The gemstones do you justice," he told her huskily, kissing her.

Madison sighed as he eased from her lips. "I'm just shocked. How could you have known then?"

He pushed the mass of blond hair off her shoulder, taming it toward her back. "I knew by the time we landed at Bagram that I loved you. Knew it was too soon but was bound and determined to chase you until I caught you."

Giving him a wicked look, Madison whispered, "You're a dangerous man, Travis Cooper."

"Soon, I won't be," he said, holding her, resting his brow against her cheek. Madison slid her arms around his shoulders.

"I'll bet Mom and Dad will want us to set a date," she said.

"What do you think of two weddings? One at Coronado, because my whole platoon wants to be there when we get married. The other here at your parents' home?"

"That works for me. I know how close you are to your friends."

"Yeah, we've bled for one another. Literally."

Madison hugged him gently. "I know," she whispered, her voice strained. He'd lost six men in his platoon over the years. Six friends who had bled and fought at one another's sides. Madison knew Travis would always be in touch with his brothers, whether he was a SEAL or not. "Maybe a week before you get out? You're officially on leave and won't most of them be there getting ready to deploy back to Afghanistan?"

Travis nodded. "That's a good idea. Everyone will be back at Coronado, ready to pack and deploy." Sometimes, SEALs had to wait four or six months before their brothers could be at the same time and place to see them married. Travis wouldn't have that problem. And he wanted to share his joy with his brothers. So often they dealt in death and grief. A wedding was a godsend.

Twenty-four Months Later

"Travis?" Madison called as she climbed out of the pickup truck. It was nearly noon and the blisteringly hot August sun made her want to duck beneath the shade of the overhanging roof of the tack house. She pushed her sunglasses up on her head, her blond hair in a braid down the center of her back.

Where was her husband? Excited, she halted near the corner of the building, in the shade, and looked around.

Her mother had told Madison she'd seen Travis down at the main arena working with a six-month-old Trakehner colt earlier. Craning her neck, she saw the arena was empty. It was too hot to work a horse, anyway. She hurried back to the pickup to get her bottle of water. She could barely contain her excitement.

Her father chugged by on a John Deere green tractor, pulling a load of baled alfalfa hay that would be put in their main barn. She lifted her hand to him, and he smiled and waved in return. Drinking more of the water, she waited until the tractor rolled by before turning the corner and leaping up onto the wooden porch.

"Travis?" she called.

"In here…" His voice drifted through the screen door of the tack room.

The heat was stifling as she pulled it open and saw him cleaning a bridle with some saddle soap on the floor. He was dressed in a black T-shirt that showed off his powerful upper body, very dusty jeans and a pair of cowboy boots.

"Hey, where did you go?" he asked. Travis smiled, thinking how, even six months after getting married, she hadn't changed one bit. Just grown more beautiful. He swore he could see a glow in her face.

"Umm, I had to go into town," she hedged. "God, it's hot in here, Travis. How do you stand it?" She came and sat down on a bench near where he was working.

"Afghanistan," he said dryly, putting the final touches to Odin's leather bridle. He took a clean, soft cloth and gave the tobacco-brown leather a final buff. Holding it up, he was pleased with his work.

Snorting softly, Madison finished off the bottle of water. She could barely sit still, dying to tell Travis the good news. "That looks nice."

It was Travis's turn to snort as he unwound from the floor and carried the bridle over to the wall, hanging it on a hook. "Yeah, it'll stay that way for a week."

Wiping her damp brow with the back of her arm, she said, "Let's go out to the porch swing. At least there's a breeze out there, and it isn't so hot."

He picked up his black baseball cap and settled it on his head. "Since when did you start whining about the temperature?" he teased, cupping her elbow and walking her to the door.

"I'm not doing so well in the heat, of late," she agreed. Travis stopped at the small refrigerator and pulled out two cold bottles of water. He handed one to her before sitting down. "You do look flushed." Her cheeks were bright red and she was perspiring more than usual. "Are you feeling all right?" he asked, drinking half the bottle of water.

She curled up in the swing, one leg beneath her, the other lightly pushing the swing. "I'm fine. Fine."

He wiped his mouth and looked at his watch. "Your mom said you had to go into town. I was looking for you earlier."

"I had an appointment," she said, holding the cold, frosty bottle between her hands.

"With?"

She reached out and slid her hand along his upper arm and resting it on his broad shoulder. "Dr. Marls." For a moment, she held her breath and watched the expression on his face. Even though it had been six months since Travis had left the Navy, his hair was just as short as ever. The hard, physical work on the farm had kept him just as toned and hard as when he'd been a SEAL. His brows dipped as he considered the name.

"Are you okay?" His voice dropped.

"I couldn't be better." She was almost to the point of bursting. "I'm pregnant."

Travis felt his heart thud in his chest. Momentarily at a loss for words, he said, "You are?" Seeing the joy dancing in Madison's blue eyes, wriggling like a happy puppy, unable to sit still, he blinked and assimilated what she'd just said.

"Pregnant."

"Yes."

"Two months?"

"Yes. Right after I stopped taking the pill."

"That was fast."

"Well, Cooper, given how you never leave me alone at night, it was inevitable."

Travis grinned and touched her cheek. "You could have told me stop."

Pouting, Madison admitted, "That wouldn't have been any fun." Closing her eyes, she sighed, feeling his work-roughened hands, the wild tingles sliding downward, making her breasts grow tight.

"I'll be damned," he breathed. "We're going to be parents."

"Yes." Madison opened her eyes and drowned in his intense green gaze. "Are you happy, Travis?" They'd discussed starting a family sooner, not later. She was twenty-eight and they wanted to be young enough to enjoy whatever children they would have.

Leaning down, Travis kissed her smiling mouth tenderly. "Crazy happy," he murmured against her lips. Easing away, he released her and brought her into his arms.

Travis moved his large hand across her belly. "You need to take extra good care of yourself, darlin'." She was carrying their baby. A good shock flowed through him. He leaned over and kissed her lips again. "I wonder what color of hair she'll have? Blond? Like yours?"

"I don't know." Madison sighed, loving his hand across her belly. It was such a loving and protective gesture on his part. "What do you want?" she asked him, tipping her head up and meeting his warm green gaze.

"Don't care as long as the mother and baby are healthy," he murmured. "You?"

She stretched against him, sliding her hand across the T-shirt that fit him like a loving second skin. "Dr. Marls said women usually know what they're carrying."

"Do you?" Travis was always stunned by women's intuition. It wasn't something to make fun of.

"I feel like it's a little boy." Her eyes sparkled with humor.

"Sounds good to me." He chuckled. Travis gazed at their new home that was nearly finished on the other side of the arena facility. Since they'd arrived home, he worked daily with several construction workers to get the rambling, single-story house completed for him and Madison. "Good thing we built four bedrooms into that house of ours," he said.

"Yes, it is." The house would be done in another two months. "We'll paint one bedroom blue and the other pink."

Travis smiled and kissed her brow. He inhaled the jasmine fragrance of her gold hair and her special feminine scent. "Just in case," he teased.

"Just in case," Madison agreed, hugging him, absorbing the strength of his arms around her.

"Life is good," Travis said. Better than he'd ever thought it would be. He was the first of the Sidewinders to leave the military. And over the past half year, he'd remained in touch with his football friends who were scattered around the world in black ops. He'd come a long way since age eighteen, when he'd joined the Navy a day after he'd graduated from high school.

And now he held an incredibly tender-hearted woman in his arms who loved him with fierce passion.

Travis moved his mouth near her ear, tendrils tickling his nose. "You know what? Life is good because you're sharing it with me. Forever…"

Epilogue

On St. Patrick's Day, Daniel Travis Cooper was born in College Station, Texas. He had his father's black hair and green eyes, and weighed eight pounds, three ounces. Madison Cooper welcomed him into the world with the help of two smiling midwives at their new home. Travis got to birth his son, who slipped from his mother and into his gloved hands, squalling and ready to take on the world. Mother was tired but happy, holding her lusty son to her breast for his first feeding. Father sat nearby, smiling, tears in his eyes.

* * * * *

ANY TIME, ANY PLACE

ANY PLACE

—

Merline Lovelace

This story is for all who have served their country, in uniform or in civvies. And most especially for the Air Commandos who blazed their way into history during WWII and still fight the good fight!

Chapter 1

USAF Master Sergeant Dave "Duke" Carmichael leaned against the scarred Formica bar, and took a long pull from his beer. As the cold brew slid down his throat, he acknowledged the simple truth. He was a leg man. Always had been. Probably always would be.

Some of his Special Forces pals vectored straight in on a woman's breasts. A few might try to claim they'd been hooked by a seductive smile or a glance from laughing eyes. Duke had never bothered to disguise the fact that slender, curvaceous legs displayed to perfection in tight jeans stirred the beast in him.

He suspected that had a lot to do with growing up in West Texas and spending his horny teen years surrounded by nubile young females in stone-washed jeans with rips and tears in all the right places. That, and being one of the infamous six Sidewinders—so dubbed due to their lightning speed and ability to strike without warning on the football field. Duke and his pals had ruled the Rush Springs High School babe scene.

They hadn't done all that bad in the years since, either. All six Sidewinders had joined the military right after high school. Although they opted for different branches of the service, they all eventually ended up in special ops. Their paths had crossed often enough that they could still keep up a joking, running count of who'd scored the most over the years. Duke didn't top the chart, but he was damned close.

Despite that vast reservoir of expertise to draw from, he had to admit the legs he now perused were in a class by themselves. And they came packaged with a nice, trim butt, a hand-spanable waist and a waterfall of glossy, mink-dark hair.

The front view was just as good as the rear. Duke should know. He'd scoped it out the first day he'd arrived in Colorado Springs to serve as the USAF adviser for the first joint Russian-U.S. exercises to be conducted on American soil in more than a decade.

Adviser. Christ!

His fist tightened on his dew-streaked beer bottle. The noise of the bar faded. His gaze shifted to a flickering neon sign across the room, and Duke felt it take him to another time, another place. He could almost see the red tracers streaking down from dark, forbidding peaks a half a world away. Hear the shouts, the deadly whir. His stomach knotted, and he cursed again the machine-gun round that had carved off a piece of his hip bone.

He should be with his squad high in the mountains

east of Kabul, dammit! Coordinating air strikes against entrenched Taliban positions. Conducting helicopter infiltrations with the Afghan commandos he'd helped train. Instead he'd been shipped back to the States for long weeks of rehab, followed by more weeks of light duty at Air Force Special Operations Command headquarters in the Florida Panhandle.

Then a tour he'd served at the American embassy in Moscow almost a decade ago had jumped up to bite him in the ass. Some weenie at headquarters remembered he'd attended the Defense Language Institute prior to his Moscow assignment, and that he'd picked up a more-or-less working knowledge of Russian during his tour. He'd forgotten most of it, but that didn't matter to the desk jockeys at headquarters. Now he was playing nursemaid to a bunch of Russians until the docs reviewed his latest medical eval. Then Duke would either be returned to full duty or…

A burst of laughter jerked him back to the noisy present. His grip on the beer easing, he skimmed a glance over the crowd. Pete's Place was even more jammed tonight than usual. The ramshackle bar was popular with Special Forces troops attending the advanced mountain operations school here at Fort Carson, just outside Colorado Springs. With a senior mountaineering class due to graduate tomorrow, the air inside the bar reverberated with the raucous relief of those who'd made it through the brutal four-week course.

Duke listened with only half an ear to the mildly exaggerated tales of rappelling ice-coated cliffs and packhorses sliding ass-backward down impossibly steep slopes. He knew from personal experience the high-

Alpine hell these guys had endured. He'd attended the course himself what seemed like a lifetime ago. When he was young and studly and totally immune to fear.

Now…

With a fierce effort of will, he concentrated on the brunette. She was slinging her purse over her shoulder, heading for the door.

Time to make his move. Again.

Duke pushed away from the bar and bit back a wince. The pain had dulled to a sharp ache, but if he twisted the wrong way it could still put a hitch in his stride. Even with the hitch, he got to the exit two steps ahead of his target.

"Allow me, ma'am."

He accompanied his best West Texas drawl with a slow grin and an even slower reach for the push-bar. She was forced to stop and wait, and flicked him an impatient glance. When the door finally yielded to a blast of cold, she skewered him with a look that said she knew exactly what kind of game he played.

"Thanks."

Undaunted by her less than friendly attitude, Duke followed her into the rapidly deepening dusk. This wasn't the first time he'd been shot down. Although he still held the record among the Sidewinders for finessing a woman into bed in the shortest time, he'd long ago learned to accept defeat at female hands gracefully and move on to the next challenge.

He'd also learned from his friends' mistakes. His buddy Travis's ex-wife had carved out his heart with a dull knife. Travis was doing just fine now with feisty Madison Duncan, but he'd trekked a long, painful road to get there. Duke didn't plan on going down that same road.

He would sure as hell consider a side trip with someone like Anna Solkov, though. The woman had intrigued him from day one with her high, slashing cheekbones and ripe mouth. Her tip-tilted chin hinted at a stubborn streak, but he was willing to take that minor defect in stride.

She was also smart as hell. A civilian analyst with the Defense Intelligence Agency, she specialized in central and eastern European languages. Duke had checked her credentials, knew she was fluent in Polish and Ukrainian and spoke four or five Russian dialects. The woman had earned her pay and then some these past few weeks by facilitating communications between the Americans and Russians. Unfortunately, she hadn't been as willing to facilitate with Duke on a person-to-person basis.

He knew she wasn't married or recently divorced. He had enough contacts in Washington to have confirmed those basics. One of those contacts thought there was a boyfriend or fiancé somewhere in the background but she didn't wear a ring. That made her fair game in Duke's book.

Determined to break through the professional barrier she insisted on maintaining, he caught up with her at her car.

"I know a great rib place not far from here. How 'bout we grab some dinner?"

She paused with her lock clicker in hand and looked him up and down. Inch by deliberate inch. He rolled his shoulders under the down vest he wore to counter the chill of late September in the Rockies. Pretty much like a cock puffing out his chest and ruffling his feather to impress a hen, he acknowledged in silent amusement.

This one remained unimpressed. She finished her inspection and finally got around to responding to his invitation.

"How 'bout we don't grab anything, cowboy."

Duke blinked. She'd echoed his deep baritone and Texas drawl with uncanny precision. It sounded as though one of the Sidewinders was channeling through this luscious, long-legged brunette.

"If I didn't know better," he said in real admiration, "I'd swear you hailed from Rush Springs."

Anna almost laughed at his look of surprise. Probably would have, if the man didn't irritate her so much. It wasn't his looks that bothered her. Those were just short of spectacular. Assuming, of course, you were into buzz-cut blond hair, skin weathered to dark oak by the sun, white squint lines at the corners of electric blue eyes and a collection of cut muscles that not even Air Force BDUs could disguise.

Anna wasn't. Nor was she attracted by the cocky male confidence so endemic to the special ops community. Particularly when it came wrapped in blatantly sexual overtones.

For a moment, a blind moment, she let herself remember the kind of man that did attract her. Quiet, funny, self-deprecating Jeremy South was the exact opposite of Duke Carmichael. Or rather, he *had* been the exact opposite. The ache that three long years couldn't erase stripped away any desire to be polite.

"Do me a favor, Sergeant Carmichael…"

"Duke."

"Do me a favor, Sergeant Carmichael, and drop the aw-shucks act."

A sun-bleached brow hooked. He looked more amused than offended. "What makes you think it's an act?"

"I'm a linguist. I'm trained to recognize individual speech pattern." She should have left it there, but honesty compelled her to add a kicker. "I also watched the video of when you were awarded the Air Force Cross."

The Air Force Cross was that service's second highest award for valor in the face of the enemy, ranking right below the Medal of Honor. Carmichael's speech after the commanding general of the USAF Special Operations Command pinned the award on his chest had been brief and incredibly moving. He'd played down how he'd exposed himself to withering enemy fire to call in an air strike, paying tribute instead to the men who'd died trying to take out entrenched enemy positions. The speech had also been crisp, clear and articulate.

"You didn't drop a single *G* or roll one diphthong," she remarked.

"I didn't, huh?"

The twinkle reappeared. With a vengeance. Anna swallowed a sigh. "You did not. Now if you don't mind, I'll…"

The sharp buzz of a cell phone cut her off. Carmichael fished his phone out of his pocket and glanced at the number on the screen. Despite the rapidly deepening dusk, Anna caught the leap of excitement in his eyes.

"'Scuse me. I've been expecting the results of my medical eval board. I need to take this call."

He moved away, the phone pinned to his ear. The message he received was short and succinct and evidently had nothing to do with his medical status. She was trying to interpret his flat, unrevealing expression when she also received a call.

Her conversation was even briefer than his. Frowning, Anna disconnected. "There's a Code Six inbound tomorrow at oh-seven-hundred," she said slowly. "We're supposed to meet him at base ops. You and I."

"Yeah, I just got the word."

"What's going on?"

"Damned if I know."

Dawn was beginning to streak the horizon when Duke left his quarters at Fort Carson the next morning. He wore his uniform, but not the ninety plus pounds of combat gear he and his fellow combat controllers carried on missions. His woodland camo BDUs blended with the shadows. His rubber-treaded boots barely disturbed the quiet as he let himself out and into the frigid predawn air.

The dark bulk of Cheyenne Mountain loomed directly ahead as he drove across the sprawling Army post. Established during WWII and named for General Kit Carson, the legendary Army scout and frontiersman, Fort Carson was home to a host of units. Among them was A Company, Second Battalion, First Special Warfare Training Group, Airborne. The battle-tested veterans of A Company were the U.S. Army's elite mountaineers. The best of the best. They taught

Special Forces from all branches of the service and a good number of foreign countries how to conduct—and survive—mountain warfare. For the past few weeks, they'd served as the host unit for the counterterrorism exercise being conducted jointly by U.S. Special Forces and Russian Spetsnaz troops.

Duke had been working out of A Company during that time. So had Anna Solkov. This morning, though, that strange phone call had instructed them to meet an incoming Code Six—military jargon for someone with the rank of colonel—at Butts Army Airfield. Like Fort Carson, the airfield was named for another Army hero. Medal of Honor winner Second Lieutenant John Butts had died in Normandy in June 1994 after exposing himself to intense fire so his men could make a flanking movement and overrun the enemy position.

Courage was pretty much duty supercharged by sheer guts, Duke thought as he pulled into a parking space in front of base ops. The credo of special operations. The need to be with his unit hit him again, hard and raw. The dead weight of it went with him into the base ops.

Anna was already there, pacing the small waiting room with coffee in hand. "Have you learned any more what this is all about?" she asked by way of greeting.

"Negative."

"Well, I guess we'll find out soon enough."

Nodding, Duke tugged off his scarlet beret. A badge of distinction, the beret was awarded only to combat controllers—the small, tight breed of warriors inserted behind enemy lines first so they could lead the way for other forces to follow.

Combat controllers went through much the same training as Navy SEALs and United States Army Special Forces. Duke could put a 7.62 NATO rifle round dead center at nine hundred yards, free-fall from twenty-five thousand feet, rappel or fast-rope sheer cliffs, scuba into hostile areas and perform emergency medical procedures with the same skill as an EMT.

What distinguished combat controllers from other branches of special ops, however, was that they were also certified at FAA level to direct air traffic. Being inserted behind enemy lines to establish assault zones and airfields was a tough job at the best of times. Directing air traffic in those zones was even dicier with enemy fire raining down and 500-pound bombs cratering the earth all around.

Folding the scarlet beret into a leg pocket of his ABUs, Duke snagged a cup of thick, black sludge from base ops' coffee maker and joined Anna. Last night's jeans were gone. He mourned their snug-fitting loss, but couldn't fault her pleated black slacks, turquoise blouse and neat charcoal blazer. She looked cool, composed and all business.

Appreciating the view, Duke took a swig of what the airfield guys obviously mistook for coffee. "Good God. This is worse than the stuff my granny used to pour down my throat when she thought I was coming down with the croup."

For the first time he could recall, Anna relaxed into a genuine smile. It softened her face, and hit Duke about six inches below the belt line.

"You've got one of those grandmothers, too?"

"Granny Jones was the terror of my youth. Still

scares the snot out of me every time I go back to Texas," he admitted ruefully.

"Ha! You should meet my babushka. She could go ten rounds with your granny and never break a sweat."

Duke had to laugh. The rich, deep chuckle seemed to crack some of the ice between him and this brown-eyed honey. With a little luck and some good, old-fashioned persistence, he might just punch right through it.

The small, sleek jet swooped out of the clouds mere moments later. Its engines had barely shut down before the side hatch popped up and Colonel Lloyd Haggarty hit the tarmac. A command pilot with twenty-three years in special ops, he was known and pretty much feared on five continents. Ramrod-straight, flinty-eyed, he strode across the apron as Duke and Anna stepped outside to greet him.

Duke had served under the colonel a number of times, the latest during his stint of enforced light duty at USAF Special Ops headquarters. The possibility that Haggarty had flown out to Colorado to deliver the results of the medical eval in person settled like a pile of bricks on Duke's chest.

The colonel's first words after he'd returned Duke's salute added another brick to the load.

"You still on meds?"

"No, sir."

"Good."

The crushing weight lifted. Haggarty seemed to understand because he gave Duke a brief nod before his razor glance cut to Anna. "We have a situation brewing, Ms. Solkov. The DIA says you're the best person to help defuse it."

She had to be as curious as Duke but knew better than to ask for details out here in the open. "I'll do my best, sir."

"Come inside. I'll brief you both while the plane refuels."

The C-21's pilot had obviously radioed ahead. The major in charge of flight ops met them at the door and ushered them to his private office. After producing coffee for the three of them, he retreated. Haggarty waited only until the door closed behind him to strike.

"What do you know about the terrorist known as Nikolai Varno?"

Anna sucked in a sharp breath. "Aka Vasili Fedak, Petr Burda, Maurel Baranski and a half-dozen other aliases. No one knows his real name, only that he has ties to both the Russian mafia and Chechen extremists. I've read the dossier on him but it's far from complete. He's as elusive as he is vicious."

"One of our listening posts intercepted a brief cell-phone transmission. It hinted that he may be en route to a village called Rasliva, high in the Carpathian mountains."

"That's in the Ukraine! My grandmother was born in a village nearby."

"So I've been informed."

"I visited that area once with my grandparents." Her forehead creased. "I was only a kid at the time, but I remember the villages are small and remote. Why would Varno go there?"

Haggarty held Anna's intent gaze. "Intelligence indicates he may be recruiting disgruntled locals to help blow up a section of the Soyuz pipeline."

"Oh, my God!"

Her shocked response had Duke dredging through his memory bank. The Soyuz line was one of three or four monster pipelines that ran from Russia through the Ukraine to different parts of Europe. Best he could recall, those lines supplied something like 80 percent of Europe's oil and natural gas. A disruption in that flow would have devastating consequences for those EU nations already teetering on the brink of economic disaster. Worse—or better from a terrorist's view—blowing up such a huge pipeline could cause horrific loss of life if the explosion occurred in a populated area.

"As you know," Haggarty continued grimly, "relations between Russia and its former satellite state have hit an all-time low as a result of disagreements over how much the Ukraine should pay for the oil and natural gas passing through its territory."

Anna nodded, obviously still trying to take all this in. "The Ukrainians shut down the pipelines in 2006, and the Russians threatened to invade," she said slowly. "The situation calmed for a while, but recent disputes have gone all the way to the international court in Stockholm for resolution."

"Correct."

Duke recognized the expression in the colonel's steel-gray eyes. He should. He'd seen it often enough. Usually just before Haggarty sent a contingent of his troops into harm's way.

Christ! They were going to send her after this Varno!

"Sir…"

Haggarty held up a hand to cut off his instinctive protest. The colonel's gaze remained locked on Anna.

"Those disputes are why the Ukraine has turned to the U.S. for assistance. They don't want to authorize a covert Russian operation in their country, but neither can they risk the loss of the Soyuz pipeline. As a result, we intend to insert a small team to verify the intel and, if possible, take Varno down. You know the area, can speak the local dialect. We want you to be part of that team."

She didn't hesitate. "Of course. When do I leave?"

"Immediately."

"Sir!"

Duke leaned forward, blocking Anna from the colonel's line of sight.

"The Carpathians aren't as high as the Alps but they're every bit as rugged and damned near inaccessible in places. More to the point, this Varno is a known killer. You can't send an untrained civilian without..."

"Excuse me?" With an icy look at Duke, Anna reinserted herself in the mix. "I'm hardly untrained. And I'm familiar with both the area and the language."

Haggarty signaled his agreement with both sides of the argument. "We're counting on that knowledge, but we appreciate the risks involved. That's why I'm sending Sergeant Carmichael in with you."

She opened her mouth, then shut it as the colonel's gaze shifted and drilled into his subordinate.

"*If* you're not still hurting. The truth, Carmichael. You back to one hundred percent?"

It didn't occur to Duke to lie. He'd spent too many years in special ops, where survival could and often did depend as much on endurance as on war-fighting skill. He wouldn't risk his life or those of his men by minimizing risks. He did, however, put an air-commando spin on his response.

"I'm ninety-eight percent, sir. On a civilian scale, that translates to…"

"A hundred and ninety-eight percent," the colonel finished dryly. He kept his steely gaze trained on Duke's for another moment. "Are you up to a mission like this?"

"Yes."

"All right, you've convinced me. Besides which, I talked to the docs before we put this op together."

"I figured as much, sir."

"They said the brutal exercise regimen you've designed for yourself has done more to strengthen and heal that hip than any physical therapist ever could. So I'm good with you and Ms. Solkov going in together. If she is."

Two pairs of eyes turned to Anna. One was narrow and gray and rock-hard. The other blue and almost as unyielding. It took her all of three seconds to decide. To quote one her babushka's many sayings, better the wolf you can see than the hungry pack lurking in the woods.

"I'm good."

A curt nod signaled his approval. All brisk business now, he outlined.

"The code name for this mission is Operation Condor. A CIA team is in the air as we speak. You'll rendezvous with them in Florida for in-depth briefings, then we'll put you on a transport to England. The 352nd special ops group at RAF Mildenhall will exercise tactical control of the mission. They'll provide logistical support, conduct the insertion and maintain twenty-four-hour command and control while you're in country."

"Roger that, sir."

He paused, looked from Duke to Anna and back again. "I don't have to tell either of you how dangerous this mission is. Or the political implications of the U.S. conducting a covert operation in a nation that Russia still considers part of its orbit. The White House wants daily updates."

"Yes, sir."

Chapter 2

It seemed to Anna that the next few hours sped by with the speed of light. One minute she was throwing a few things into a carryall and rushing back to base ops. The next, she was climbing aboard the C-21 and being whisked back to USAF Special Operations Command Headquarters with Colonel Haggarty and Sergeant Duke Carmichael.

She stepped off the plane into the muggy afternoon heat of the Florida Panhandle. USAF Special Ops Command was headquartered at Hurlburt Air Force Base, once an auxiliary training field of the much larger Eglin Air Force Base some fifteen miles away. Together, the two bases ate up more than 800 square miles of Northern Florida.

It was at Eglin that Lieutenant Colonel Jimmy Doolittle secretly assembled B-25 bomber crews in 1942.

After intensive training in simulated carrier deck take-offs, low-level and night flying, over-water navigation and low-altitude bombing, the B-25s were later launched from U.S. aircraft carriers in the Pacific and conducted the first attack of the war on the Japanese homeland.

And it was Hurlburt that eventually became home to the first air-commando group, which won historical fame by providing fighter cover, air strikes and airlift for Wingate's Raiders, then operating behind the lines in Burma during WWII. Called the "Burma Bridge Busters" the air commandos earned a reputation for unorthodox air fighters and formed an aerial lifeline to Wingate's Raiders that was never broken.

Hurlburt AFB had gone through many iterations in its mission and assigned units since that day, but it never lost its association with Special Forces. Air commandos had operated in Korea, Vietnam, Iraq, Bosnia and Somalia, and provided humanitarian relief to disaster-stricken peoples in every corner of the globe. And, as Anna knew well, they were the spearhead of the global war on terrorism. Units assigned to USAF Special Ops Command had racked up one of the highest casualty rates in Iraq and Afghanistan.

She couldn't help letting her gaze roam Duke Carmichael's tall, muscular frame as he hefted their bags and led the way to the Jeep waiting at the edge of the ramp. He walked with only a slight limp, but she knew he'd been wounded in the vicious firefight that had left so many dead and earned Carmichael the Air Force Cross. Seriously wounded, judging by Colonel Haggarty's demand to know if he was up to this mission.

She struggled with a moment of doubt about her swift agreement that Carmichael be included in this little team. Was he honestly good to go, or had his assertion that he was fit merely been the macho bragging of a special ops type who couldn't admit any weakness?

She got the answer to that question some five hours later. Four of those were spent locked in a classified briefing room, being fed updates from various intelligence sources about the activities of the shadowy, faceless terrorist known as Nikolai Varno. Their initial briefer was a tall, balding CIA analyst Anna knew only by reputation. From all reports, Terry Johnson was good at his job but his briefing style was dry and flat-toned. Not that he needed to inject drama. The subject matter provided that.

"We suspect Varno was involved in the 2004 Belsan massacre," he said, flashing up a series of grim photos.

The Belsan massacre had happened several years before Anna was recruited by the Defense Intelligence Agency, but she knew the details. It began when a group of armed Chechen separatists entered a school and took over a thousand hostages, almost eight hundred of them children. They demanded recognition of Chechnya as a separate nation at the UN and immediate withdrawal of Russian forces in that state. The siege ended three days later, when Russian security forces used tanks, incendiary rockets and assault weapons to attack the school. Over three hundred hostages died in the assault, almost two hundred of them children. Hundreds more were injured.

The stark photos Terry Johnson flashed up on the

screen showed mangled, bloody bodies lying everywhere. As often as Anna had studied reports of the
brutal massacre, it still had the power to make her seriously question the human race's chances of survival.

"We also know Varno helped mastermind the 2010
Moscow subway bombing," Johnson continued.

Anna was more familiar with this attack. It had
happened shortly after she joined the DIA. She and
her fellow analysts had spent long hours and days and
weeks sifting through intelligence feeds from the attack, desperately hoping the knowledge they gleaned
of the terrorists' methodology would prevent a similar
incident in the U.S. Although she could have recited
most of the details by heart, she listened intently as the
briefer laid them out.

"In this instance, the attack was perpetrated by
two female suicide bombers. One was identified as
the widow of a terrorist killed by Russian forces the
previous year. The other was a twenty-nine-year-old
schoolteacher whose brother was supposedly linked to
the Chechen separatist movement. The attack was carried out at the height of the morning rush hour, when
an estimated half a million people were in the subway
system. The bombing killed at least forty people, and
injured a hundred more."

More photos, more devastation. The thought of
going up against the perpetrator of such evil sent a
shiver rippling down Anna's spine. She glanced at Carmichael, saw him staring at the screen with his jaw
tight.

He'd pulled an embassy tour in Moscow some years

back, she remembered from his career brief. He must have had friends, acquaintances, who used the subway.

"Intelligence suggests Varno may now be targeting the Russian oil and natural gas pipelines that feed Europe."

A map of Europe flashed up on the screen. There was Mother Russia, not the great lumbering bear it had been during the years of the Soviet Union, but still big and powerful enough to cast its shadow over its former satellite states. Those states now formed a buffer between Russia's western border and her European neighbors—from Estonia in the far north, through Latvia, Lithuania, Poland, Belarus, Hungary and Romania, to the Ukraine in the south.

Approximately the size of Texas, the Ukraine straddled the Black Sea. It was a country with a wide variance in topographical characteristics: the fertile grasslands of the Steppes in the north; the mountains in the east and west; the fifteen-hundred-mile-long Dnieper River, Europe's third longest, flowing all the way across the country to empty into the Black Sea; the marshy delta of the Danube.

Given its strategic location as a gateway to Europe, the Ukraine had become a major conduit for the Russian oil and natural gas that fed Europe. The pipelines dropped from oil fields in Russia's frozen north, traveled south for thousands of miles and spidered across the Ukraine.

Anna knew those red lines represented more than just a conduit for natural resources. They were Europe's lifelines. Not only was natural gas a major source of residential and commercial heat, but it was also used in the manufacture of everything from fertilizers and plastics to pharmaceuticals and fabrics. Any disruption to the flow of a major line could have devastating economic and political consequences, which was no doubt why Varno was targeting it. That, and the catastrophic loss of life that could result from a major explosion.

"For a number of reasons," Johnson continued, tracing one of the spider legs with a laser pointer, "the Ukrainian antiterrorism division believes Varno's target may be the Soyuz line."

Anna leaned forward, her brows knotted in concentration as she studied the Soyuz route. It bisected the Ukraine from east to west. A spur dropped down to Odessa, the country's major seaport on the Black Sea. And there, close to the Ukraine's border with Romania, the Soyuz skirted the mountains her grandmother had grown up in.

Where Varno was now believed to be operating.

Intent on the rumpled brown that represented the mountains, Anna didn't realize Johnson had wrapped up this portion of his presentation until he snapped the lights on. Startled, she saw they'd been at it for almost four hours. A glance at the clock on the briefing room wall showed it was now past 7:00 p.m.

"We'll take an hour break," the CIA analyst announced. "Stretch your legs, chow down on the sandwiches in the other room. Then my counterpart from field ops will detail your cover for this mission. After that, you'll board a transport for the flight over to RAF Mildenhall."

Anna pushed away from the table, bumping elbows with Duke in the process. "Sorry."

"No problem. I'll see you back here in an hour."

"Aren't you going to grab a sandwich?"

"I've been sitting too long. The base gym's right across the street. I'm going to work out some kinks before we get on the plane for England."

He hefted the gear bag he'd hurriedly packed before leaving Colorado and started for the door.

"Wait, I'll go with you."

Anna wasn't an exercise fanatic but she hit the gym more or less regularly. All right, mostly less. She hadn't anticipated having any time to exercise during this mission, but she'd stuffed several tank tops and a cherry-red exercise suit in her duffel, thinking the drawstring pants and lightweight jacket would be good for the flight to England. Military transports weren't known for their comfort or convenience.

"We've got a long flight ahead," she said when Carmichael raised a politely skeptical brow. "I might as well work out a few kinks, too."

When they walked into the ultramodern facility, they were greeted with the familiar scents of rubber mats, the antiseptic used to wipe down the equipment and the acrid tang of perspiration. The display of sweaty, gleaming muscle power, however, was *very* different from what Anna normally encountered back at her own gym. Of necessity, military personnel were required to maintain a higher level of physical fitness than their civilian counterparts. Since Hurlburt was home to USAF Special Ops, the military at this base took fitness to an entirely different plane.

So, apparently, did Duke Carmichael. He'd emerged

from the men's locker room before Anna came out of the women's. She spotted him in the weights area, bending and stretching and twisting at the waist to loosen up. His black lycra shorts encased hard, muscled thighs. Below the shorts, his legs were dusted with hair the same tawny gold as that on his arms. His sleeveless, wick-away gym shirt was silvery gray and stretched across what looked to Anna like a half acre of chest.

She couldn't help but note the tattoo that circled his upper arm. It looked like a snake, coiled and ready to strike. The tat didn't show when he was in uniform. She would have noticed it before. She certainly noticed it now, as she headed for one of the fifteen or so stair-steppers lined up on one side of the aerobic workout area. Each came with its own TV screen. She turned hers off, wanting to process the details of the briefings she'd just had. To her profound annoyance, both her attention and her glance kept wandering to the weights area.

Carmichael was doing curls. He'd straddled a bench and planted an elbow on one knee. His head was bent and his face a study in fierce concentration as he slowly, rhythmically raised and lowered his arm. He must have been using a forty- or fifty-pound dumbbell. His biceps bulged each time he raised the weight, stretched hard and sleek each time he lowered it.

Okay. All right. Anna might not particularly care for the man's cocky grin or the lazy twang he turned on and off like a faucet, but she could appreciate a prime male specimen when she saw one. And Carmichael was most definitely prime!

When he progressed from one-armed curls to

squats, she found herself pumping the stair-stepper harder and faster. Although he didn't favor either hip, she knew the up-and-down exercise had to pull at his still-healing wound. His jaw locked tighter with each squat. The tendons in his neck corded. Sweat glistened on his shoulders and arrowed down the front of his shirt.

For some reason, the sight of Carmichael pushing himself to the limits of his endurance drove her, as well. As if she had to prove she was up for this mission, to herself as much to him. She pumped harder. Stepped faster. Within moments, her breath rasped and her lungs screamed for air.

Wiggling out her exercise suit jacket, she draped it over a handle. The air-conditioned gym air raised goose bumps on arms and back left bare by her scoop-necked tank. The bumps went away fast as the damned stair-stepper became an instrument of torture.

Anna wanted to sob with relief when she hit the end of her programmed workout and went into cool-down mode. Three minutes later, she almost fell off the machine. Her legs felt like wet rags. Gasping, she staggered toward the locker rooms. She had less than eight minutes to shower, change and hotfoot it back across the street.

She felt rather than saw Carmichael come up behind her. Amusement and what she chose to interpret as a touch of admiration colored the drawl that drifted over her shoulder.

"I saw you givin' those stairs a run for their money. You look a little wobbly right now, though. Need some help soaping down?"

She didn't bother to answer. Nor did she do more than flick him a cool glance when she emerged from the locker room and found him waiting to escort her back across the street.

A soft Florida dusk had gathered during their brief sojourn in the gym. Anna drew in the heavy, sea-tinged air, thinking how different it was from the thin, crisp Colorado air she'd breathed mere hours ago. Different, too, from the mountain air she'd be sucking in once she and Carmichael landed in the Ukraine.

With their departure looming closer by the minute, she wavered between impatience to board the transport and nagging worry at how she and Carmichael would function as a team once they landed in the Ukraine. That worry exploded into disbelief when she learned the cover devised for the mission.

Tom Hancock, their second CIA briefer, was all nervous energy. He paced back and forth constantly while he talked, shooting information at Anna and Carmichael like bullets.

"Here's the deal. You two got to know each other while working together in Colorado. Fell in love. Got married on the spur of the moment. Decided to spend your honeymoon…"

"Wait a minute!" Anna shot upright in her chair. "You're kidding about the married part, right?"

"Do I look like I'm kidding?" Hancock stabbed a finger at the bags under his reddened eyes. "Neither Johnson nor I have slept since the Ukrainians alerted us to Varno's possible presence in their country. We have to get you two in, and fast. We also have to make sure you can communicate privately, day or night, without raising suspicion."

Her jaw set. "We can communicate without posing as a married couple."

"Not as well or as securely. Christ, Solkov, we've weighed every option. This is the best, and the safest for you."

"Safest?"

"You're not trained in field ops. Carmichael is."

Bristling with impatience, Hancock slapped a baggie containing two gold wedding bands on the table in front of her.

"Are you in or out?"

Anna stared at the rings, her throat constricting. He couldn't know… None of these people could know how the mere idea of sliding one of those bands on her finger ripped a hole in her heart.

It was three years since Jeremy had taken her to dinner at their favorite Washington bistro and suggested in his quiet, unassuming way that they get married. Three years since a drunk diver had almost decapitated him. Three years since Anna had buried her heart.

Her breath stuttered. Her chest ached. Slowly, she nodded.

"I'm in."

She forced herself to look at Carmichael, sure she'd find him grinning like some damned tomcat. The grin was there, but it came with a glint of laughter in his blue eyes that invited her to share in the joke.

Stone-faced, she turned away and dragged the baggie toward her. One quick yank had it unzipped. When she reached inside and extracted the smaller of the two rings, Carmichael stirred.

Anna couldn't bear the thought that he might make a big production out of sliding a wedding ring on her finger. Aching inside, she jammed the gold band over her knuckle.

Chapter 3

Thirty-eight hours and nine time zones later, Anna peered through the side hatch of a HH-60 Pave Hawk helicopter at the granite peaks of Europe's second longest mountain range.

The sight of the Carpathians' pine- and birch-covered slopes kicked her jet-lagged mind into gear. She was just moments now from entering the operational phase of this mission. The prep work was behind her: the intense briefings in Florida; the long flight across the Atlantic; the brief stop at RAF Mildenhall to be outfitted and equipped; the hop from England to a classified forward operating location; this jump over the mountains. The cumulative effect of those activities had taxed both her nerves and her strength.

So had the effort required to adjust to her new identity. Even now, just moments away from touch-

ing down, she had to repeat a stern mantra. She was a
new bride. Spending her honeymoon driving through
Europe. Eager to share some of her heritage with her
groom.

She dragged her gaze from the mountains below to
the narrow band circling her ring finger. The glinting
gold was a cruel reminder of what might have been.
Tears stung her tired eyes, but she blinked them back
with fierce determination and slanted a glance at the
man sprawled in the adjoining web seat.

Her…

She gritted her teeth. Forced her protesting mind
to shape the word.

Her *husband* appeared oblivious to the deafening
whap-whap-whap of rotor blades. His head lolled back
against the bulkhead. His long legs were outstretched
and crossed at the ankle. In keeping with their cover
of having meandered across eastern Europe, he hadn't
shaved since leaving Florida. Golden bristles shadowed
his cheeks. His red down vest showed several grass
stains. Beneath the vest he wore a long-sleeved, zip-
neck microfiber T-shirt, jeans and well-worn boots.
The ultrathin T-shirt and snug jeans molded his long,
muscled body.

Before she could block them, Anna's thoughts
zinged back to that brief, punishing session at the Hurlburt base gym. She'd had a glimpse then of the brutal self-discipline Carmichael employed to keep those
muscles honed. Seen, too, how he pushed himself to the
limit. Would he push her as hard during their mission?

The panic she'd struggled to suppress at various
times across all those time zones rose up again. She

was an analyst, for God's sake! A data cruncher. She was well aware that the thousands of bits of intelligence she collected and analyzed and disseminated impacted military operations. This was the first time she'd directly participated in one of those ops, however.

And she was going after one of the world's most dangerous terrorists! Nikolai Varno ranked near the top of the United Nations' list of most wanted. In his fanatical determination to wrest Chechnya's independence from Russia, Varno had resorted to horrific violence. Now he could be targeting the pipeline that ran through the country Anna's grandparents had emigrated from so many decades ago.

The thought of those grandparents steadied her. She'd spent so many summers with her poppa and babushka, had grown up on stories of these mountains, had visited them once as a child. Even now she could recite from memory many of the Ukrainian folk tales her grandmother had embellished with dramatic pauses and extravagant gestures.

Anna knew the area. She spoke the language. She could do this mission. She *had* to do it. Still, she wasn't surprised that her pulse skipped several beats when the chopper banked and began a steep descent.

The maneuver woke Carmichael…Duke… Dammit, she had to remember to call him Duke.

He transitioned from semisnoring to full awareness in a single blink. After a quick glance at the granite peaks filling the helo's side hatch window he turned those electric blue eyes on Anna. He must have read the nervousness turning her insides to mush. A teasing grin sketched across his face.

"Ready to start the honeymoon, sweet thang?"

The exaggerated drawl and hokey endearment grated like fingernails on a chalkboard. Irritated, Anna almost forgot for a moment they were here to hunt down a stone-cold killer. The fact that Carmichael—*Duke!*—had intended exactly that didn't lessen the grate.

Batting her lashes like flyswatters, she poured a gallon of pure syrup into her reply. "Ah'm ready, honeypot."

His grin morphed into a wince. "Honeypot?"

"Would yah prefer sweetikins?"

"Oh, come on. I don't really shovel it on that thick, do I?"

"As a matter of fact, you do."

"Okay, okay. I'll lay the shovel aside."

He surrendered with good-natured grace. In the next moment, he turned dead serious.

"But that's all I'll lay aside. We're in this together, Anna. I'm going to rely on your skills, and you have to rely on mine. If I say down, you eat dirt. Instantly. No questions, no arguments. Agreed?"

She'd already accepted that they each brought separate and distinct skills to the op and saw no need to pound it into the ground. Since he didn't look ready to let go of the matter, however, she gave a curt nod.

"Agreed."

"So what do you want me to call you?" he asked, circling back to the start of this discussion. "We're married, sweetheart. I need to use something more familiar than 'hey, you.'"

"Okay, fine. Use that."

"Sweetheart?"

"Yes."

The response was curt and showed her annoyance but satisfied Duke. He counted it as a small victory in his ongoing battle to loosen up this woman. She'd been torqued tighter than a lug nut since briefings in Florida. Not that she'd been particularly loose before that.

A movement from the front of the chopper caught his attention. He turned to see the flight engineer weaving his way through the equipment strapped down in the Pave Hawk's cargo bay. Christ! The kid looked like he just started shaving last week.

"Five minutes to TD," he shouted over the roar of the engines.

"Roger."

Duke had coordinated the insertion site with the Pave Hawk's pilot. The narrow valley was a good fifty miles from their target destination but shielded by near vertical slopes that would allow the Pave Hawk to swoop in and out again with minimal chance of detection.

The flight engineer might look like a high-schooler, but he knew his stuff. The moment the chopper's skids touched down on the floor of the steep-sided valley, he slid back the side hatch. Duke jumped out, keeping his head down, and helped Anna dismount. When they were clear of the whirling rotors, the younger engineer activated the lift arm to swing out their pallet of equipment.

The pallet thudded down, and Duke ducked under the still-turning blades to help him remove the cargo webbing. Working with smooth coordination, they had the pallet and webbing stashed back aboard in mere minutes. The engineer jumped back into the cargo bay and radioed the all clear to his pilot. Hanging from a safety harness, he shouted through the whine of the revving engines.

"Good luck!"

Duke nodded his thanks and hunched his shoulders against the downdraft when the Pave Hawk lifted off. The powerful wash beat the tall, tough native grasses to the ground. A quick tilt of the rotors angled the chopper's nose and sent it arrowing down the valley. The thick stands of pine and birch blanketing the slopes acted like sponges to absorb the sound of its blades slicing the air.

When the Pave Hawk rounded a jutting crag and disappeared, Duke extracted his cell phone from a zippered pocket in his down vest. The instrument looked like an ordinary cell but CIA wizards had ramped it up with the latest in ultrasophisticated technology. The damned thing could bounce a signal off Mars if necessary.

He didn't need to bounce a signal off Mars. Just off the military satellite communications network. From there it would travel via secure downlink to their control at the 352nd special ops group.

"Condor Base, this is Condor One."

The phone felt small and insignificant compared to the handheld military radios Duke was used to, but Mildenhall's reply came back lightning fast and without the usual tinny crackle.

"This is Condor Base. Go ahead, Condor One."

"Be advised we have boots on the ground."

"Acknowledged."

"We're preparing to proceed to the objective."

"Roger that, Condor One. We'll send a sitrep up-channel. Good hunting."

"Thanks. Condor One out."

In the sudden stillness that followed the brief transmission, Duke did a quick three-sixty. He saw no signs of life other than a faint curl of smoke from the farmhouse at the distant entrance to the valley. He and Anna might have been alone in this cradle of pine-covered slopes slashed with the brilliant gold of birches.

Anna made a slower circuit. Her gaze lingered on the stands of birches blazing their way up the steep slopes. "I'd forgotten how beautiful these mountains are," she murmured.

"No surprise there. You were, what? Six or seven when your grandparents brought you for a visit?"

"Seven."

She drew in the sharp, clean mountain air, her gaze still on the spectacular views. Duke had to admit he preferred the scenery a little closer in. The wind whistling through the valley put spots of color high in her cheeks and teased the ends of the ponytail she'd tugged through the back opening of her ball cap.

The folks at the 352nd had suited her out with a rainproof windbreaker in easy-to-spot yellow, a warm thermal turtleneck and lightweight hiking boots. The jeans were hers, though. Stone-washed and snug, they curved over hip and thigh and calf. The sight of those long legs shot Duke back to the study he'd given them that evening at Pete's Place, just moments before they'd been tagged for this mission.

She'd iced him good that evening. Now, just three nights later, they'd be snuggling up like honeymooners. Three nights was nowhere close to Duke's record for sweet-talking a female into bed, of course. Still, it was pretty damned good considering Anna's less than enthusiastic response to his initial overtures.

He knew the other Sidewinders wouldn't let him take credit for this one, though. Not when the snuggling-up part came with serious restrictions. He was on a mission. His buddies would know he couldn't risk the distraction of a tumble between the sheets. If Duke and Anna had to cuddle—and he sincerely hoped they would—they'd do it just to maintain their cover. Or in the words of that hyperactive CIA type, to facilitate private communication.

That didn't mean he couldn't enjoy the delectable Ms. Solkov's company, however. And continue his campaign to loosen her up a few notches whenever the opportunity presented itself.

"We better get loaded and move out."

Nodding, she tore her gaze from the swaths of brilliant gold and moved to their mound of equipment. The largest item was a mud-spattered Arturo, the European version of a Jeep Wrangler. It came equipped with four-wheel drive, reinforced suspension, a roll bar and removable side doors. Tough and reliable, the jeep could ford fast-flowing steams and climb near vertical inclines with the sure-footedness of a mountain goat.

The papers in the dash indicated it had been rented at the Budapest airport three days ago by David S.

Carmichael. The stamps in his and Anna's passports showed they had subsequently made a leisurely journey through Hungary and Romania before crossing into the Ukraine earlier this morning. Anna's passport was still in her own name, the rationale being that a newlywed wouldn't have had time to submit a name change.

To reinforce the impression of a couple enjoying a rustic honeymoon, they'd stuffed their spare clothing into a single, commercial-style duffel to give it the rumpled look of three days of travel. Their backpacks contained only the bare necessities: personal hygiene products, extra socks, maps, water bottles, energy bars, binoculars and their seemingly ordinary cell phones.

Duke had gone into more than one tight situation without the luxury of personal hygiene products. He wouldn't go in without weapons, however. Normally he clipped the KA-BAR with its lethal, drop-point blade to his utility belt. For this mission, he folded the blade into its handle and tucked it in the inside pocket of his vest. The Heckler and Koch .45 concealed in a false bottom of his backpack was a favorite of USAF special ops. The grip was molded to Duke's hand, and a single shot from its ten-round clip could take down one of the Ukraine's notoriously fierce brown bears.

Hoping to hell he'd get a shot at Nikolai Varno instead of a bear, Duke loaded their gear into the vehicle. He twisted wrong when he hefted the duffel and felt the pull on his still-healing hip muscles. The ache went deep, but brought nowhere near the stabbing pain it had a few weeks ago.

Ignoring the ache, Duke nodded approval as Anna filled the cup holders and side pockets with enough miscellaneous items to make it look as though they'd lived out of the vehicle for several days.

When they were ready to roll, he automatically started for the driver's side. A raised brow stopped him.

"Sorry," he said with a shrug. "I'm used to taking charge. You want to drive?"

Anna conducted a swift, silent debate. In theory they were equal partners in this endeavor. Just moments ago Duke himself had stressed how they'd have to rely on each other's skills. But it would be stupid to take the wheel just to score a win in a minor power struggle.

"The maps and road signs are all in Ukrainian. I'll navigate."

The plan was to drive up to the village her grandmother had come from and use that as a base of operations to scout out the neighboring villages. Although Anna wouldn't admit it, she was more than happy to let Duke tackle the narrow, unpaved road leading out of the valley. Ditto the dizzying series of switchbacks they started up some miles later.

The hairpin turns sent her heart into her throat. The unprotected drop-offs mere inches from the passenger-side wheels had her gripping her seat. Even the shimmering beauty of the birches lost its allure. Their slender white trunks crowded the narrow road on one side. On the other, their pointed tips speared up from below like sharpened stakes.

"I don't remember the road being this bad," Anna muttered during a short, straight stretch. "I... *Look out!*"

Her shriek flushed a covey of red-crested blackbirds from the birches. It also startled the horse plod-ding around the curve in their direction.

The shaggy beast skittered and pushed back against the straps harnessing him between the shafts of a wooden logging cart. The cart's rear wheel scraped the crumbly road edge. Its heavy load of logs tilted dan-gerously. Swearing profusely, the driver fought to keep the cart from taking him and his horse over the side.

Anna was out and running before Duke slammed the vehicle into Park. She got a grip on the horse's har-ness, adding her pull to the driver's grim efforts to urge it forward. For a few frantic seconds she thought they would lose the tug-of-war. Then the cart's rear wheel caught. Inch by inch, it regained solid ground.

Once his swaying load had settled, the driver glared at Anna. Wisps of sparse white hair poked from under his flat-brimmed felt cap and framed a face mottled with anger.

"Why did you screech like that?"

She identified his dialect immediately. It was the same mix of Polish, Romanian and Ukrainian her ba-bushka had spoken as a child.

"I'm sorry. We didn't see you until it was almost too late."

The swift, idiomatic reply added curiosity to the anger still simmering in his eyes. "How do you speak Hutsul? And why do you come up this road? It leads nowhere."

Anna stroked the horse's shaggy mane. The ani-mal stood no higher than her shoulder. It was from the tough, stocky breed that had originated here in the Car-pathians, developed over the centuries for hacking and pulling timber. It was still a primary means of transport for logs harvested on the more inaccessible slopes.

"This road leads to the village of my grandmother," she told the driver. "She taught me her language when I was young."

"Your grandmother, eh? Who is she?"

"Her name is Katerina Solkov. Katerina Baustus before she married my grandfather."

"I don't know her."

The suspicion that accompanied the flat statement didn't surprise Anna. Isolated and clannish, the people of these mountains were known for their distrust of outsiders. Once they accepted a stranger into their midst, however, they would share their last crust of bread with him.

"My grandmother was born in the mountains but moved to Kiev as a young girl."

"So why do you come?"

"I want to show the land of my ancestors to my… to my husband."

Annoyed, she delivered a swift, mental kick for stumbling over the word. And for the flush that crept up her cheeks as the husband under discussion ambled up and slid a possessive arm around her waist.

"Is there a problem, sweetheart?"

The question was easy, the meaning behind it not so much.

"No problem."

She tried for a honeymoonish smile. The effort hurt her cheeks. Exercising what she considered admirable restraint, she didn't twitch away from Duke's loose embrace.

"I'm just satisfying this gentleman's curiosity about the tourists who nearly ran him off the road."

The driver watched their exchange from the cart, waiting only until it was done to issue a gruff request. "You will move your car so I may pass, yes?"

"Yes, of course."

Easier said than done, Anna soon discovered. She held her breath while Duke backed up, foot by careful foot, until the road widened enough for the cart to squeeze by. Even then Duke had to pull dangerously close to the edge.

"Don't stay in the jeep," Anna pleaded.

"There should be enough room. But just in case…"

He climbed out and hauled their backpacks from the rear seat. Dropping them beside her, he went back to help guide the cart past the precariously parked vehicle.

The driver tipped Anna a grudging nod as he passed. She returned it, holding her breath as he inched by. She was just beginning to relax when she heard a crunch. One of the logs protruding from the back end of the cart had put a deep crease in the jeep's fender.

"Damn." Duke surveyed the damage and shook his head. "Hope I don't have to foot the bill for the repairs."

"Surely not! You're on official business. If you explain how…"

The white squint lines at the corners of his eyes crinkled, and the slow grin she was beginning to recognize as an intrinsic component of his personality tipped the corners of his mouth.

"I'm kidding, Anna."

"Oh."

"If special ops personnel had to pay for every piece

of equipment they dropped, blew up or otherwise destroyed, we'd have to mortgage our homes and sell our wives and children. Speaking of wives…"

He glanced at the cart disappearing slowly down the steep grade. The driver was just visible, staring back at them over his shoulder. Duke recognized a perfect opportunity when it smacked him in the face.

"The driver still looks suspicious." He slid a hand under Anna's ponytail and cupped her nape. "We'd better make this look good."

Chapter 4

Duke intended the kiss as a blind. A tactical move to allay the driver's suspicion of the strangers in his mountains. Maneuvering the seductive Anna Solkov into his arms was merely a secondary objective.

Yeah, right! He recognized that for the lie it was the moment his mouth covered hers. One taste, and he was in a free fall. A long, slow glide that picked up speed and intensity with every second he had her in his arms. Instinct said he'd better yank the ripcord. Raw hunger overrode instinct.

Shifting his stance, he brought her closer and deepened the kiss. She stiffened for a moment. Two. Then her mouth opened under his.

Yes! A surge of pure male triumph shot through him. But despite the need that kinked his gut, he kept his hold loose. He fully expected her to pull away at any moment. When she didn't, the last remaining corner of his mind that hadn't imploded from the taste and the scent and feel of her finally told him that he needed to end it.

Reluctantly, he broke contact and raised his head. Her lids lifted. He expected—hoped!—to see the slumberous smile of a well-kissed woman in her cinnamon-brown eyes. Instead they met his with a cool disdain that punched an asteroid-sized hole in his ego.

"You've been wanting to do that since that night in Pete's Place, haven't you?"

"Pretty much," he admitted.

"Then it's just as well we got it out of the way."

Still cool, still maddeningly aloof, she pushed out of his arms and picked up her backpack.

"Now we can focus on the mission."

Duke had been shot down before. Not often, though, and not with such casual disdain. His only consolation was that she'd responded. Just for a second or two, but she'd responded. He'd felt her body lose its stiffness, caught the hitch in her breath before her mouth opened under his. Still, as he hooked the strap of his backpack and trailed her to the jeep, he tried to convince himself he wasn't leaving a big chunk of his manhood lying in the dirt road. It was a tough sell.

"Better let me pull away from the edge before you get in," he warned gruffly.

Anna managed to maintain her air of nonchalance until he had the jeep repositioned. Once she climbed in and they were headed back up the steep grade, the facade almost crumbled.

She could still taste him! Still feel his taut, muscled

body against hers! And every time she succeeded in blocking the sensations, the vehicle would hit an incline. The muscles in Duke's thigh corded as he worked the clutch. His arm grazed hers as he shifted. Anna edged as close as she could to her side of the jeep but the seat belt wouldn't let her escape him completely.

She didn't want these wild sensations. And she certainly didn't need the distraction they were causing. Granted, some of her antipathy to Duke Carmichael had faded. And yes, she'd almost swallowed her tongue when she'd seen him working out at the gym. Despite the increasingly chill mountain air, the memory of his rippling muscles and hard body made her sweat a little under her turtleneck. Thoroughly annoyed with herself, she whipped up the map and studied their tortuous route.

A little less than an hour later they rounded a turn and her grandmother's village came into view. The cluster of dwellings was strung along a narrow shelf carved out of the timber. The valley dropped off below, and the mountains towered above.

"It hasn't changed at all!"

The exclamation burst out of Anna before she noticed the satellite dishes. They sprouted from the steeply slanting roofs of a few dwellings and perched on balconies of several others. Everything else looked very much the same, though.

One main street bisected the village. Faded Cyrillic letters on the sign above the only shop indicated it still did double duty as a post office. Chickens pecked in the dirt outside the houses scattered along both sides of the street. The homes were predominantly clapboard and small but brightly painted—to be more visible in the deep winter snow.

The road into the village led past a church, with its twin spires topped by onion domes. Wreaths of dried wildflowers hung from the rusting Greek-Catholic iron crosses in the cemetery.

"My great-grandparents are buried there," Anna told Duke. "And that's the house where my babushka was born. I think a cousin five or six times removed lives there now."

She nodded to a rectangular, single-story dwelling. Its brilliant blue paint was flaking off, baring the weathered boards beneath, but its window boxes were filled with late season flowers that defied the cold fall nights. A wreath with a profusion of colorful streamers decorated the front door.

As expected, their arrival generated intense scrutiny by the few locals out and about. A bearded shepherd driving his flock through town stared at them with narrowed eyes. A woman beating a carpet hung on a clothesline halted in midswing. The two young children with her stopped playing to gape. The boy wore a knitted sweater and a miniature version of the black, flat-brimmed cap Anna always thought of as a Zorba-the-Greek hat. The little girl had round blue eyes and a thumb stuck in her mouth. Her long braids were woven with bright ribbons.

That was another thing Anna suddenly remembered. The Hutsuls' love of color. They expressed it in their brightly painted houses and in the clothing they donned for weddings and other special events. On those occasions, the women topped rainbow-colored skirts with exquisitely embroidered and beaded blouses. The men tucked their pants legs into their boots Cossack-style and cinched their equally colorful shirts with wide leather belts. She was recalling one especially flamboyant party when she caught sight of a familiar face.

"Stop!"

Duke hit the brakes for the second time, and Anna swung out of the jeep. Although she and the stoop-shouldered woman just emerging from the village store were actually cousins several times removed, she used the time-honored title bestowed on older women by younger generations.

"Auntie? Auntie Oksana?"

Her cry caught the other woman by surprise. Turning a wrinkled walnut of a face, she squinted through cataract-clouded eyes as Anna rushed forward.

"It's Anya. Katerina Solkov's granddaughter. Do you remember me?"

"Anya? Little Anya?"

"Yes, although I'm not so little anymore."

Her eyes widening beneath her flowered kerchief, Oksana beamed a smile that almost got lost in her wrinkles. "You've come for another visit?" She peered eagerly in the direction of the jeep. "With my dear, dear cousin Katerina?"

"No, Auntie, my grandmother is well but too frail to make such a long trip. I've come with, uh, my husband."

Oh, for God's sake! She had to stop stumbling over that word.

Okay, it wasn't the word itself. It was the intimacy

it implied. Anna had worried enough about playing the role of love-struck bride *before* Duke pulled her into his arms. Now...

Now the prospect of lying close to him for the next few nights had her all tangled up in knots of nervousness and rigidly suppressed need.

"So you have married at last!" the older woman exclaimed. "In her last letter, your grandmother said she feared this would never happen."

"Yes, well..."

Before Anna could spiel out her carefully scripted cover story, Oksana's blurred eyes dipped to her belly.

"But you're not yet pregnant?"

"No, not yet."

"Ahhh." She wagged a knowing finger. "You must not waste too much time, Anya. You're not as young as most brides. If you nibble the fruit but spit out the seeds, you will never give your babushka babies to kiss and cuddle."

Laughing, Anna acknowledged the age-old lament of Ukrainian mothers and grandmothers. "The babies will come, Auntie, in time."

"If you say." Her squinty gaze shifted to the jeep. "So this is your husband?"

"It is."

"You! Come here!"

The order was in Ukrainian but Duke had no trouble interpreting the imperiously crooked finger. Dutifully, he climbed out of the jeep.

"This is my grandmother's cousin," Anna told him. "My Auntie Oksana."

He smiled a greeting, which the old lady didn't return. Instead, she subjected him to an up-and-down that left him feeling pretty much like a raw recruit being sized up by a lantern-jawed drill sergeant. Correction. Make that a prize stud about to be put up for auction. Auntie's gaze lingered on his crotch long enough to make him acutely uncomfortable.

Duke figured he'd read her narrow-eyed assessment right when she cackled something in Ukrainian and Anna turned a dull pink. He had to ask.

"Did I pass inspection?"

"Auntie wants to reserve judgment until she, uh, sees how the big knob grows on the branch. It's an old Ukrainian saying," she added, not meeting his eyes. "It means…"

"I get the drift."

Another exchange between Anna and her auntie followed. Both women employed gestures and a series of vigorous head-shakes, but Duke could tell who won the debate.

"She insists we stay at her house," Anna said, confirming his guess. "She says her spare bedroom is empty since her grandson left for the university."

"Sounds good to me."

"You sure? She's kin to my babushka. Either one of them could give that granny you told me about a run for her money."

"I'm sure."

Three hours later Duke admitted he might have committed a tactical error. Granny Jones had nothing on Auntie Oksana. The woman was relentless.

First, she insisted on feeding them. Boiled mutton.

Stuffed cabbage leaves. Beets simmered with onions. Crunchy, sugared fried dough.

"This is called *hvorost*," Anna said as she savored a bite. "It's a traditional Ukrainian dessert that's been passed down for untold generations."

Duke thought *hvorost* tasted pretty much like deep-fried newspaper but he manfully consumed several pieces.

Once Auntie had stuffed her guests to the groaning point, she invited what seemed like the entire village to greet them. Her tiny four-room house was soon jam-packed. A pungent combination of leather and sweat permeated every room, and lethal, home-brewed vodka flowed like spring water.

Her guests accepted Anna warmly but were obviously reserving judgment on Duke. The women eyed him with assessing glances that turned to smirks and knowing nods when they put their heads together. On learning that he was a sergeant in the U.S. Air Force and a former star football player, the men engaged him in a somewhat one-sided discussion over the differences between American and European-style football.

All of the guests appeared to have donned at least a portion of their Sunday best for the impromptu gathering. Duke couldn't remember when—or *if*—he'd ever seen such a collection of colorful shirts and intricately embroidered blouses. He was commenting on the bright plumage to Anna when Auntie shouted from across the room.

"Anya!"

Waving an arthritic claw, the old woman negotiated the crowd with a younger one in tow. A distant memory tugged at Anna as she eyed the slender, green-eyed blonde but she couldn't pin it down until Oksana announced her name.

"Do you remember Elena? The daughter of my sister's third son? You and Elena played together when last you visited."

"It's been too many years," the blonde protested. "Anya won't remember."

"But I do!"

The years rolled back and a disjointed sequence of events spilled out of Anna's memory bank.

"You shared your dolls with me. And you were in love," she reflected with a grin. "Seven or eight years old, and so much in love with that handsome little boy we both tagged after. The one with the cowlick. What was his name?"

Elena's friendly smile evaporated. "Marko," she said stiffly. "His name was Marko. He was my husband."

The *was* indicated trouble, but Anna wasn't sure what kind until Auntie tsked and shook her head.

"Such a young man, such a terrible accident."

"It was no accident!" Fire blazed hot and green in Elena's eyes. "He was murdered, I tell you!"

Her sharp retort rifled through the crowded rooms. Heads turned, a few women sighed audibly and more than one set of male eyes rolled. Elena caught the reaction and cursed. Spinning on a heel, she thrust her way through the crowd and out the door.

"I'm so sorry, Auntie." Stricken, Anna apologized for her unintentional gaffe. "I didn't mean to upset her."

"How could you know? She still hurts, that one, and doesn't want to let go of it." Oksana sighed and pushed away the sadness. "Come, meet the wife of my nephew's brother-in-law."

Duke snared Anna's arm as her honorary aunt forged a path through the crowd. "What was that about?"

"I'll tell you later."

Later didn't come for several hours. Darkness had dropped like a curtain. The temperature dropped with it. Cold air whooshed in every time the door opened and yet another guest trooped out.

By the time the last one exited, Anna had started to sag with fatigue and Duke was feeling the vodka's kick. He'd understood only one word in a dozen aimed in his direction. His Russian was ten years old and of the Moscow variety. Nothing like the dialect of the Carpathian mountain people. He couldn't mistake Auntie Oksana's sly expression, though, when she insisted they leave the cleaning-up for morning. With a shooing motion of her gnarled hands, she herded them to her closet-size second bedroom.

Duke had brought the backpacks and duffel in earlier so he was prepared for the room's minuscule dimensions. The twin bed was a problem, though. The only way he and Anna could both fit in it was if they spooned, and spooned tight.

The bed was shoved against the far wall, leaving barely enough space on the near side for a skinny nightstand with a lamp and vase of dried flowers. Above the bed Auntie had hung an elaborately punched tin icon containing a picture of the Virgin Mary. Crowded against the foot of the bed was a collection of garments hung on a wooden pole below a shelf nailed to the wall.

Auntie had pushed the clothing to one end of the pole to carve out room for their backpacks. Wedging herself into the tiny room, she pointed to a zippered cloth bag on the shelf above the pole.

"She wants you to lift it down," Anna explained.

"No problem."

Duke placed the cloth bag on the bed and backed out the door to give the women room to maneuver. Auntie caressed the bag with her gnarled hands for a moment, then tugged at the zipper. Duke was sure as hell no expert on quilts, but in his untutored opinion the one she drew out of its protective bag qualified as a work of art. Birds and flowers and vines formed rings of brilliant color. Centered among them were large, entwined initials.

Auntie smiled wistfully and spoke a few soft words. Anna's expression seemed to fold in on itself. For a moment she looked so lost that Duke felt something twist inside his chest.

Auntie broke the moment with a spate of lively chatter. Her head bobbed in Duke's direction several times, obviously demanding a translation.

"It's her wedding quilt," Anna explained, coming back from wherever she'd been. "Auntie says she and Uncle made many babies under it. She, uh, hopes we will, too."

"Right." Duke knew an exit line when he heard one. Deciding discretion was the better part of valor, he stretched an arm into his backpack and extracted his shaving kit. "I'll hit the head first."

The bathroom opened off the kitchen and was barely big enough for a sink, stool and shower with plastic accordion-style doors. He didn't try to squeeze into the stall, opting instead for a quick shave and scrub down.

When he left the bathroom, the door to Auntie's bedroom was closed and Anna waited for him in theirs. Duke checked at the sight of the nightgown that draped her from neck to ankle. Like the spread, it was beautifully embroidered. *Unlike* the spread, it was damned near transparent.

"It's Auntie's," she said with a forced shrug. "She insisted."

She edged past him with toothbrush in hand. Duke tried to keep his eyes off her backside and long, slender legs silhouetted through the thin linen. He really tried.

When the door closed behind her, he shed his boots and downy vest. He retrieved the KA-BAR from the inner vest pocket and slid it between the mattress and the bed frame. That done, he edged the bed a few inches away from the far wall.

"It's the only way this is going to work," he said when Anna returned and frowned at the crack between the mattress and the wall. "We won't both fit otherwise."

"This is crazy. I should have told Auntie we would just spread our sleeping bags on the floor in the other room." Still frowning, she yanked back the quilt. "If we stay another night, I will."

Duke couldn't resist. "Good luck with that. She'll tell you it's hard to make babies zipped up in separate sleeping bags."

She shot him a venomous look and slid under the quilt and top sheet. Wiggling, she spanned the gap with her hips and wedged her butt against the wall.

"Get in."

She peeled back the quilt, but not the sheet. The thin barrier was merely symbolic. She knew it. Duke knew it. The kiss this afternoon had altered the chemistry between them. Before that kiss, brown-eyed, brown-haired Anna Solkov had stirred his interest and unabashed lust. Here, with her dark, silky hair fanning across the pillow and those doe eyes tempting him to sin, she stirred a helluva lot more than interest.

Forcibly reminding himself they were here to search out and destroy a known terrorist, he shed his boots, long-sleeved microfiber shirt and jeans. The weight he'd lost during rehab left his skivvies riding low on his hips.

A small frown creased Anna's forehead as she studied the still-red scar from his wound. A second or two later her gaze slid up to the snake tattooed around his biceps. She didn't mention either, though, and Duke backed into the bed. Hanging half off the near edge, he reached for the switch to the lamp.

"Talk to me," he instructed when darkness engulfed them. "Tell me what you picked up from all that chatter tonight."

"Not much. Someone—the grandson of Auntie's friend Tasha, I think—mentioned that the logging company that employs half of the men in the village recently cut back. Several locals lost their jobs."

"Does the company have ties to Russia?"

"I don't know. If it does, do you think laid-off loggers could be angry enough to align themselves with Chechen terrorists and blow up a section of Russian pipeline?"

"It's a stretch," he admitted.

She shifted, angling for more room. Her front was jammed against Duke's back. Her breath was warm on his neck.

This, he decided, was going to be a long night. Gritting his teeth, he tried to block the sensations coming at him from every point of contact.

"What about that woman?" he asked. "The blonde? Something sure lit her fuse. Was her husband one of the men who lost his job?"

"I don't think so. Auntie said he died in an accident. The blonde—Elena—claims it wasn't an accident. She thinks he was murdered."

"By whom?"

"She didn't say."

"Another stretch, but worth looking into."

He felt Anna's nod. The slight movement, hardly more than the dip of her chin against his shoulder blade, shot fire along his nerves.

"I'll talk to her tomorrow."

"What about strangers in the area? Anyone mention a man fitting Varno's description?"

"No."

Silence wrapped around them, punctuated by the broken snorts and wheezes coming through the thin walls. It hadn't taken Auntie long to zone out.

"What's the story on your tattoo?" Anna asked after a few moments. "I need to have an explanation ready if someone sees and comments on it."

Duke suspected there was as much curiosity behind the request as a need to maintain their cover. He had no problem with either.

"It's a sidewinder. A breed of rattlesnakes common in the Southwest. They're lightning-fast and deadly."

He closed a fist in an unconscious gesture he and his pals had perfected back in high school. The move flexed his biceps. Although neither he nor Anna could see it in the dark, the rattler showed its fangs.

"There are six of us with this particular tat."

"All special ops?"

"All special ops," he confirmed, "although not all Air Force. We've been buddies since high school. Played football together and got a reputation for being fast on our feet."

"I bet that's not all you got a reputation for," she commented dryly.

She'd bet right. Smiling in the darkness, Duke slid into memories of shoulder pads cracking like rifle shots and cheerleaders in short little skirts performing backflips whenever one of the sidewinders tackled a receiver or intercepted a pass. They'd made a few tackles off the field, too. Dan Taylor in particular could get those sweet young things performing more than backflips.

Well, hell! Recalling those torrid encounters wasn't real smart, Duke realized as Anna shifted again. The sweaty, aching urgency of his high school days didn't come close to the hunger that grabbed him by the throat when Anna nested her thighs against his.

He had to shut this down, and fast. He couldn't afford to let both his brains and his balls turn to mush while on the hunt for Nikolai Varno.

Eyes closed, Duke tried every skill he'd been taught and a few he'd acquired the hard way to separate his mind from his body. None of them worked. He stayed awake and hurting long after Anna had gone all soft and warm against him.

Chapter 5

The strident crow of a rooster pierced Anna's hazy dreams. She lay with eyelids still glued together by sleep and winced as the rooster let loose with another raucous warble. The damned thing sounded as though it was right outside the window.

Only after his cry faded did she wake enough to record several other sensations. One, the dim light of dawn was seeping through the blinds on the room's only window. Two, her cheek rested on smooth, bare skin. Three, her nose was pressed against a whiskery chin. Four...

Four sent a spear of heat through her belly.

Sometime during the night she and Duke had dispensed with the protective barrier of the top sheet. It was now twisted around her waist. As was a heavy, hair-roughened arm. And instead of facing the solid wall of Duke's back, she was cradled against his side.

She inched back, slowly, carefully. When she put some space between her nose and the golden bristles, however, she saw his eyes were open and ridiculously clear. Hers still felt gritty with sleep, but she couldn't miss the smile that crinkled those squint lines.

"Mornin'."

She pushed back another inch or so, trying to ignore the smooth skin and taut muscle beneath her cheek.

"How long have you been awake?" she asked.

"Awhile."

The dry response left room for several interpretations. Anna chose to ignore the most obvious—that the same erotic sensations she was now experiencing had pulled him from sleep—and went with an alternative.

"We have to call in an update this morning. Have you decided what to report?"

"Not much *to* report, other than we're in the AO and have initiated queries, but I'll call it in."

"Okay. Well, ah, I'd better get up. I hear Auntie making noises in the kitchen."

She wiggled, intending to extricate her rear end from the gap between the mattress and the wall and climb over him. A terse command stilled her tentative movements.

"Hold still. I'll go first."

He slid his arm out from under her and rolled off the bed. Anna made a determined effort not to watch as he dressed in the same clothes he'd worn yesterday. He helped by keeping his back to her. Mostly. When he zipped up his jeans, though, he angled to the side just enough to give Anna a glimpse of a world-class erection.

The prominent bulge stirred an instant response. She could feel the muscles low in her belly tighten. Feel herself getting wet. The hunger that grabbed her was instinctive and unthinking. For the first time in longer than she could remember, she let herself imagine the feel of a man thrusting into her.

No! Not just any man. This man.

The intensity of her reaction to Duke Carmichael dismayed her. It was only their enforced proximity that stirred this absurd hunger, she told herself sternly. That, and the fact that he was six feet two inches of raw masculinity.

So different from Jeremy.

The thought hit with a punch and made her feel like a traitor to the man she'd once planned to spend the rest of her life with. Scowling, she waited only until the door closed behind Duke to scramble off the bed and into her clothes.

Auntie Oksana insisted on preparing breakfast for her guests. Duke's belly rumbled in appreciation when she plunked a heaping plate down in front of him. Four eggs sunny-side up. Four fat black sausages. A stack of sliced tomatoes. A wedge of pungent goat cheese. And thick chunks of dark, grainy bread to spread it on.

Duke cleaned everything up but had to hold up a hand when Auntie tried to spear more sausages onto his plate.

"No, no more. *Dakoyu.*"

That "thank you" pretty much exhausted the

Ukrainian he'd picked up so far. He turned to Anna for the rest.

"Tell her she puts my Granny Jones's biscuits and gravy to shame."

Smiling, Anna complied. She still felt a little uncomfortable from that moment in the bedroom, but she was determined to get past it. Duke's compliment helped. It led to an interested query from Oksana on how this granny of his made the biscuits and gravy he spoke of. After they'd exhausted that subject, Anna took a sip of her coffee and turned the conversation to Elena.

"I feel terrible that I upset her last night, Auntie. I thought I would go see her this morning and apologize."

"She upsets easily, that one." Sadness seemed to pull the older woman's wrinkles into long folds. "Ever since Marko died, she grows more and more angry."

"What happened to him?"

"An accident, as I said." Sighing, Oksana poked a wisp of white hair under her flowered kerchief. "He learns to drive the big tractors and bulldozers in the Army, yes? After the Army he comes home to the mountains but there are no jobs, so he tells Elena they must wait until he finds work to have babies."

"And that upset her?"

"Of course! Every wife wants babies."

Anna left that part out when she translated the conversation for Duke.

"Marko grows tired of her weeping and goes to Odessa," Auntie continued. "He finds work with a construction company, but his bulldozer hits something…. A cable or a power line or some such. There is an explosion, and Marko dies. Elena cannot blame herself for sending him to Odessa so she blames the company that hired him."

"Do you know the name of the company?"

"No."

"What kind of construction project he was working on perhaps?"

"What does it matter what the project was?" Oksana gave a gusty sigh and voiced a saying Anna had heard many times from her babushka. "The wind will blow whether the dog barks or not."

"I don't get it," Duke said when she caught him up on the conversation. "What does a barking dog have to do with the wind?"

"Beats me." She pushed away from the table and started to gather the empty plates. "But I might as well follow up with Elena."

"Sounds good. I'll help clean up and we can go."

"Not we. Me."

"I don't think so, babe."

"Elena doesn't know you. She's not as likely to talk with a stranger present. Besides, Auntie intends to parade you through the village."

"Huh?"

She took genuine delight in his sudden, deer-in-the-headlights expression. "She wants to show you off to the few folks who didn't cram in here last night. I know your Russian's rusty, but most of the older folks here still speak it. You might pick up some useful information while I'm at Elena's."

She paused with the stack of plates in hand, her face

thoughtful. "Auntie says Elena's husband, Marko, was in the Army. We know there are factions within the Ukrainian armed forces who believe the Russian pipelines are a slap in the face to their national sovereignty. Maybe Marko was aligned with one of these factions. Maybe his death is in some way connected to the plot to blow one up."

"Maybe," Duke agreed reluctantly as he cleared the rest of the table. "Just be sure you keep your cell phone with you. Call if you turn up anything, *anything,* that feels off to you."

"Will do."

They put the dishes in the sink and Anna got ready to leave. When she pulled on her windbreaker, she caught Auntie watching them with a knowing smile. Sighing, she went up on tiptoe to do her wifely duty.

"This is just for show," she murmured as her lips brushed Duke's.

She should have known he'd take full advantage of the situation. Sure enough, his arm came around her waist and a wicked glint lit his eyes.

"That little peck won't fool anyone, sweetheart. You need to show a little more enthusiasm."

"Careful, cowboy."

Ignoring her low warning, he brought her up against him. "Okay, I'm ready. Give it another shot."

With a look that promised serious retribution, Anna used both hands to grab the collar of his vest. She yanked him down and delivered a kiss that left her breathless, Duke grinning and Auntie cackling with delight.

Thrown off balance by her reaction to Duke Carmichael yet again, Anna zipped up the yellow windbreaker and stepped out into a mountain morning. The sun had crested the higher peaks but had yet to burn away the morning mist. Spirals of gray rose from the frost-rimmed ground and cloaked the birches like a lover's kiss. The cold fog carried with the scent of woodsmoke that spiraled from the chimneys of the houses Anna passed on her way out of town.

She barely noticed the fog or the chill. Auntie said Elena lived in a house about five kilometers outside the village. She needed every one of those kilometers to clear her head.

She wanted to talk to Elena, true, but the driving force behind her insistence that she go it alone was the need to get away from Duke. They'd been in each other's company almost around the clock for the past five days. The line between reality and the role they'd assumed for this mission was beginning to blur.

Those damned kisses didn't help. Or waking up to find herself cradled against his naked chest. Or the all-too-visual evidence that he was feeling the same effect of their enforced proximity. The mere memory sent heat spearing through her belly.

She shook her head. This was ridiculous. She needed to analyze her growing hunger for Duke Carmichael with the same dispassionate objectivity she brought to her job. Looked at that way, she didn't have to search hard to find the root cause for her edginess. The simple fact was that it had been too long since she'd had sex.

Jeremy would always occupy a corner of her heart. Anna knew that. She also knew that she'd used sixteen-hour workdays to help her get through the past three years. Ironic that the career she'd thrown herself into night and day had landed her in another man's arms. Worse, it had stirred a need she hadn't felt in far too long.

So what could she do about it? She had the answer even before the question fully formed in her mind. She couldn't do a damned thing. Neither could Duke. Not while they were here in the Ukraine. Maybe not anywhere.

They were too different. His career took him all over the world at a moment's notice. Hers was rooted in Washington. Normally rooted in Washington, anyway. The point was, she wanted stability and monogamy in a mate. From the first moment Duke had come on to her in Colorado, she'd known darn well it was because she represented a challenge. Certainly not because of any desire on his part for a serious relationship.

To be brutally honest, he'd never shown any indication he was interested in any kind of a relationship, serious or otherwise. Not back in Colorado. Not here. Anna had to give him that. The intimate moments they'd shared had all been for show.

Hadn't they?

She was damned if she knew, but the question occupied her for the rest of the trek to Elena's home.

That turned out to be a prefab structure set in a small clearing. As colorful as the other dwellings in these mountains, this one boasted pale aqua siding and red wooden shutters decorated with an explosion of brightly painted wildflowers. Tall grasses crowded the front stoop, though, and tightly drawn curtains gave the house a brooding air. A car was parked in front of the house, one of those toy-sized European minis that Duke couldn't have shoehorned into.

Afraid she might have come too early, Anna was debating whether to return later when the front door opened and Elena emerged. She was in jeans and sturdy work boots, with her hair caught back by a kerchief and a dented tin pail in her hand. She came down the front steps, whistled shrilly and started for the shed at the edge of the clearing.

No, not a shed, Anna saw. A small barn with an attached corral defined by split birch rails. Obviously home to the shaggy mountain pony that whinnied an eager greeting.

"Ahh, Succi, you're a greedy little beast." Elena knuckled the horse's forehead affectionately. "You want your breakfast, eh? Well, I…"

She broke off when the horse raised its head, ears pricked forward. Spinning, the blonde glared at her uninvited visitor.

"What do you want?"

The naked hostility stopped Anna in her tracks. "I came to apologize for upsetting you last night. I didn't know about Marko."

"Fine. Good. You have apologized. Now go."

"Elena, I'm so sorry…."

"For what? That those bastards in Odessa murdered my husband? You're no more sorry than I, Anya. No more…"

Her voice cracked, wavered.

"No more than I," she finished on a broken sob.

The pail clattered to the ground. The young widow

buried her face in her hands. Anna rushed forward and tried to put an arm around her shoulders.

"No!" The blonde flung off her hold. Tears streaked her face, but her eyes sparked now with fury. "I don't want comfort. I want only justice for my Marko."

"But…"

"It was no accident, I tell you! It was murder. They didn't mark the feeder line as they should have. They killed him. They killed my husband."

Anna hated to play on the woman's grief. Feeling like the worst kind of voyeur, she probed deeper into Elena's raw, weeping wound.

"Marko hit a feeder line?"

"To the Soyuz pipeline."

Anna's pulse tripped. "Your husband worked on the Soyuz?"

"You know it? You know the Russian company that owns it?"

"I know of it."

Elena's lip curled. "They want only to make a profit. They care nothing for the people who work for them, nothing for the land and seas they pollute. Well, they will soon *have* to care."

"Why?" Her heart was banging against her rib cage like a trapped bird. "What will make them…?"

"Who is this, Elena?"

The deep, sensual voice brought both women around. Elena's face went dead white as she faced the newcomer, and Anna looked into the ice-blue eyes of a killer.

Chapter 6

"Who's this?" Varno repeated, his eyes on Anna.

"This is… This is…"

Fury or fear or maybe her storm of weeping had robbed Elena of breath. As the blonde fought to get it back, Anna gathered every ounce of courage she possessed and thrust out her hand.

"Anya Solkov. I'm visiting from America."

God knew how she managed that cool, polite smile with spiders of fear crawling up her spine! Or how she kept from snatching her hand back when Varno held it several moments too long.

"You're an American, yet you speak like a native. How is that, Anya Solkov?"

"My grandmother was born in this village. She and my grandfather immigrated to the States, and I spent my summers with them when I was young. I grew up speaking both Russian and Ukrainian. And you are...?"

"Ah, forgive me. I am Gregor Zak, a friend of Elena's husband. As you can no doubt tell from *my* accent, I, too, am visiting this area."

In a desperate attempt to control her terror, she catalogued his features. Those pale, icy eyes. The slanting black brows. Skin showing the faint pock mocks of old acne. A full, sensual mouth set above a chin with a dent in the center.

That dimple would tag him, she thought exultantly. He could wear contacts or dye his hair, but unless he underwent cosmetic surgery, antiterrorism units around the world would now have a distinguishing feature to associate with Nikolai Varno.

Assuming Anna lived to report it.

"I don't remember seeing you at the party last night," she commented with a nonchalance that almost choked her. "Were you at Auntie Oksana's?"

"No, I had business to attend to and got back late." His pale eyes conveyed a show of disappointment as they shifted to Elena. "You didn't tell me there was to be a party."

"Anya and her husband arrived only yesterday afternoon. Auntie invited everyone to meet them. I would have told you about it this morning," she added with a hint of desperation that Anna picked up on immediately, "but you were still sleeping when I came out to feed Succi."

"I see." Varno's gaze lingered on Elena's mottled face for a moment before turning back to Anna. "So your husband is with you. Is he also an American?"

"He is. If you come into the village today, stop by Auntie Oksana's and I'll introduce you."

"Perhaps I'll do that."

"Great." She made a show of checking her watch. "I'd better get back. I left him and Auntie trying to communicate with hand signals."

She hesitated, unsure how much Varno had overheard, and went with the truth. "I'm sorry about Marko, Elena. Very sorry."

Her reply was low and bitter. "So am I."

The walk from the barn to the road was the longest of Anna's life. She kept her shoulders loose and stride easy, but more cold sweat gathered at the base of her spine with each step. Her hands shook so bad she jammed them in the pockets of her windbreaker. Her fist closed around her cell phone and squeezed it like a vise.

Had she asked too many questions? Too few? Was Varno suspicious?

Stupid, stupid, *stupid!* Of course he'd be suspicious. The man had killed or helped kill hundreds of innocent people. Police and militia forces in a dozen countries were hunting him.

She reached the edge of the clearing. Started down the dirt road. Forced herself to turn and wave to the two standing motionless, watching her. Neither returned the wave.

Her sweaty fist gripped the phone. Not yet. She couldn't contact Duke yet. Birches lined either side of the road, but she was still visible through the wickerwork of their slender white trunks.

Dried leaves crunched under her boots. The road took a curve up ahead. She strained to hear sounds from behind, was terrified that she would. To keep herself from bolting, she counted her steps. Five. Six. Seven…

She risked a quick look over her shoulder, and was jabbing at the phone's keyboard almost before she completed the sweep. Her heart dropped to her boot tops when the phone rang and rang.

Answer! Answer, dammit!

She jerked the instrument down from her ear, checked the number on the display and was about punch to redial when a laconic greeting came through the speaker.

"Hey, sweetheart."

"Where are you?"

He picked up on her urgency instantly. His own voice altered. Not enough to alert anyone listening to his end of the conversation, but Anna's trained ear caught the subtle change.

"I'm with Auntie at the store. Did you see Elena?"

"I saw her." Her heart pounded so hard and fast she could barely breathe. "I saw Varno, too. He's here, Duke. At Elena's place."

"Are you there now?"

Nothing subtle in that. It came at her with the speed and force of a bullet.

"No, I'm on the road, walking back to the village."

"Keep moving, and keep this line open!"

Duke threw out an excuse in mangled Russian and barged out of the small, cluttered shop. He left Auntie and the two old men he'd been trying to pump for information gaping after him.

Swearing viciously, he raced to Auntie's house to retrieve his weapons. He shouldn't have let Anna go off on her own. Shouldn't have accepted Auntie's assertion that he and Anna were the only strangers to show up in the village in recent weeks.

All right. Enough recriminations, dammit!

He needed to shut down, retool, focus.

Eyes flat, thoughts narrowed, he extracted the .45 from its hiding place, ejected the clip and made sure it was fully loaded before snapping it back in and chambering a round. The pistol went into the right pocket of his vest, a second clip and the KA-BAR into the left.

The jeep kicked over on the first try. Duke rocked it into a two-wheeled turn. The goat in Auntie's neighbor's yard bleated and jumped to the end of its tether to avoid bouncing off a fender. Chickens flapped their useless wings, squawking and scattering as Duke tore down the village's only street.

He earned a shouted curse from the housewife whose compost pile the jeep's rear wheel plowed through. An up-thrust finger from the sheep herder he sent diving for the side of the road. Then the village fell behind and the road dipped and curved ahead.

The leaves still clinging to the birches flashed by in flickers of orange and yellow and brown, like a DVD in fast forward. The jeep's tires spit up dirt and rock with every sharp turn. His eyes on the road, Duke kept his ears tuned to the phone stuffed in his shirt pocket and both hands on the wheel.

He didn't pull in a full breath until he spotted Anna's

canary-yellow windbreaker. She was coming toward him at a dead run, her dark hair trailing in the wind.

"It's Varno," she gasped as he skidded to a stop. "He claims he was a friend of Elena's husband, but she's nervous around him. Too nervous."

Duke threw the jeep into Park and swung out. "Where's the house?"

"About a kilometer and a half straight down this road."

"Right. Here's the plan. You go back to the village. I'll circle…"

"No way!"

"Remember our agreement?"

"Yes, but…"

"Listen up!" The command lashed like a whip. "I don't have time to argue with you and I damn sure can't go in worrying about whether Varno will frame you in his sights. Get in the jeep and haul ass, woman."

She bit down on her lip, hard, but did as ordered. He waited only until she'd put the jeep in gear and executed a screeching Y-turn before he palmed the .45 and took off.

Damned good thing he'd spent the weeks before this mission in Colorado Springs. The Carpathians didn't come close to the Rockies for oxygen deprivation. Duke's still-healing wound tugged at his hip like a sulky child demanding attention but he ran fast and he ran low.

He'd covered just over a half kilometer when he spotted the smoke rising above the tree line. It coiled into the blue sky, too thick for chimney smoke, too dark for a wood fire. A hundred yards later, he caught the stench. It came at him through the trees, carried on the wind with the stink of burning wood and melted plastic.

Duke's gut knotted. Anyone who'd ever pulled a buddy from a blazing armored vehicle or had to identify their charred remains could recognize the smell of burnt flesh. Savagely suppressing the memories of the times he'd had to search a still-smoking corpse for ID tags, Duke broke into an all-out sprint.

Mere moments later he spotted the flames leaping up to join the thickening column of smoke. A turn in the road brought the farmhouse into view. Fire licked at its windows. Heat from the inside was already buckling its exterior siding. More smoke poured through the open front door, almost concealing the body sprawled half-in, half-out of the house. She was on her stomach, with her face buried in a bent arm, but the blond hair spilling across the front stoop identified her.

"Dammit!"

Duke raced for the burning house. His weapon at the ready, he made constant sweeps to either side as he ran. He was halfway across the clearing when a loud thud pierced the fire's deadly crackle. Dropping into a shooter's crouch, he spun toward the sound and took two-handed aim at a wooden shed attached to the far end the house. His heart stayed square in his throat even after he spotted the panicked horse backing away from the burning house and thumping its haunches against the shed's wall.

Duke's priority was the woman. His gut told him she was too far gone to save, but he had to try. Shoving the .45 into the waistband of his jeans, he ripped off his vest as he closed the last few yards to the house.

Smoke boiled through the open door and windows shattered by the heat. Flames shot through the melted siding. A part of the roof crashed down even as Duke locked air in his lungs and ducked under the thick, suffocating smoke. Using the down vest to smother the flames licking at Elena's head and shoulders, he dragged her clear of the house.

As gently as he could, he rolled her onto her back. Her hair was gone now. Her scalp was black and blistered. Her bent elbow had protected her face from the fire. Might even have saved her life if someone hadn't sliced open her jugular.

Jaw locked, Duke retrieved the .45 from his waistband and pushed to his feet. Instinct as much as common sense told him Varno was gone. The bastard wouldn't have hung around until someone spotted the smoke and came running. Still, Duke kicked in the door to the shed and made a thorough sweep before going back outside to free the panicked horse. He slammed a shoulder against the top rail of the pen and aimed a vicious kick at the second to send it tumbling to the ground. The short, shaggy horse rolled its eyes, whinnied and sailed above the remaining rail. Hooves thundering, it took off at a gallop.

When Duke kneeled beside Elena again, her green eyes stared sightlessly at the sky. He closed them gently, battling a mix of cold fury and raging self-disgust. He should have accompanied Anna to Elena's house this morning. Should never have left her alone. He wouldn't make that mistake again.

Still kneeling beside Elena's body, he brought up his phone and thumbed in a code to uplink him to the military comm-sat net.

"Condor Main, this is Condor One."

He expected at least a token resistance from Anna to his flat declaration that they would operate in tandem from here on out. She surprised him by accepting the dictum with barely a nod. Elena's gruesome death had shaken her. Shaken Auntie Oksana and the rest of the village, too.

Word of the murder spread with the speed of light. Every resident of the village knew the gory details long before two *militsiya* officers from the Ministry of Internal Affairs arrived. They'd driven up from Khmelnytskyi, the nearest town of any size, and took over the investigation from the local constable.

Duke thought he might have to do some tap dancing given the murky justification for his and Anna's presence in the area. Auntie Oksana took care of that. With wringing hands and tear-streaked cheeks, she overcame whatever doubts the *militsiya* might have about dear, dear Anya and her husband.

While the Ukrainian police detectives conducted their investigation, the sitrep Duke called in to the 352nd at RAF Mildenhall was already producing results.

He'd supplied the name Varno had given Anna and her description of his appearance, along with a description of the car she'd spotted parked at Elena's. Armed with that information, the DIA and DOD had sent a joint emergency request to the National Reconnaissance Office in Chantilly, Virginia.

The NRO was one of the U.S.'s five "big" intelligence collection organizations. A sister agency to the CIA, NSA, DIA and NGA—the National Geospatial-Intelligence Agency—the NRO designed, built and operated the spy satellites that provided vital intelligence to senior military and civilian decision makers.

The decision maker in this instance sat smack atop the chain of command. The president himself had ordered the NRO to redirect satellite surveillance to this remote corner of the Carpathians. If Varno was tackling these winding mountain roads in a pearl-gray mini, Duke should get word any moment. So should the president.

At that point, the commander-in-chief would have two options. He could give the CIA the green light to pulverize the mini with a laser-guided missile launched from a drone. Or he could send word through secure channels for Duke to track Varno to his lair and call in a strike to take out not just the terrorist, but the rest of his cell. In either case, he would coordinate with the Ukrainian premier, who'd requested U.S. assistance.

The flash message came through just after noon. Duke excused himself from the crowd jammed into Auntie's house and went outside. He reentered the house a few minutes later and signaled to Anna to join him in their bedroom.

"They located the car," he told her quietly. "It was abandoned about forty clicks from here."

"Varno?"

"No sign."

"Dammit! Someone *has* to have seen him!"

"Yeah, well, with any luck someone will."

"What do we do in the meantime?"

"We pack up. We're leaving."

"We can't leave! Not with Varno still on the loose."

Anna's protest came straight from her gut. Going toe-to-toe with a known terrorist this morning had scared the crap out of her. All she'd wanted then was to get away from the man and call in the heavy artillery.

But Elena's brutal murder had altered her perspective on every aspect of this mission. Made it personal in a way that none of the hundreds and hundreds of hours she'd spent poring through intelligence data could.

"Orders are orders," Duke said calmly.

"And you always follow them?"

It wasn't so much of a question as an accusation, but she answered herself anyway.

"Yes, of course you follow them. The military's your life."

"Anna…"

"Get back on the phone. Contact Condor Main. We can't leave." She chopped a hand through the air to emphasize her point. "We know what Varno looks like now, but I'm the only one who's seen him up close and personal."

Too close and personal. She countered the shiver that raced up her spine with a stubborn tilt to her chin.

"I can ID the man, Duke. I want to stay until he's found."

"Use your head. He won't remain in this area. The consensus now is that Varno came to the mountains specifically to recruit Elena. Her belief that the greedy bastards who operate the pipeline killed her husband made her putty in his hands. Which is why," he continued, cutting off another protest, "we've been ordered to Odessa."

"What?"

"Think about it. The gas company's headquarters are in Kiev, but the accident that killed Elena's husband happened in Odessa. Given her grief and bitterness, what better way to avenge her husband's death than by destroying the project that destroyed him?"

"God!"

Her protests stilled, Anna's heart seemed to freeze inside her chest.

"Odessa's a huge city," she said with a swallow. "An explosion could cause massive casualties."

"Which is Varno's specialty," Duke agreed grimly. "And why two officers from the Ukrainian Ministry of Interior's Counterterrorism Division are flying down from Kiev to meet us in Odessa. So pack up. We need to make tracks."

Chapter 7

Auntie Oksana saw them off with teary eyes and the gift of her precious wedding quilt. Anna tried to refuse, protesting that the beautifully embroidered quilt was a family heirloom.

"You're the granddaughter of my dear, dear cousin Katerina. You *are* family."

The older woman kissed her on both cheeks before turning to Duke. With a mock scowl, she wagged an arthritic finger.

"You. Get to work. Make some babies. Tell him what I say, Anya."

She did, with great reluctance, and wasn't surprised by the grin that came crooked and slow and all male.

"I'll give it my best shot, ma'am."

The older woman was no more immune to the wicked delight in his blue eyes than the younger. Anna had to forcibly repress a flutter in the vicinity of her stomach. Auntie cackled and motioned for him to bend down before kissing him soundly on both cheeks.

"Now go." Her face fell into sober folds. "Find the one who killed Elena."

The road leading down out of the mountains was as twisty and knuckle-whitening as the way up. Once they hit the small town of Maiaky, however, they picked up E-87 and a straight shot into Odessa.

The air lost a little more of its nip with each kilometer. Not surprising, since they were headed toward a popular Black Sea resort city. Anna pulled up the unclassified DIA file on Odessa and scrolled through it, filling in Duke on the city's turbulent history as they sped along the modern motorway.

"Odessa started life way back in the day as a Tartar settlement, one of their few warm water seaports. The Lithuanians took control of it for several centuries, then the Ottoman Turks. After the Russians defeated the Turks in 1793, Catherine the Great granted Odessa an imperial charter. Many of the city's most elegant hotels and private residences date from that golden era."

"From 1793?" Duke whipped around a slow-moving truck. "Hope to hell they've updated the plumbing since then."

Anna ignored the sardonic comment and continued scrolling. "Odessa was the fourth largest city of Imperial Russia after Moscow, St. Petersburg and Warsaw. During the Soviet period it served as one of the USSR's most important ports and trade centers."

Duke was more conversant with the city's recent

history than its imperial past. "The Soviets established a major Navy base there, didn't they?"

"They did. Which made Odessa a prime target during WWII." She scrolled up another page and grimaced at the grim statistics. "The Germans and Romanians captured the city in 1942 after a brutal, two-month siege. They rounded up and massacred an estimated ninety thousand civilians, most of them Jews."

Chewing on her lower lip, she skimmed the recap of the atrocities. Thousands upon thousands of men, women and children had been marched to fields outside the city and machine-gunned where they stood. Thousands more were herded into nine separate powder warehouses, which were then set afire. Untold numbers were deported to concentration camps and never heard from again.

Anna dropped her hands to her lap and let the cell phone screen go dim. She was an intelligence officer. She read and analyzed reports every day that gave ample evidence of the seething hatred that drove human beings to commit the most despicable acts. Yet the massive scope of these atrocities was almost beyond comprehension.

At least until she compared them to atrocities Nikolai Varno reportedly had a hand in. Varno didn't shy away from murder, either, although on a smaller scale. Any means justified the ends in his view—including outfitting the widows of martyred subordinates with explosives and sending them into a Moscow subway at the height of rush hour.

He'd used the same cold-blooded approach with Elena, Anna thought grimly. Exploiting her grief. Firing her with a desperate need for vengeance. Had he contacted other women widowed by the accident that took Marko's life?

The thought brought Anna upright in her seat. Swiftly, she cleared her phone screen and punched in the code for the secure military satellite link.

"What are you doing?" Duke asked curiously.

She held up a finger and listened for the tone signaling her to go ahead. "Condor Main, this is Condor Two."

When the 352nd responded, she was ready with her request.

"Can you patch me through to JITF-CT at DIA headquarters?"

The acronym stood for the Joint Intelligence Task Force—Combating Terrorism. DIA had set up the task force several years ago to better integrate the vast array of intel collected from such varied sources as prisoner interrogations, spy satellites and military attachés serving at embassies around the world. Driven by her sudden thought, Anna was desperate to get hold of someone in the task force.

"Do you copy, Condor Main?"

"I copy, Condor Two. JITF-CT at DIA HQ. Hang on."

In the few moments it took to make the patch, she ran through a mental list of the civilian and military analysts detailed to the DIA task force. To her relief, the one who came on the line was a Navy lieutenant she knew personally.

"What can I do for you, Solkov?"

"I need everything you can dig up on the explosion that took the life of a Ukrainian construction worker by the name of Marko Rushenko. The explosion occurred four or five months ago near the city of Odessa. He was working on a project to upgrade a feeder line for the Soyuz pipeline."

"The Russian natural gas line that runs through the Ukraine?"

"Affirmative."

The lieutenant didn't audibly suck wind, but Anna knew he wanted to. She would, too, if hit with a request like this.

"We'll have to tap into highly classified sources. And if we turn up any information, we'll need top-level clearance to release it."

"I understand. What I want are the names and family data of any other men killed or injured in the same accident."

"Noted. I'll get back to you if we can find the info and get the green light to release it."

"They'll get the green," Duke drawled when she filled him in on the other end of her brief exchange. "Although I suspect the Ukrainian agents meeting us in Odessa could get the information faster."

"Maybe," Anna said with unshakable faith in the superior capabilities of the U.S. intel community, "and maybe not."

"In any case, that was good thinking."

She basked in the small glow of his approval for the last thirty kilometers before they hit the outskirts of Odessa. Using SatCom mapping directions, Anna guided them through the urban sprawl.

The half-light of early evening wasn't kind to the Soviet-era apartment buildings ringing the outer city. The long, unadorned, eminently functional stretches of concrete looked like prison blocks. Obviously recent attempts to add color and small green parks did little to soften their bleak exteriors. Only after Anna and Duke had penetrated the outer rings did the elegance of Catherine the Great's favorite seaside resort begin to emerge.

The streets widened and became tree-shaded boulevards. Unadorned concrete gave way to crumbling, not-yet-restored 18th and 19th facades. These in turn led to palaces and public buildings meticulously returned to their baroque glory. At the heart of the city, Odessa's famed Opera and Ballet House stood resplendent in gilt and white marble. Illuminated niches containing statues of the world's most famous composers encircled the neoclassical structure. Riveted by its beauty, Anna flicked her thumbs again to bring up the building's history.

"It says here the acoustics are so incredible that the softest whisper can be heard throughout the horseshoe-shaped hall," she relayed to a semi-interested Duke. "Tchaikovsky and Rachmaninoff conducted here. The great Enrico Caruso, among others, performed on stage, and Isadora Duncan danced here."

"I've heard of her," Duke commented as he negotiated the traffic circle in front of the Opera House. "Isn't she the one who was strangled when her long, billowing silk scarf got caught in the spokes of her Model T's tires?"

Leave it to a special ops type to have picked up that arcane bit of history.

"I think so."

Anna craned around for a last glimpse of the building *Forbes* magazine listed as one of the most important sights in Eastern Europe. When she flopped back into her seat, her breath caught at the lavishly adorned stucco palaces that lined the boulevard spearing out from the theater. Painted pink and turquoise and pale yellow, they'd been lovingly, gloriously restored.

At the very heart of the city was a larger-than-life-size statue of Catherine the Great. The empress dominated an elegant square and gazed toward the Black Sea, which could be accessed by what looked like a steep set of steps that seemed to drop straight down to the harbor.

"Those are the *Potemkin* steps," Anna informed Duke. "Once the formal entrance to the city for all visitors."

"Never mind the steps. Just get us to the hotel."

"It's supposed to be right here, on the square."

Their instructions were to check in, and the agents from the Ministry of Interior's Counterterrorism Division in Kiev would contact them at the hotel.

Anna and Duke spotted their designated destination at the same time. He gave a low whistle. She gulped.

"I don't think we're dressed for this."

It was all pink stucco and white marble columns, with elaborate pediments crowning every window in what looked like a mile-long facade. A half-dozen limos were lined up near the entrance. Doormen in white periwigs and frogged-and-braided blue coats stood ready to welcome guests.

The bewigged doormen were too well-trained to show anything but welcoming smiles for the two scruffy tourists who pulled up in an open jeep with mud-coated wheels. Duke gave them the jeep's keys but declined help with the luggage.

"We've got it," he said easily.

His pistol was back in its concealed compartment. Anna knew he wasn't about to let it out of his hands. He hefted the duffel and his backpack. She carried hers. The doormen held the door for them, and they entered a lobby screaming with marble and money. The crystal chandeliers alone must have cost a prince's ransom.

Although Anna guessed the average price of a room in Odessa was probably half that of a comparable room in Paris or London or Washington, the knowledge did little to ease her bureaucrat's conscience. Duke might have been joking about being required to pay for the damage to the jeep caused by the logging cart. Her years working in Washington, however, had given her a front-row seat to the sordid spectacle of high-ranking elected officials being sanctioned for extravagant boondoggles made at taxpayers' expense.

Her first impression of the lobby they walked into did little to soothe the prick of her conscience. The men strolling the marble floors or occupying one of the massive leather armchairs scattered amid feathery palms looked as though the cost of a room was the least of their concerns. They were executives for the most part, some in three-piece suits, some in jeans topped by sports coats, but all exuding the assurance that they belonged to an exclusive club. The women accompanying them were young and sleek. *Very* sleek. Unlike the males, few if any of the females sported wedding rings.

"What happens in Vegas," Anna murmured, eyeing one tall, particularly attentive companion.

"Or in Odessa," Duke agreed dryly.

The receptionist manning the marble counter greeted them with the same polite disregard for their casual attire as the doormen.

"Good evening. May I help you?"

"Mr. and Mrs. Carmichael," Duke told him. "I believe you have a reservation for us."

"Yes, indeed, Mr. Carmichael. We have you and your wife in a lovely two-bedroom suite overlooking the square."

If the receptionist wondered why a married couple needed two bedrooms, he certainly wasn't going to ask. With brisk efficiency he swiped their passports and took an imprint of Duke's credit card before handing them the key cards for their suite.

With a word of thanks, they made for the elevators. They'd discussed at some length the need to continue their cover during the drive into the city. Anna's passport carried her own name. The agents they would meet with shortly knew their real status. She could have checked into a separate room.

Duke had insisted they maintain the charade of a married couple, however. They didn't know if Varno was, in fact, headed for Odessa. Or if he'd relayed information about the American woman who'd talked to Elena to other members of his cell. If he had, they might come looking for Anna. So Duke wanted to keep her close. A two-bedroom suite was as much distance as he would allow between them.

She'd agreed to the compromise with a swamping sense of relief. The intensity of her response to Duke Carmichael had made her question whether she'd closed off too much of herself after Jeremy's death. The crush of Duke's mouth on hers, the feel of his arm banding her waist, brought needs too long dormant roaring back to life. The erection she'd glimpsed only this morning had added to the simmering and very volatile mix.

That very impressive bulge told her it wasn't all one-sided. She was having the same effect on him he had on her. Well, maybe not the same. With that lazy, come-hither grin and unshakable confidence, the man had probably racked up more trophies than a big-game hunter. Anna would just be one more to add to his wall.

Still, between the hunger he roused and the urgency of their mission, she felt more alive, more in-the-moment, than she had in longer than she could remember. The realization both tantalized and disturbed her. Hopefully, their separate sleeping quarters would give her a breather from Duke's overwhelming presence and help her decide how best to act—or not act—on the physical desire she couldn't seem to suppress no matter how hard she tried.

She was still wrestling with the conflicting emotions Duke roused when the elevator doors opened onto a hallway carpeted in royal-red. Sconces dripping crystal tears illuminated the corridor. Anna noticed Duke scoping out the security cameras mounted at strategic intervals. He also tested the crash bar on the stairwell as they passed.

Once inside their suite, he gave another low whistle. The sitting room was larger than Auntie Oksana's entire house. The furnishings blended exquisite antique with high-tech. Duke's eyes lit at the sight of a 55-inch plasma TV hanging above a well-stocked minibar. Anna zeroed in on the view of the main square framed by a pair of French doors.

"Ohhhh."

Enchanted, she nudged the doors open and stepped onto a balcony enclosed by a waist-high wrought-iron railing. Equally elaborate iron streetlamps lit up Odessa's main square, while carefully placed floodlights illuminated the ornate facades of the palaces lining the plaza.

The effect was magical. A visual masterpiece. One that must have delighted the sensual, hedonistic Catherine the Great, who'd indulged her love of beauty by taking dozens of handsome young lovers and amassing one of the world's greatest collections of art.

Duke was on the MilSat link when Anna went back inside. After confirming their arrival in Odessa, he listened a moment and nodded. "Roger that. We'll stand by."

"Stand by for what?" she asked when he signed off.

"The agents from Kiev have been delayed. They won't get here until morning."

She shrugged to dispel the tiredness that dragged at her like an anchor. "Well, I guess we might as well go hunt up dinner."

Going out was the last thing she wanted to do right

now. She was not only weary, but she also felt grubby beyond words. Duke, thank God, shared her sentiments.

"I could use some downtime. Why don't we clean up, then order from room service?"

"Deal!" She grabbed her backpack. "Which bedroom do you want?"

"Doesn't matter. I checked both while you were on the balcony. One has a tub," he related, manfully restraining a grimace, "the other a shower."

"You can have the shower. Right now I can think of nothing more seductive than wallowing in a tub of fragrant bubbles."

"Nothing?"

An all-too-familiar glint came into his eyes, and Anna kicked herself for giving him the perfect opening line.

"Don't say it."

She hesitated for a few moments, then decided it was time to be honest.

"As you might have noticed, I'm out of practice when it comes to sexual repartee."

"I don't know 'bout that, sweetheart."

"Duke. Please. Take my word for it. I haven't… I'm not… Oh, crap!"

She blinked furiously to stem the tears that welled up without warning. She couldn't stop them. She knew they were due to accumulated stress. Knew, too, they were nothing more than a release valve. All the rationalization in the world couldn't stop her from being completely mortified, however.

The tears surprised Duke almost as much as they

did her. He recovered faster than Anna, though. The teasing glint evaporated, and his voice gentled.

"Go take your bath. Wallow as long as you like. We'll order dinner when you get out."

She fled before she embarrassed herself further. The bedroom door slammed behind her.

Way to go, Carmichael!

Disgusted, Duke slung the duffel onto the bench at the foot of his bed. His backpack slammed down on top of it.

Throw out the same glib lines, why don't you? Lay on the smarmy grins and sexual innuendoes. What the hell are you? A walking, talking penis?

He didn't want to answer that one. Still thoroughly disgusted with himself, he stripped and turned the shower to full blast. The hard, hot stream bulleted his face. Angry pellets needled his body. Bracing both hands against the tiles, he let the water pound into him.

The pummeling didn't help. He was still blaming himself for Anna's minor meltdown as he rummaged through the carryall for clean jeans and a shirt. He left the shirttail out and was working the buttons when he finally acknowledged the truth.

He was damned close to falling in love with Anna Solkov. Had been teetering on the edge since the first time he'd imagined those long, curvy legs wrapped around his. Only now he was more interested in the total package.

Interested, hell. He wanted her with a primal need that struck deeper and harder than any he'd felt before. Duke knew damned well that need was all tied up with the urgency of their mission and his raw, visceral fear this morning when he found out she'd wandered smack into Varno's sights.

Yet...

Even without the adrenaline spike of their mission, Anna Solkov attracted him on more levels than any other woman he'd known. There were her smarts, for one thing. Duke didn't know anyone else who could converse fluently in four languages and speak several variants of each one. Then there was her precise, logical approach to problems. She broke every issue down, analyzed the underlying factors and viewed the reassembled whole with a clear eye.

He admired both of those qualities, but in his warrior's mind they paled in comparison to her courage under fire. She'd recognized Varno instantly. Knew she faced a stone-cold killer. Yet she'd maintained her cool, extricated herself from the dangerous situation and called for backup. To Duke, that kind of grit stirred feelings that went deeper than any physical attraction.

Or so he thought. Right up until Anna strolled out of her bathroom almost forty minutes later. Her face was flushed from the steamy heat of her bath. A towel was wrapped around her damp hair turban-style. And the hotel's plush, terrycloth robe gave glimpses of just enough sleek, damp flesh to put an instant kink in Duke's gut.

Chapter 8

Obviously unaware of her impact on his entire system, Anna dropped onto the sofa and tucked her legs under her. Duke made a concentrated effort to get his mind out of the gutter and off the question of what she might or might not have on under that robe. Remembering her surprising bout of tears aided in the effort.

"Did you check out the room service menu?" she asked.

"I did. It's right there on the coffee table if you want to take a look."

She leafed through the embossed leather folder and made a quick decision. "The borscht looks good to me. How about you?"

"Steak, medium, with all the trimmings."

"If you'll pour me a glass of red wine, I'll call the order in."

"Deal."

While he opened one of the splits in the minibar, Anna punched the button for room service on the house phone. It must have been left on speaker, as a pleasant male voice floated into the room.

"How may I help you, Mr. Carmichael?"

"This is, uh, Mrs. Carmichael. We'd like to order dinner."

"Yes, madam."

Duke hid a smile as he poured wine for her and a pale, light lager for himself. She'd probably get used to that *Mrs.* about the time they turned in their wedding rings.

Unless they didn't turn them in.

The thought came hurtling at him from out in left field. *Way* out in left field. Along with it came the reminder that he owed Anna an apology.

He handed her the wine and took one of the armchairs set at an angle to the sofa. Leaning forward, he rested his elbows on his knees and cradled the cold beer in his hands.

"Look, Anna, I'm sorry about earlier. I tend to come on a little strong at times."

"A little?"

"You know it's ninety percent hot air and ten percent wishful thinking, don't you?"

"I'm not sure I agree with the proportions but I won't argue the point."

"Good, because the last thing I want is to make you uncomfortable." The self-disgust he'd felt earlier rolled back with a vengeance. "I apologize for overplaying this husband bit and..."

And what? Turning what should have been a couple of casual pecks on the cheek into full-body contact? Taking advantage of her surprise to coax a response she never intended to give?

"For initiating physical contact," he finished lamely. "It won't happen again."

"It won't?"

"No, ma'am."

He was dead serious. No twang. No drawl. She acknowledged as much with a small nod. Then she raised the glass, took a sip and knocked him back on his ass.

"That's too bad."

He blinked. "Come again?"

"I did some thinking while I soaked. There are a few things I need to say, too. First, I owe you an explanation for going all girly earlier."

"Girly's okay," he said, scrambling to recover. "Girly's good."

"No, it's not. And it's not me. I can't remember the last time I fell apart like that. Wait. That's not true."

She looked down at her wine and let out a slow breath.

"I do remember. It was three years ago last month." She ran a fingertip around the rim of the glass. Once. Twice. "I'd just gotten engaged. Jeremy proposed over dinner at our favorite restaurant in Washington, D.C. I had an early briefing in the morning, so he left my apartment around midnight. He didn't make it home."

"What happened?"

She lifted her gaze, met his. The pain in her brown eyes stabbed into Duke like a bayonet.

"A drunk driver plowed across a median on the GW

Parkway going more than ninety miles an hour. He slammed into Jeremy's car head-on."

"Christ!"

Duke could guess how little was left of her fiancé when they'd pried him out of the wreckage. He ached to scoop her into his arms and comfort her. Just comfort her. Ironic, given his recent promise to cease and desist all physical contact.

Unless…

His thoughts arrowed back to her previous that's-too-bad comment. Did she *want* to be held? Want contact? He got his answer when she set aside her glass and looked him square in the eye.

"That's why I said I was out of practice. I haven't dated much in the past three years. I haven't had sex at all."

Good God! Three years? Duke gulped and tried to sound rational and sympathetic.

"Understandable. You're still grieving."

"Not as much as I was," she replied with brutal honesty. "I don't know if it's the urgency of our mission or being here in the Ukraine or squeezing up next to you last night. But for the first time in a long time I feel alive and—" she pulled in a deep breath "—hungry."

Carefully, very carefully, Duke avoided looking at the creamy flesh exposed by that deep drag.

"Also understandable," he said with a calm he was light-years from feeling. "Situations like this generate intense emotions. You don't need to be embarrassed by them."

"I'm not embarrassed."

Whoa! Remember. You are not *a walking penis. You*

will not *pounce*. This situation called for understanding. Sympathy. Restraint.

"There's a name for what you're feeling." He forced a friendly, professorial tone. "It's called situational response. Sun Tzu wrote about it in *The Art of War*. He was referring to the thousands of factors that have to be assimilated in a combat situation to make the right decision but…"

"Oh, for pity's sake!" Exasperated, she thunked her wineglass onto the coffee table. "Do you want to have sex or don't you?"

Screw restraint!

"Yes, ma'am, I surely do. Any time, any place."

"What?"

"That's the motto of the air commandos," he growled as he slammed his beer down on the side table. "Not the same as the combat controllers, but it sure works in this instance."

Leaning forward, he wrapped a hand around her wrist. All the reasons this was a bad idea flashed into his head as he tugged her off the sofa and into his lap. He countered each of them just as swiftly.

They were in a secure location. He'd mapped out ingress and emergency egress routes. The doors were double-locked, the windows bolted, the drapes pulled. His comm device sat within easy reach, his weapons were less than ten steps away.

"I wanted you the first moment you sashayed into my line of sight, sweetheart."

And he was back, Anna thought on a swift, jolting thrill. The cocky cowboy with the exaggerated drawl and the unmistakable invitation in his blue eyes. Oddly, those traits didn't irritate her now. Just the opposite. Her blood pounding fast and hard, she hooked her arms around his neck.

"How long do you think we have before room service gets here?"

"Not long enough." He nuzzled a spot just behind her right ear. "Nothing says we can't fire up the APU while we wait, though."

"APU?"

"Auxiliary power unit. Engines. F-16s."

"Right."

She knew what an APU was. Would have remembered that maintenance personnel rolled out the cart to jump-start jet engines in another moment or two. Sooner, if Duke hadn't distracted her by trailing hot, stinging kisses from her ear to her chin to her mouth.

He nudged her lips open with his. Nudged her robe open a few moments later. His growl when he cupped her bare breast triggered an atavistic response in Anna.

Everything that was female in her seemed to spring to life. She ached for him, craved the feel of him on and over and in her. Her senses soared, registering vivid impressions. She breathed in the clean, soapy scent of his skin. Reveled in the feel of hard muscle under his shirt. Tasted hops and hunger on his breath.

She was wondering wildly what Sun Tzu had to say about situational responses in these particular circumstances when Duke's thumb grazed her nipple. Small darts of pleasure streaked from her breast to her belly. Then he hiked her up a few inches and replaced his thumb with his mouth. The darts became fire-bursts of delight.

When he'd teased and tortured her nipple to an aching peak, he jerked the robe off her shoulder and bared the other breast. Half embarrassed, wholly aroused, Anna arched her back and offered herself like some pagan sacrifice.

The towel wrapped around her hair dropped to the floor in a damp heap. Her robe opened at the waist, and the sight of her no-nonsense cotton panties produced a smothered chuckle.

"These look like the ones my Granny Jones used to hang on the line."

"Hey, I didn't think I would need a thong when I packed for this little excursion."

"Thongs?" His blue eyes lit with delight. "You wear thongs?"

"On occasion."

Groaning, he angled his head and pressed his forehead against hers. "Oh, babe, you're killing me here. We may not make it to the bedroom."

"Well…"

The doorbell buzzed, and Anna spit out a curse. Duke's oath was considerably more colorful.

"I'll get it," he groaned. "Don't forget where we were."

Like she could?

Still breathing hard, Anna drew the front of her robe together and followed Duke's swift detour to the bedroom. When he returned, she knew the .45 rode under his shirt at the small of his back.

The reminder of where they were and why sobered her. So did his careful check through the peep hole before he opened the door. He followed that with a narrow-eyed assessment of the waiter who rolled in a trolley.

"Shall I set up at the table by the window, sir?"

"That's fine."

The prospect of dining with a view of Odessa's lamplit main square sounded lovely to Anna. Duke disagreed. After he signed the check and added a tip that made the waiter thank him profusely, he nixed her suggestion they open the drapes.

"Too dark outside," he said with a shrug as he reset the door locks, "and too bright inside. Urban guerrilla warfare 101. You never want to present an illuminated target."

That pretty much doused the last of Anna's sexual sizzle. Deflated, she tightened the belt of her robe and raked back her damp, tangled hair before joining him at the table.

He sensed the change in mood even before she lifted the cover on her bowl of soup. His mouth tipped into a wry grin.

"Something tells me I'm going to regret opening the door to that waiter. I should have just told him to leave the trolley in the hall."

"Maybe." She played her spoon around the dollop of sour cream floating atop the rich, red borscht. "And maybe it was just the time-out we needed. Correction, make that the time-out *I* needed."

"Having second thoughts?"

"Second, third and fourth."

"Ouch." He faked a wince. "Doesn't say much for my technique."

His deliberate attempt to lighten the mood drew a reluctant smile. "Your technique is excellent, cowboy."

"Good to know."

Duke sawed off a corner of steak. It was tender and juicy and went down a whole lot easier than Anna's change of heart.

"So the problem is…?" he asked, feeling her out.

"The problem is I let myself forget where we are, why we're here."

"I didn't."

Not entirely true. There were a few moments back there when the taste of her, the feel of her, blocked every conscious thought. Not real smart in these circumstances, but Duke had learned to trust the subliminal instinct that operated just below the consciousness level. God knew it had jerked him from deep sleep to full alert too many times not to.

"I have to be honest." She laid the spoon aside, her borscht untasted. "There's more."

He figured there was. Judging by the way her brows straight-lined into a frown, he also figured he wasn't going to like it.

"I decided to use you," she confessed slowly, reluctantly. "As I told you earlier, I haven't had sex in a long time. You… This situation…"

"Make you feel alive again. Yeah, I got it the first time."

The sardonic reply set her back in her chair, frowning. It set Duke back, too. Who the hell was he to come all indignant at the idea of being used by a woman? And why should it dent his ego that this particular woman considered him a half step up from a vibrator?

For the second time that night, he delivered a swift mental kick to his own ass. What was with him? Anna had opened up for the first time. Given him a glimpse of the pain she'd lived with for three years. The least he could do was acknowledge that hurt.

"That came out wrong," he said gruffly. "I appreciate you telling me about your fiancé. Not all scars are on the outside, and I'm glad yours are finally starting to heal."

He considered adding that he was available 24/7 to speed the healing process. Just as quickly, he axed the thought. He was done dishing out sexual quips.

"Healing is a slow process, Anna. Mental or physical. You can't force it. Some scars just take longer than others to fade."

As he knew all too well.

"What you can do, though, is eat your soup before it gets cold. Then we'd better grab some sleep. I suspect our friends from Kiev will want an early start tomorrow morning."

They did.

Duke's bedroom was pitch-dark when the house phone on his nightstand jangled. He caught it on the second ring, noting the faintly glowing 6:32 a.m. on the digital clock-radio.

"Carmichael."

A man answered in heavily accented English. "This is Special Agent Anatoly Yallin. When can you and Ms. Solkov be downstairs?"

"Give us a half hour."

"I will have a car waiting."

"To take us where?"

"The Central Office of the Ministry of Internal Affairs here in Odessa. I will meet you there."

Duke pulled on his jeans and went to tell Anna about the call. She was already up, tying the belt to her robe as she met him in the sitting room.

"I heard the phone. What's up?"

"Our contact from Kiev wants an early session. Can you be ready to go in thirty minutes?"

"I can if you'll make some coffee."

He got the sleek European coffeemaker going, then went to splash water on his face and give his teeth a quick scrub. No time to shave or do more than shove his feet into his boots and his arms into the sleeves of the same shirt he'd dug out of the duffel last night. He tucked the tails in this time, though, and added his down vest for warmth.

After some debate, he secured his .45 in the room safe. MI headquarters would be swarming with officers, uniformed and plainclothes. Chances were they screened all visitors, probably had them go through full-body scanners. The pistol would set off all kinds of alarms.

So would the KA-BAR, but Duke wasn't going out naked. Special Agent Yallin would just have to get the knife past the gatekeepers.

A call from the driver alerted Yallin to their arrival. When they pulled up at the entrance to the pale yellow, stucco-and-brick edifice that housed Odessa's central police headquarters, he was waiting on the front steps.

Anatoly Yallin turned out to be a small, very intense

man with a tilt to his eyes that suggested Tartar ancestry. He wore the gray-blue, military-style uniform of the Ministry of Internal Affairs. The insignia on the uniform's collar indicated he held the rank of major, and the sharpshooter's badge mounted above a rack of ribbons indicated he hadn't spent his career behind a desk. With him was another officer he introduced as chief of the Ukrainian Interpol Bureau.

"Please, come with us."

As Duke had anticipated, access to the headquarters was through a security checkpoint that included a full-body scan. Anna went first. After sending her shoulder bag through the conveyor, she stepped into the booth and raised both arms. Duke watched the face of the uniformed cop behind the screen. The man's smarmy expression said he was thoroughly enjoying the view.

Even without the body scan, she drew admiring attention. Her mink-brown hair was swept up to reveal shell-shaped ears, and her cream-colored turtleneck molded her breasts. A primitive possessiveness Duke never knew he had in him curled his hands into fists. He was a half step way from punching out the lights of the leering cop when a terse order from Yallin ended the display.

Anna lowered her arms and reclaimed her purse. Not bothering to disguise her icy disdain, she skewered the voyeur with a look that said she hoped he'd enjoyed the peep show. Duke guessed the caustic remark she subsequently addressed to the man put that sentiment into words.

Her zinger flustered the cop so much he almost forgot to wave Duke into the scanner. Another sharp exclamation recalled him to his duty. Duke dumped his phone, loose change and folded knife into a plastic tray. He'd reached the scanning booth before the cop even noticed the knife rattling along on the conveyor.

His startled exclamation brought two associates rushing over. They snatched the tray off the conveyor and engaged in a heated debate with Yallin. The counterterrorism agent finally cut it off and motioned Duke through the scanner with an impatient gesture.

"Why did you bring this?" he asked in his thick, guttural English as he returned the folded blade.

"Same reason you've got a holster tucked under your left armpit. We're both after a killer. One Ms. Solkov has not only seen, but spoken to. And right now she's the only one who can ID him."

"The Ukrainian authorities are well aware of that!"

Still irate, Yallin made a visible effort to rein in his temper.

"Not all of us in the Ministry of Internal Affairs agreed with the decision to ask the Americans for help in this matter," he admitted. "My division is responsible for the capture of Nikolai Varno. It is our number-one priority."

"Understand. And Ms. Solkov's safety is mine."

Yallin accepted the comeback with a curt nod and led the way down a tiled corridor.

Chapter 9

Anna and Duke spent the entire morning at the Ministry of Internal Affairs. The first two hours involved an exhaustive review of the events at Elena's place. Blurred jurisdictional lines magnified the number of participants in this session. Nine officials—eight men, one woman—of different ranks and different areas of responsibility sat in. Some were military, some were police officers. Two were civilian with vaguely defined political jobs. Yallin and his associate from the Interpol Bureau had flown in from Kiev, which didn't sit well with the Odessa locals. Most of the attendees spoke basic English, thankfully. Where there were gaps or questions, Anna acted as translator.

As the session went on, the size and diversity of the group nagged at Duke. His Moscow embassy tour hadn't left him with a warm fuzzy, as the bureaucracy had grown to such power during the heyday of the USSR. Graft was a way of life among civilian officials, the police and the military. The Russian mafia operated with near impunity.

He didn't want to ascribe the same systemic weaknesses to the Ukrainians. They'd admitted they needed help nailing Varno. Had requested that the U.S. set up this covert op. Still...

Duke looked around the table, studying each face, listening to their questions and opinions on what options to pursue at this point. All the time, he kept trying to gauge where their loyalties lay. The discussion of the accident that killed Elena's husband caused a sharp rift in those loyalties.

One of the civilians at the table was a rep from what Duke guessed was the Ukrainian equivalent of the U.S. Department of Commerce. The man apparently served as a midlevel flunky in the division that monitored the construction, operation and maintenance of the pipelines that cut through the Ukraine. Heavy-set and red-faced, with a thatch of salt-and-pepper hair and bushy white eyebrows set above protruding eyes, the bureaucrat became defensive when Anna related Elena's contention that her husband's bulldozer had hit an unmarked feeder line.

"It was not so! We investigate that explosion, yes? The fault was the operator's." He beetled his brows and scowled at Anna. "When you say otherwise you insult my department."

"I didn't say it," she replied coolly. "Elena did. She was convinced the Russian company that owns the pipeline cut corners to increase their profits."

"Cut corners?" the official blustered. "What is this cut corners?"

"They sacrificed safety to save money. Or," she added with a bland expression, "perhaps paid bribes to Ukrainian inspectors to look the other way at shoddy workmanship."

The man's eyes bulged as if they were trying to jump out of their sockets. "This is not so!"

The other female at the table gave a snort, which she quickly converted to a cough. Two of the uniformed officers exchanged openly sardonic glances.

"Were there other workers killed in this accident?" Anna asked.

"Two," the bureaucrat conceded stiffly.

"You have their names? The names of their family members?"

"I do not carry them in my head," he huffed.

"You might want to look them up. We suspect Nikolai Varno was attempting to exploit Elena's grief and recruit her as a suicide bomber. He may try to do the same with someone else who lost a loved one in that explosion."

The civilian started to bluster again. Special Agent Yallin cut him off with a curt comment in Ukrainian and addressed Anna directly.

"Making bombs and convincing women to strap them on is indeed Varno's area of expertise. We will obtain the names of the other men who died in the accident and talk to their families."

The session broke up soon after that. The civilian charged with overseeing the Russian pipeline left red-faced with anger. Eyes hard, Yallin watched him go before turning to Anna.

"We have a—how do you call them?—a graphics artist standing by. Will you work with him to provide a picture of what Varno looks like now?"

"Of course. He may have changed his appearance since I saw him, though."

"We must hope he has not had time."

It was past noon by the time Anna and the police artist assigned to work with her had produced an image of Nikolai Varno. Yallin immediately had it digitized and sent it with an alert to every national and international agency involved in the hunt for terrorists.

"You must take a copy, too, Ms. Solkov." He handed her a printed version of the alert along with his business card. "Look at the image again later, with fresh eyes. If you wish to add anything or make a change, please notify me at once."

Anna slid both the image and his card into her purse. "I will."

"We cannot thank you enough for your assistance in this matter. And you, Sergeant Carmichael." He gave Duke one of his cards, as well. "Perhaps you will allow me to take you to dinner as a small gesture of my government's gratitude."

"Thanks, but that's not necessary."

"Please, I insist. We should fix a time. When do you return home?"

"We haven't arranged that yet."

"I understand. You must wait for termination orders to come down through your chain of command. You will receive them shortly. Now that we know what Varno looks like and that he's most likely here, in Odessa, my government has instructed me and my department to assume full responsibility for his capture."

Yallin's polite expression gave no hint of what he thought about the decision, but Duke suspected politics had played a major role in it. The Ukrainian government had asked the U.S. to conduct a secret, undercover op in their country to help ID and, hopefully, take down the vicious but elusive Varno. Now that the noose appeared to be tightening around the bastard, the Ukrainians obviously wanted to take full credit for the kill.

Duke hated the thought of being yanked off the op at this crucial point. Elena's burned body cried for justice. It was the Ukrainians' call, however. If they wanted to pick up the ball at this point and run with it, Duke would get word soon enough.

And there was Anna to consider. As she and Duke followed Yallin down to the exit, he found himself hoping to hell the stand-down order came soon. He'd worried that Varno might target Anna to prevent her from ID'ing him. Now that she'd provided a description, there was the revenge factor to consider.

The faster Duke put an ocean between her and the terrorist, the happier he'd be. And once he had her home, he thought with a sudden tightening in his belly, the two of them had some unfinished personal business to take care of.

* * *

Various methods for taking care of that business occupied Duke's mind during lunch at the hotel's restaurant. Anna spooned down a hearty potato soup. On her recommendation, he feasted on Kiev-style fish cutlets cut into fine strips, served with green beans and potatoes. They followed the main courses with coffee and a dessert Anna called *vergun.*

"I used to help my babushka make these," she commented as the waiter deposited a platter containing spears of braided and fried dough dusted with powdered sugar. "We had them every Sunday after we got home from church."

"They look good." Duke bit into one of the still-warm pastries. He tasted honey and rum and butter. Lots of butter. "They *are* good."

Anna took a bite, savored the taste and rendered judgment. "They're okay."

"Just not in the same league as your babushka's," he teased.

"Not anywhere *near* the same league."

She polished off her pastry. Duke did the same and would have reached for another if the sight of Anna daintily licking her fingers hadn't sent his thoughts zinging back to their unfinished business.

He was hungry all over again when they left the table. Even hungrier when the elevator doors closed behind them and he spotted a trace of white on her upper lip.

"You're sporting a sugar mustache."

"I am?" She swiped her fingers over her mouth. "Did that get it?"

"Not quite."

He cupped her chin and brushed his thumb across her lips. Once. Twice. And again, more slowly.

Anna's eyes widened, and the air between them suddenly went static. Like electrical charges that needed grounding, the unseen sparks leaped from her lips to Duke's thumb and shot straight to his groin.

He flattened his free palm against the wall behind her head and tilted her chin with the other. He had to have a taste of her. Just one.

"Anna…"

He'd waited too long. The damned elevator glided to a stop before he could make his move. Smothering a curse, he dropped his hand, waited for the doors to ping open and did a quick visual of the hall.

She didn't say a word as they walked to their suite. Duke keyed the door and entered first. After a quick sweep, he gave her the okay. She crossed to the overstuffed sofa and dropped her purse. A flush rode high in her cheeks when she faced him with arms crossed.

"I thought we decided last night to put this…this… whatever it is between us on hold."

"More or less," he agreed.

"So what was that about in the elevator?"

"That was the less."

The laconic reply didn't satisfy either of them. She frowned, and Duke scrubbed a palm across the back of his neck.

"Turns out I'm having a harder time keeping my hands off you than I thought I would," he admitted ruefully. "I'll work on it, sweetheart."

He'd have to work hard. Damned hard. Starting now.

"I didn't have time to shave or shower this morning. 'Scuse me while I go take a long, cold one."

Anna remained where she was for long moments after he'd retreated to his bedroom. She heard him moving around and picked up the faint zip of the duffel followed by the drum of water against the shower stall.

A calm, rational corner of her mind said she'd done the right thing by putting the brakes on last night. The rest of her screamed with the need to strip off her clothes and join him in the shower to finish what they'd started.

She went with the need.

Duke was just reaching into the glass shower stall to adjust the temperature. His discarded clothing lay in a heap on the bathroom floor. His shaving kit sat open and ready on the marble counter.

"Duke."

He spun around, his muscles tensing. His narrowed eyes did a lightning sweep of her face, her hands, the room behind her. Whatever he saw—or didn't see—relieved some of his tension but put a sharp edge to his voice.

"What's wrong?"

"I've been thinking…"

Too much, she realized. She'd been thinking too damned much. When all this time she should have been listening to what her body and her heart were telling her.

"I don't want you to keep your hands off me."

His shoulders went taut again. It was a different kind of tension this time, and Anna's pulse began to pound.

He seemed unconcerned or oblivious to the fact that he was naked. She was neither, however.

Her greedy gaze roamed from his face to the snake coiled around his biceps to the still-healing scar on his hip. Neither the tattoo nor the scar could detract from the symmetry and sheer male beauty of his body. What had he said? Healing was a slow process, and some scars took longer than others to fade.

Anna knew now that hers had healed. She would always hold Jeremy's memory in her heart, but he was her past. Duke Carmichael was her present. Possibly her future. The absolute rightness of what she was feeling made her whole body shiver with anticipation. Slowly, she reached for the hem of her turtleneck and tugged it upward.

Duke stood like a rock. Steam curled out of the shower behind him, unnoticed and unimportant.

"Are you sure about this?" he growled.

"I'm sure. I told myself…and I told *you* that the adrenaline rush of the mission was what made me feel alive again. That I could ride the high and use you for sex, then we'd go our separate ways."

She unzipped her jeans. Shimmied them over her hips. Saw his blue eyes flame.

"I discovered several problems with my analysis," she said, her voice husky. "First, our mission's over. According to Yallin, his government has the stick now. And yet my adrenaline's still pumping."

She bent her arms behind her and unhooked her bra.

"Second, I don't want just sex. I want *you,* Duke. *You* make me feel alive again. *You* make my blood pound and my heart sing and my…"

That was all she got out. All she needed to get out. In the next instant, his hands were at her waist. One swift move disposed of her panties. Another planted her bottom on the cool marble of the bathroom counter.

"I can't even begin to tell you what you do to me, little Anya."

His mouth came down on hers, hot and hungry. The bristles on his cheeks scraped hers. His hands raked into her hair, anchoring her for his kiss.

Anna thought briefly about suggesting that he turn off the shower. Then he nudged her knees apart and she had no thought for anything but this moment, this man.

She opened for him, spreading her legs wide. She could feel him rock-hard against her thigh. Feel the heat scorching his skin as she hooked an arm around his neck and returned his kiss with greedy hunger.

She was panting with need when she wedged her other arm between their straining bodies. Her fingers closed around his jutting erection. She slid her hand up, down, up again, feeling him pulse with each stroke, then cupped his tight sac.

Grunting, he pulled out of her hold. "Hang on a minute."

"For *what?*"

He answered by reaching over to grab the shaving kit he'd tossed on the counter. Moving at the speed of light, he dug out a condom, ripped it open and sheathed himself.

"Now," he said, angling her hips so he pressed hard against her hot, wet center, "where were we?"

Wiggling, she increased the pressure. Her breath came in quick, eager pants.

"Right..."

She wiggled again and felt a spasm of pure sensation.

"About..."

She twisted her arms around his neck and locked her ankles around his hips. With a thrust of her hips, she pulled him into her.

"Here!"

Anna had made the initial thrust, but Duke set the rhythm. Slow at first. Maddeningly slow. She tried to increase the pace but he delivered an exquisite torture. Stretching her, filling her, lifting her half off the counter with a bunch of his powerful thigh muscles. Then pulling out an inch, two inches, four. All the while he used his hands and his mouth on her throat, her breasts, her nipples. And when he pressed a thumb against the tight, aching flesh at her center, he drove Anna to a spinning, screaming climax.

She stiffened, riding the wild waves, slowly drifting down. Then the thrusts got faster, harder, and she soared again until his neck corded and his body went rigid.

When she opened her eyes, steam from the shower was curled around them. Every mirror and glass surface in the bathroom had fogged, and the counter beneath her was slick to the touch.

Smiling, Anna stroked Duke's whiskery cheek. "I think your water's hot."

"Looks like," he agreed with a grin. "Want to scrub my back?"

"I'm not sure I can stand," she admitted ruefully, "much less scrub."

She slid off the counter and discovered getting her legs to hold her upright was, in fact, an iffy proposition.

"I need time to recover," she told Duke. "Take your shower. And shave those bristles," she added when she noticed a prominent whisker burn on her left breast.

"Yes, ma'am."

She gathered her clothes and left him whistling happily in the steamed-up glass cubicle.

She made a quick trip to her bedroom and emerged wearing clean underwear and the comfortable, cherry-red exercise suit with a short-sleeved white tank. She was tightening the drawstrings of the pants when the purse she'd tossed on the sofa table emitted a loud buzz.

Startled, Anna fished her phone out and checked the digital display. It showed the coded number for Condor Main. Thumbing in the answering code, she jammed the instrument to her ear.

"This is Condor Two, go ahead, Condor Main."

"We have a data file to transmit from JITF-CT."

Yes! The lieutenant had come through!

"Go ahead, Condor Main."

"Please switch from voice to data mode, Condor Two, and advise on receipt."

Anna made the switch, silently giving thanks for the technology that made it possible to zip files up to satellites, across oceans and down again with the speed of light. Or sound. Or whatever.

Mere seconds later she'd saved the file to her phone's encrypted memory board and confirmed receipt. When she tried to read the contents, though, the print was too minuscule to decipher without a magnifying glass.

"Dammit."

Frustrated, she took the phone to the desk set against one wall of the sitting room. Maybe she could print the file using a larger font.

Like the rest of the suite, the desk offered a blend of gilded antique and high tech. Not that high tech, unfortunately. The combination fax/scanner/printer on the credenza behind the desk didn't do wireless, and a search of all drawers failed to produce a USB cord.

"Great. Just great!"

The USB cord had probably gone home in the briefcase of the last exec who'd stayed in this suite. Or whatever high-priced companion he'd brought up here with him. Anxious to decipher the data, she picked up the house phone and punched the button for the business center.

"How may I help you, Mr. Carmichael?"

"This is Mrs. Carmichael," Anna corrected with no stumble this time. She was getting used to the title. "I need to print a document from my cell phone, but I can't find a USB cord for the printer."

"It should be in the top center drawer of the credenza, madam."

"It's not."

"I apologize for the inconvenience. I'll search out a replacement and send it up to you."

Anna shifted her cell phone from hand to hand. Impatience bit at her. The transmission could contain vital data that should be shared with Yallin.

"That's okay," she told the business center manager. "We'll come down there."

She hurried back into the bedroom and shoved her feet into the high-tops she'd worn for most of the trip.

When she reentered Duke's bathroom, he greeted her with a smile.

"Change your mind about scrubbing my back?" he called over the whoosh of the shower.

"You wish!" She held up the phone for him to see. "The JITF data just came through. We need to review it."

"Okay." He reached for the miniature shampoo bottle supplied by the hotel. "Give me five minutes."

She returned to the sitting room and paced. After two minutes, she'd almost decided to make a quick jog down to the business center herself. At three, another buzz stopped her in her tracks.

It was the doorbell this time. The business center must have sent up a USB connector, after all. She detoured to the door but wasn't about to open it until she verified who stood on the other side. She put her eye to the peephole and got a distorted view of bulging eyeballs topped by fuzzy white eyebrows.

They identified the visitor immediately as the testy civilian bureaucrat from this morning's meeting. Frowning, Anna unlocked the dead bolt but kept the chain guard on.

"Yes?"

The man was beet-red and sweating profusely. She couldn't keep from staring at his protruding eyeballs. They looked like they were about to pop out of their sockets at any minute.

"I…I have uncovered some disturbing information about the accident," he stuttered. "Special Agent Yallin said I should come speak with you about it."

"Okay. Just a sec."

She closed the door and released the chain, then opened the heavy oak panel again. If the man in the hallway was red-faced and sweating before, he looked like he was about to stroke out now. She reached instinctively for his arm.

"Are you okay?"

Before he could answer, a dark shadow separated from the wall beside the door. There was a glint of steel, and a flash of terror on the fat official's face. In the next instant, a gaping maw opened in his throat.

Blood gushed like an uncapped oil well, splattering Anna's face and chest. Before she could stumble back, before the gurgling bureaucrat had even sunk to his knees, a brutal hand was buried in her hair and a bloodied blade tip cut into the underside of her jaw.

"Don't scream!" Varno dug the tip deeper, slicing skin, drawing blood. "Don't scream, or I will kill you."

Her head was angled so far back that all she could see were his eyes. They turned her bowels to water.

"You'll…" She hated herself for whimpering. "You'll kill me anyway."

"Not unless you force me to. You're more valuable alive than dead right now. Do as I say, and you may survive."

She didn't believe him. Not for a second. But she fought to breathe through her terror and listened desperately to the sounds from Duke's bathroom. She had to warn him. Had to…

"Let's go."

In a lightning move, Varno switched his brutal grip

from her hair to her arm. The knife was still there, pressed against her jugular, as she stumbled over the corpse now sprawled half-in, half-out of the suite.

Chapter 10

Like most combat veterans, Duke had racked up too many memories that still gave him night sweats. He'd seen men blown apart, others set ablaze. Heard them cry for their mothers, their wives, their God. He'd edged too close to the fine line between interrogation and torture to extract desperately needed information from a sobbing, terrified prisoner. On one grim occasion, he'd called in an air strike, then watched in horror when the NATO pilot missed his grid and splashed his 500-pounder less than two hundred meters from an Afghan village school.

Those soul-searing moments would always remain etched on his psyche. So would the moment he strolled out of the bathroom and spotted the blood-drenched body sprawled across the threshold of their suite. It wasn't Anna. That registered instantly, and he was through the door almost before his heart kick-started again. There was no one in the hall. No sound, no movement, no dark smears in the plush carpet or bloody handprints on the wall. One of the digital displays above the elevators was blank, indicating no movement. The other was stopped at lobby level.

Duke raced the few yards to the emergency exit. Slamming the crash bar, he burst into the concrete-block stairwell. With a vicious effort of will, he shut down the fury and fear roaring in his ears and forced himself to listen. Just listen. No footsteps thudding up or clattering down. No gasps or grunts or harsh breathing other than his own.

Varno, he acknowledged savagely. It had to be Varno or his accomplices. Wherever they'd taken Anna, though, he knew in his gut it wasn't to another floor or room in the hotel. They had to anticipate that the entire building would go into lockdown while the police conducted a room-to-room search. No, they had to get her out of the hotel, and fast.

Acting on pure instinct, he leaped down four flights of stairs. A crash door opened onto each floor, then into the lobby.

He bypassed the lobby exit with only a moment's hesitation. They wouldn't take her through the front entrance. Too many eyes, too much risk someone might see her terror, smell her fear. There had to be another exit, some way for guests to escape in the event of fire or evacuation.

There was. Another half flight down, a crash door opened onto a back alley. It was permeated with the stink of overflowing Dumpsters. The cars parked bumper to bumper along one side of the narrow passageway left barely enough space for other vehicles to squeeze by.

None were trying to at the moment. No delivery vans, no garbage trucks, no drivers attempting to unwedge their parked car. But Duke did find two items that got his heart pumping pure adrenaline. The first was a small greenish splotch of coolant, still wet and shimmering, which suggested a vehicle had idled right outside the exit recently. *Very* recently. The second was the surveillance camera mounted on the hotel's elaborate cornice. Its eye pointed straight down the alley.

Duke raced back up the half flight and hit the lobby at a dead run. Shoving past a couple waiting to check in, he barked at the receptionist.

"Where's your security office?"

Startled, she gave the man she'd been helping an apologetic glance before addressing Duke.

"I'm sorry, sir, if you'll just let me finish with this gentleman, I'll be happy to..."

"Your security office! Where is it?"

"Uh, down the hall and to the left." She reached for her phone. "I'll call the security officer on duty, shall I, and ask him to come..."

Duke left her with the phone halfway to her ear.

The hotel's security center sat hunched between the business office and the exercise room. Duke might have missed it completely if not for the discreet placard lettered in English, Japanese and Cyrillic. Inside the office was a reception area with a desk and comfortable chairs for guests coming in to report a lost watch or stolen credit card. Behind that was a glass partition separating the reception area from the flickering, black-and-white world of surveillance monitors.

The security officer on duty looked to be in his late thirties, with a half-eaten sandwich in his hand and a bored look on his thin, almost cadaverous, face.

"May I help…?"

Duke shoved past him and aimed for the area behind the partitions. His narrowed eyes skimmed the bank of monitors stacked six to a row.

"Sir!"

"David Carmichael," he rapped out in answer to the indignant protest. "Suite 306. My wife's been kidnapped."

"Wh-what do you say?"

"There."

He jabbed a finger at a still view of the hall leading to their suite. Their room was halfway down the hall. The open door showed clearly the lower half of a crumpled body.

"If you'd been doing your damned job you might have noticed you have a dead man on your hands."

The security officer gaped at the screen, goggle-eyed. His bony fingers clamped down on his sandwich. A pinkish goo of some kind of sauce mixed with mayonnaise sprayed across his sleeve and just missed the business card Duke whipped out of his wallet.

"Call this number. Tell Special Agent Yallin we need him here, fast. Then run the disk for the security camera covering the alley behind the hotel."

Yallin arrived less than twenty minutes later. By then a small phalanx of police and hotel security personnel had converged on the hotel. Half of them had treated Duke with naked suspicion. The other half was still trying to understand just how this big, burly American and his missing wife were tied to the dead official.

Yallin cut them all off with a curt order in Ukrainian. His shoulders were rigid under his blue-gray uniform, his Tartar eyes as black as ice as he faced Duke.

"What has happened?"

"I was in the shower."

Duke kept his reply as hard and flat as Yallin's expression. He'd rack up the self-recriminations later. Right now he didn't have the luxury of excoriating himself for the extra few minutes he'd taken to soap down.

"Anna must have answered the door because the chain's off and there's no sign of forced entry. I'm guessing she recognized him…."

Duke gestured to the view still up on one of the screens. The body hadn't been moved, but another small troop of uniformed and plain-clothed officials had taken up positions in the hall.

"Who is it?"

"The civilian who attended our meeting this morning. The one who got so hot at the idea his office would take bribes."

The Ukrainian special agent muttered something in his native language. The tone didn't convey a sense of regret for the bureaucrat's demise.

"His throat's slashed," Duke continued. "It couldn't have happened more than four or five minutes before I found him."

"And Ms. Solkov?"

"Gone."

"In four or five minutes? How is that possible?"

"Like this."

He motioned to the bone-thin security officer. Still shaken by everything that had come down on him in the past half hour, the scarecrow keyed his console. His equipment wasn't exactly high-tech but it was good enough to capture a grainy, black-and-white image of the small delivery van idling in the alley. Iridescent waves of exhaust rose from the van's tailpipe. Rust streaked its roof. Caked-on mud obscured its front tag.

Although Duke had played and replayed the next sequence a half-dozen times, his stomach still knotted when the hotel's back door kicked open. There was Anna, a thin stream of blood trickling from the underside of her chin, staining her white tank top. Varno had her arm twisted at a vicious angle behind her back and a five-inch blade at her throat.

The van's back door opened. Varno shoved Anna inside and climbed in behind her. The door slammed. The van jerked into motion, then tore down the alley with reckless disregard for the Dumpsters and vehicles crowding it on either side.

"Run that again," Yallin ordered.

He leaned into the monitor, scrutinizing the sequence with narrowed eyes, and had them freeze on the frame just before the van took off.

"The driver is a woman."

"Yeah." His jaw clenching, Duke stared the pale, blurred oval. "Varno's weapon of choice."

His already knotted stomach took another twist. An image filled his mind of the women who'd carried out the Moscow bombing. He pictured Anna draped in a heavy black burka. Her face was all but obscured by a veil. Only her eyes showed, flat and dulled by drugs as she walked into a crowded metro station wearing a heavy belt packed with explosives under the conceal-ing black folds.

No! He couldn't go there. Not when there was a hope they could run Varno to ground before the son of a bitch turned Anna into one of his instruments.

"Ms. Solkov received some data just before she was abducted," he growled.

Yallin looked up sharply. "Concerning?"

"The other men killed or hurt in the accident that took Elena's husband."

The special agent's eyes sharpened to dark lasers. "I've requested the same data but have not yet received it. How…?" He scrubbed a hand over his chin. "Never mind. Some things are best not explained. Where is this information now?"

"On Anna's phone."

"Her phone?" The look of a hunter spotting its prey lit Yallin's face. "She has it with her?"

"No. It's upstairs in our suite."

Duke watched the agent's hope of tracking the signal die with the same visceral disappointment he'd expe-rienced when he'd tasked the 352nd to run an emer-gency trace.

"I've had the data fed in here, however."

He passed Yallin the printed version of the DIA transmission. The single page contained the name and nationality of the second man who died in the explosion that killed Elena's husband. It also listed the other five workers injured in the blast.

"The second victim was Vietnamese," Yallin noted with a shake of his head. "Brought in by Russia to slave on their pipeline. He was probably paid no more than a hundred rubles a day. Even if his papers were in order, it will take time to track down his survivors."

"Several others, however, live in Odessa. Including this one."

Duke pointed to a name midlist. The brief entry indicated the injured man was twenty-six and recently married. Also that the blast had left him paralyzed from the neck down.

"Young, just married, completely incapacitated. Enough to turn any bride vengeful."

"Our people will talk to her and the others on this list. They will also trace the van," Yallin said with a glance at the vehicle still frozen on the screen. "In the meantime…"

"In the meantime?"

"All we can do is wait."

"I'm not waiting!"

The Ukrainian agent stiffened. He started to retort, caught himself and issued a curt order to the hotel's security officer. The man left the screen room without a word.

"I understand your frustration, Sergeant Carmichael," Yallin said carefully. "I share it."

"Then you know I'm not about to sit around on my ass while you take over this hunt."

"I'm afraid that is not your choice. My government has forwarded a request to yours to terminate Operation Condor. Your covert mission is over. And now that an American citizen has been kidnapped, it becomes even more imperative that we employ every resource within the Ministry of Internal Affairs to recover her safely. We cannot do that covertly."

"Yeah, that's obvious."

The sarcastic drawl raised a flush on Yallin's high cheekbones. "We will, of course, keep you informed and..."

"Informed, hell!"

Duke had had enough. The man facing him might hold officer's rank. He might have the power of his government behind him. He might even be right about the termination of Operation Condor.

None of that meant squat to Duke. With or without orders, with or without either government's approval, he was *not* standing down until Anna was safe.

"Listen to me, Special Agent Yallin. We work together on this or we work alone. Either way, I'm going to track Varno to his lair. And when I do, he's a dead man."

Chapter 11

"You're a dead man."

Anna shifted on the backless workbench. Plastic restraints cut into her wrists and tethered her arms around a rusted pipe that ran from the cement floor into the ceiling. Dried blood caked the underside of her chin and neck. Her eyes were locked on Varno as he entered through a side door and crossed the cluttered shop.

"You know that, right?" Her lip curled in what she hoped was a credible show of disdain. "If you don't let me go, my husband will hunt you down like a rabid dog and put a bullet between your eyes."

She didn't have any problem with *husband* in this instance. Any weapon she could use against this killer, she would.

"We all must die," he said with a shrug. "We have

no choice in that. We can, however, choose to make our deaths count for something."

"Right," she sneered. "Brave words from the coward who sends women in to do *his* killing."

She regretted the jibe when Varno changed directions. She saw the intent in his pale eyes, watched his arm swing back and braced herself for the vicious backhand that followed. Even prepared, she couldn't hold back a cry as pain exploded in the left side of her face.

"Don't overestimate your value, Mrs. Carmichael. I will let the Ukrainians negotiate for you, yes. Such negotiations will buy my friends and me the few days we need to complete our plans. But if you annoy me too much, or make any attempt to escape, I will slit your throat as I did Elena's and that fat pig who tried to take bribes from us while selling his soul to the Russians."

"The Ukrainians…" Anna swallowed the coppery taste of blood. She could hardly hear herself above the ringing in her ears. "The Ukrainians have a stated policy of non-negotiation with terrorists. So does my government. They…they won't concede to whatever demands you make."

"I don't expect them to."

How could such a handsome man project such evil? It was in his face, in the smile that looked like it might slither right off his face.

"As I said, all I need is time. You've bought me that. Neither government will take rash action as long as they think I might let you go."

"Will you?"

"You must cling to that hope."

Yeah, she'd do that. Right up until she plunged the bastard's knife into his belly and gutted him.

The savage thought sustained her while Varno hauled over a stool and busied himself at the worktable running the length of the shop. It was a garage of sorts, a mom-and-pop operation judging by the rusted tools hanging above the workbench and the assorted junk filling two stalls.

The white van occupied the third. It had been parked there since Varno hauled Anna out of its rear compartment and anchored her to this damned pipe. Five hours ago? Six? She couldn't formulate more than a rough guesstimate. The garage had no windows, only two bare bulbs dangling at the ends of long wires, so she didn't know if it was still afternoon or coming on to night.

Varno had been in and out several times. So had the woman who'd driven the van. She was young, probably in her mid-twenties, although her sunken features and the utter despair in her dark eyes made her seem decades older. All Anna had been able to extract from her before Varno cut them off was her name. Julia, pronounced *Yu-lia* in her native language.

Her cheek still burning and her ears ringing, Anna gathered her courage. "Do these plans of yours involve whatever you're tinkering with there on the workbench?"

"Actually, they do."

He swiveled on the stool and held up a palm-size circuit board with leader wires sprouting from either side like tricolored spaghetti.

"This is a timer. It's constructed from components

readily available in any electronics store." He hefted
what looked like an ordinary cell phone in his other
hand. "And this is the detonator. With these two mir-
acles of the modern age and that van packed with fer-
tilizer, I will mirror the act of one of your country's
terrorists."

"You're referring to Timothy McVeigh, the Okla-
homa City bomber?"

"I am. My death count will be considerably higher
that his, however."

For a moment Anna thought she saw something
close to regret in his ice-blue eyes.

"It's a terrible thing that so many must die before a
government admits they cannot shackle a proud people, yes?"

Keep him talking.

*Every DIA training manual said to keep a subject
talking.*

The Stockholm syndrome could work in reverse.
Not often, it was true. But in rare instances, hostages
could bend their captors' minds.

"What people?" she asked. "What government?"

"The Russians have kept Chechnya enslaved for too
long. We demand our own country. We will have it, no
matter how many we must kill to…"

The rattle of the garage's side door cut him off. Swift
as a snake, he leaped off the stool and rounded the
workbench. His knife slid from the scabbard at the
small of his back with well-oiled ease.

Weird, Anna thought in the half second before the
door opened. Really weird. The bastard wouldn't hesitate to unleash the destructive power of modern tech-

nology on innocent victims. Yet his weapon of choice was the same one that cavemen had brandished after they'd chipped the first flint to a razor's edge.

Julia nudged the door open with an elbow and entered the garage. She jumped back, the crockery on her tray banging, when she saw the flash of the blade mere inches from her face.

"Nikolai! I only bring her some soup!"

"You must knock before you enter, woman."

"Yes, yes, I know." The tray shook. Soup sloshed over the sides of an earthenware bowl. "I'm sorry."

The fear on her face prompted an abrupt change in Varno. In less than a heartbeat he went from stone-eyed to gentle.

"I, too, am sorry, Julia. What we do here, you and I, is so important. Pray God it will keep others from suffering as your husband does."

"Pray God," she echoed in an anguished whisper. Tears leaked from her eyes as she clenched the tray with white-knuckled fists. "Your...our friends wait for you in the kitchen. There's soup and bread and fresh *vergun*. You should go, eat with them. I'll feed this one."

He caressed her cheek, as sincere and caring as a viper, before exiting the garage. The man made Anna want to hurl. Resisting the urge, she scooted closer to the pipe to make room for Julia on the bench.

Talking. Get her talking.

"The goulash smells wonderful. Did you make it?"

"Yes."

Sandy lashes lowered, fanned across pale, tired eyes. Aching sadness made a desolate moonscape of her face as she raised a heaping spoonful. Anna leaned sideways to take it and tasted the instant bite of pepper and paprika.

"My husband used to brag to his friends about my goulash," Julia said, stirring the soup with the spoon. "Now he cannot so much as taste it."

"Why?"

"He cannot swallow. One sip of water, one bite of bread, and he will choke."

A sob ripped from the younger woman's throat. Tears swam in her eyes.

"He breathes only on a machine," she said in a raw whisper. "But last month the court says the company that builds the pipeline was not at fault. They no longer have to pay for the machine that keeps him alive."

She raised the spoon again, let it clatter back down.

"I cannot pay. Our families cannot pay. So my husband will die."

"And you will avenge him," Anna said, her heart aching for the soon-to-be widow. "But do you really believe blowing up a section of pipeline will change anything?"

"It must!" Her head jerked up. A martyr's fervor replaced the desolation in her voice. "This company? It's owned by the Russians but managed by their Ukrainian lackeys. They are all corrupt! Every one! They look only to get rich from the blood of others. Someone must expose their evil. If I must die to do it, I will."

"Julia…"

"No! I won't be turned away from this! Nikolai knows what must be done. He guides me."

"He's using you! Just like he used those women to

bomb the Moscow subway. They died with the innocent victims ripped apart by their explosives. But their sacrifice didn't change anything, Julia. Terrorism only strengthens resolve. I know. My country hunted Osama bin Laden and his lieutenants relentlessly. They'll hunt Nikolai, too, and…"

"Ha! They won't find him." She hesitated, anger and fear and pity warring in her eyes. "They came earlier, you know."

Anna's heart stuttered. "What?"

"Two police officers. They came to my door. Nikolai and the others hid in the bedroom. I shook like a new leaf but I answered their questions and they left."

The hope Anna had been nursing shriveled and died an agonizing death. She wanted to scream, to unleash her fear and beat her head against the pipe. It took everything she had to keep the terror from her voice.

"Listen to me, Julia. You can't let Nikolai turn you into a murderer. Do you want other women—other wives and mothers and daughters—to suffer as you have? To see their loved ones maimed or blinded or torn apart by…"

"Stop! I won't listen to you." She sprang up and slammed the tray onto the bench. "Feed yourself, or starve."

The door banged behind her. Silence fell like a hammer. Anna waited, her heart thudding, but the younger woman didn't return. Nor did Varno.

Slowly, so slowly, she started breathing again. Her glance drifted from the door to the tray. Her mind was still numb with the shock of learning that the police had been there and left. Desperately she tried to regroup, to focus on what she could here, now. She should eat. She needed to maintain her strength. Or...

Her eyes narrowed. Her pulse kicked. Her thoughts winged from eating to escape. The earthenware bowl was thick. Too thick to shatter in a simple fall. Spearing a quick glance at the door, she stretched sideways and used a hip to nudge the tray off the bench. The soup splattered on concrete. As she'd anticipated, the bowl didn't.

Feverishly, Anna worked her wrists up the pipe and pushed to her feet. Once upright, she toed the pottery bowl closer and smashed down her heel. Once. Twice. Finally, the bowl broke into thick, jagged pieces.

"Yes!"

She dropped to her knees again and fumbled for one of the shards. Angling a wrist, she got an edge of it under the plastic binding her wrists and started sawing. The restraint was tougher than she would've believed possible. Her fingers gripped the broken pottery piece so tight they got numb. Blood oozed from cuts she carved into her wrist. Hoping to God she wasn't slicing into a vein, she hacked at the plastic.

When the first shard flaked to a dull edge, she fumbled for another. Then a third. Praying, panting, almost sobbing, she sweated and sawed. Just when she was ready to rest her head against the pipe and bawl, the plastic gave.

Her arms dropped to her sides. They hung there, lifeless, while Anna sucked in air. Then she was up and running for the door.

"Condor One, this is Condor Main."

Duke stepped away from the unmarked police vehicle to take the transmission, but his eyes never wavered from the concrete block of apartments directly ahead. Yallin and another officer approached the entrance to the unit at the south end of the building. Floodlights mounted at intervals around the stark, unadorned Soviet-era complex kept the darkness at bay enough for Duke to pick out the piping on Yallin's uniform. His eyes never wavering from the Ukrainians as they approached the apartment building, he put his cell phone to his ear.

"This is Condor One, go ahead, Condor Main."

"We have the satellite imagery you requested."

"Send it!"

"Will do, but be advised there's been a change in operational command and control. We're instructed to coordinate all further field activity with the U.S. embassy in Kiev."

Duke's knuckles went white where he gripped the phone. Fury steamed in his veins. He'd done what he could to squelch the Ukrainian request to terminate Operation Condor. He'd forwarded several sitreps since Anna's kidnapping, and a personal communiqué to Colonel Haggarty. Now this!

It narrowed everything Duke had been feeling for the past few days to a single point. Anna. She was what mattered. The *only* thing that mattered. Screw following orders. Screw the Air Force. Screw his military career.

He opened his mouth, intending to advise Condor Main that the U.S. Embassy in Kiev could go to hell. They beat him to the punch.

"Also be advised that we've been instructed to dual-channel."

Dual-channel. Military-speak for sending private signals. Haggarty had come through.

"Imagery downloading, Condor One. Please acknowledge receipt."

The phone vibrated against Duke's palm. He whipped the instrument away from his ear, saw the flash that indicated a downlink.

"Receipt acknowledged, Condor Main."

"Roger that. Condor Main standing by. Let us know if you require anything else."

The screen was too damned small, the night too dark. Keeping one eye on the men now mounting the entrance steps, Duke moved into the closest circle of floodlight.

Yallin's sources had confirmed that the man paralyzed in the same accident that killed Elena's husband lived in this apartment complex. Two officers had visited him earlier, spoken to him and his young wife. She was pale, they'd reported. Nervous. But no more so than to be expected when faced with an unexpected visit from the police.

Still, the nervousness had convinced Yallin to make another visit. Personally this time. Although he'd turned up no evidence that the couple owned a van, they could have begged or borrowed one from a friend to transport the husband to his doctor's appointments.

It was a long shot, but all they had at this point. Which made the image Duke was now scanning all the more vital. If these people had access to a van, it wasn't parked on the street. It could be on a side alley, though, or in a back lot or under a protective awning.

Or in a garage. The distinctive rectangle almost leaped from the screen. Single story. Three bays, all shut tight. Old tires and rusting car parts in a jumble behind it.

It sat by itself, a separate structure some yards behind the concrete block of apartments. Duke's eyes whipped from the screen to the darkness shrouding the area beyond the complex. The garage was there, it had to be there, but he couldn't see it. Wishing to hell he had his night vision goggles, he started for the patch of darkness. The driver of the unmarked police car voiced an obvious protest in Ukrainian and gestured for him to wait for Yallin. Duke ignored him.

Instinct kicked in. Every sense went to full alert. The night sounds, the side sweeps, the dim visuals, took him to a different plane. This was the place. He could feel it.

He pocketed the phone. Palmed the .45 he'd retrieved from the hotel suite. Thumbed the safety. Caught the thud of boot soles pounding concrete.

Two people.

One heavier than the other.

Both in a dead run.

Almost before he'd differentiated the sounds, Anna burst into the circle of light shed by the streetlamp closest to the garage. She was coming straight at Duke, blocking most of the dim figure behind her. All he could see was a glint of steel raised to shoulder level behind her.

"Anna! Down!"

For a frozen second, he was sure she hadn't heard him. Swearing, he angled the .45's front site a millimeter up and to the left, aiming for a shot just over her shoulder.

Then she dropped like a stone, and Duke pumped out three rounds.

Epilogue

The wedding took place on a crisp, wintery December afternoon at the home of Anna's parents. The comfortable stone-and-brick residence sat on a one-acre lot in the rolling hills of northern Virginia, close enough to DIA headquarters that her boss and a good number of coworkers could attend.

It was also close enough for a half dozen of Duke's friends who were currently condemned to Pentagon duty to drive in. The colorful medals and polished brass on their dress uniforms vied with the bright scarlet and silver Anna had chosen for her attendants.

Combat controller scarlet, she'd declared, since she was marrying into the brotherhood.

She and Duke had talked long and hard about that. They both knew the odds. The divorce rate among special ops personnel went through the roof. Duke would've walked away from the military. *Had* almost walked away in Odessa. Anna wouldn't let him. Not until they'd at least tried to integrate their combined careers into a life together—or until she discovered she couldn't handle the worry and uncertainty every time Duke deployed.

He wanted to believe it would work. So did the three men standing shoulder to shoulder with him at the head of the aisle formed by rows of white folding chairs. Incredibly, four of the six Sidewinders had managed to convene on the same continent at the same time.

Travis Cooper, former Navy SEAL. Dan Taylor, Army Ranger. Jack Halliday, Delta Force. Josh Patterson and Chris Winborne were deployed, but both had sent Anna their congratulations for putting a ring through the Dukester's nose. They'd also suggested various strategies for keeping it there, all of which he'd ordered Anna to ignore.

The memory of one of Josh's more descriptive strategies had Duke shifting his shoulders under his dress uniform. The slight movement caught the eye of his best man. Travis, of course, pounced on it.

"Worried?" he asked with a sardonic grin. "Need some pointers on married life?"

"I'll figure it out," Duke drawled.

Although Travis could probably give him some excellent advice. One glance at the blonde beauty in the second row of seats verified that. Madison radiated happiness. The baby nestled against her shoulder only underscored her joy.

"Beats the hell out of me how you managed to convince that woman to marry you," Duke muttered.

"Me, too."

The former SEAL shook his head in unfeigned amazement before shifting his gaze to the two women who sat directly in front of Madison. They had their heads together, their iron-gray curls almost touching.

"Looks like your granny's getting on well with Anna's grandmother."

Duke shuddered. "Yeah, I know."

Either of those two could give CIA interrogators lessons. Granny Jones was particularly devious at extracting information. Not content with generalities, she'd demanded specifics. When, where, how, how often.

Anna's babushka had worked them over with equal skill. Now, according to Duke's bride-to-be, both grandmothers had put her on notice to start producing offspring ASAP. His glance shot back to Travis's baby. Duke could handle a kid like that.

Maybe.

Any doubts he might have entertained on the matter evaporated when the door leading into the spacious living room opened. His heart hammering, Duke popped to attention. The three men beside followed suit.

"Not too late," Dan muttered out of a corner of his mouth. "You've still got time for an emergency extraction."

"I'll remind you of that when some sweet young thing shoots you down in flames."

"Never happen," the Ranger asserted confidently.

Duke sent Travis a quick glance. "Yeah, well, Coop and I didn't think it would happen to us, either. Just goes to show how wrongheaded..."

He broke off, unable to push another word past the

goose egg that suddenly got stuck in his throat. The three women serving as bridal attendants were making their way down the aisle. Their ruby dresses shimmered in the afternoon sunlight. Behind them came Anna and her father.

Duke couldn't remember taking a breath during that slow procession. All he saw, all he would ever recall, was the woman with her dark hair caught up in a cascade of curls and her brown eyes smiling at him.

The wedding soon became a blur to Anna, as well. All she took away from it was the hitch in Duke's voice when he gave his response to the traditional do-you-take-this-woman?

"Any time," he vowed. "Any place."

The honeymoon, on the other hand, she would always remember in vivid detail. She and her new husband escaped the reception and the good-natured ribbing of the Sidewinders a little after seven that evening. By eight-thirty, they were checked into a suite at the ultraposh, five-star Inn at Little Washington. The canopied bed and crackling fire set an instant mood. The sheer, celery-colored silk gown Anna slithered into before emerging from a bathroom felt liquid and totally sinful against her skin.

But it was the sight of her husband minus his uniform jacket, his tie dangling, and his shirt half unbuttoned that curled her bare toes into the pinewood flooring.

"Let me do that."

Brushing his hands aside, she worked the rest of the buttons. By the time she planed her palms across his soft, cottony T-shirt and eased the dress shirt off his shoulders, her breath had gone fast and shallow. It picked up even more when he drew her into him.

His mouth was hot on hers. Hot and hungry and so skilled that Anna barely noticed when he tugged off the gown she'd slipped into just moments ago.

She noticed when he yanked down the bedcovers, though. And when he tumbled her to the mattress. And when he shed his remaining clothes. Aching for him, she opened her arms. Spread her legs to accommodate his lean hips and muscled thighs. Welcomed him into her wet, eager body.

The burning logs spit and cackled. Anna flamed right along with them. Duke used his mouth and hands and hard, driving thrusts to push her up and up and up. She was at the edge, teetering right on the brink, when he stiffened.

"Dammit!"

"What?"

"I almost forgot."

"Forgot what?"

"Just hang on a sec."

"Hang on?" It was half wail, half moan. "Please tell me you're kidding."

"We have to do this right."

"I thought we were!"

He rolled off the tangled covers and rummaged through the carryall perched next to her weekender on the bench at the foot of the bed. Raging with need, Anna levered up on one elbow.

"What on earth are you looking for?"

"This."

Her jaw dropping, she gaped at a much-folded patchwork of color and embroidery. "Is that Auntie Oksana's wedding quilt?"

"It is," he confirmed with a grin that melted her bones. "Your babushka made me promise to spread it on our bed. She says it's guaranteed to produce results."

Laughing, Anna flopped back down. "Spread it, for God's sake, and get back to work."

* * * * *

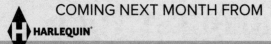

REQUEST YOUR
FREE BOOKS!

2 FREE NOVELS
FROM THE SUSPENSE COLLECTION
PLUS 2 FREE GIFTS!

YES! Please send me 2 FREE novels from the Suspense Collection and my 2 FREE gifts (gifts are worth about $10). After receiving them, if I don't wish to receive any more books, I can return the shipping statement marked "cancel." If I don't cancel, I will receive 4 brand-new novels every month and be billed just $6.24 per book in the U.S. or $6.74 per book in Canada. That's a savings of at least 22% off the cover price. It's quite a bargain! Shipping and handling is just 50¢ per book in the U.S. and 75¢ per book in Canada.* I understand that accepting the 2 free books and gifts places me under no obligation to buy anything. I can always return a shipment and cancel at any time. Even if I never buy another book, the two free books and gifts are mine to keep forever.

191/391 MDN F4XN

Name	(PLEASE PRINT)

Address	Apt. #

City	State/Prov.	Zip/Postal Code

Signature (if under 18, a parent or guardian must sign)

Mail to the **Harlequin® Reader Service:**
IN U.S.A.: P.O. Box 1867, Buffalo, NY 14240-1867
IN CANADA: P.O. Box 609, Fort Erie, Ontario L2A 5X3

Want to try two free books from another line?
Call 1-800-873-8635 or visit www.ReaderService.com.

* Terms and prices subject to change without notice. Prices do not include applicable taxes. Sales tax applicable in N.Y. Canadian residents will be charged applicable taxes. Offer not valid in Quebec. This offer is limited to one order per household. Not valid for current subscribers to the Suspense Collection or the Romance/Suspense Collection. All orders subject to credit approval. Credit or debit balances in a customer's account(s) may be offset by any other outstanding balance owed by or to the customer. Please allow 4 to 6 weeks for delivery. Offer available while quantities last.

Your Privacy—The Harlequin® Reader Service is committed to protecting your privacy. Our Privacy Policy is available online at www.ReaderService.com or upon request from the Harlequin Reader Service.

We make a portion of our mailing list available to reputable third parties that offer products we believe may interest you. If you prefer that we not exchange your name with third parties, or if you wish to clarify or modify your communication preferences, please visit us at www.ReaderService.com/consumerschoice or write to us at Harlequin Reader Service Preference Service, P.O. Box 9062, Buffalo, NY 14269. Include your complete name and address.

SUS13R

SPECIAL EXCERPT FROM

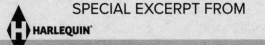

ROMANTIC suspense

When Liz Marcoli went missing from her home,
Detective Steve Kincaid had no idea that investigating
the disappearance would bring the sexy Roxy Marcoli
into his life, along with a danger from his past that
could destroy them both.

Read on for a sneak peek of

COLD CASE, HOT ACCOMPLICE

by Carla Cassidy, available December 2013 from
Harlequin® Romantic Suspense.

"I need to buy a gun," she said as Steve pulled out of the
Roadside Stop parking lot.

He nearly snapped her neck with his fast stop. He turned
in his seat and frowned at her. "You are not getting a gun.
You can be anything you want in the world, but you can't be
a gun owner. You'd wind up shooting a customer or yourself
by accident."

"Or you," she said, knowing he was right.

"There's always that, too," he agreed.

"It sucks being a target of somebody and not knowing who
they are or why they want to hurt me."

"It's odd that whoever it is hasn't succeeded yet. I mean,
instead of just locking you in the freezer, why not stab you to
death or beat you with something?"

"I know. I thought of that already."

He turned down the lane that was Amish land. "It makes me wonder again if maybe the attacker is a woman."

Roxy frowned. "I just can't imagine any woman who would want me hurt or dead." She turned and looked out the window, where young and old men in black trousers, long-sleeved white shirts and wide-brimmed straw hats worked in the fields.

Steve drove up to a modest white ranch house with a huge dairy barn behind it. "This is Tom Yoder's place. He's the bishop, and we need to check in with him before we speak to anyone else."

He pulled to a halt before the Yoder house and cut the engine. He unbuckled his seat belt and then turned to look at her. "And, Roxy, just for the record, you should never have to change a thing about yourself for any man. You're perfect just the way you are."

He didn't wait for a reply, but instead turned and got out of the car. It was at that moment Roxy realized she was more than a little bit in love with Detective Steve Kincaid.

**Don't miss
COLD CASE, HOT ACCOMPLICE
by Carla Cassidy, available December 2013 from
Harlequin® Romantic Suspense.**

HARLEQUIN®

ROMANTIC suspense

SEDUCED BY HIS TARGET
by Gail Barrett

For victims of violence, Nadira al Kahtani is
a savior in surgeon's clothing. But this time
it's Nadira who must be saved...from her own
corrupt family. Rasheed Davar—a rebellious
CIA agent seeking to avenge his wife's murder—
could risk his undercover mission to save her.
But will he? Things are heating up off
Columbia's coast, and Rasheed can't deny
the mounting tension. Nadira is beautiful.
She is brave. And she's just the kind of
high-stakes hostage who could lure him
directly into terrorist crosshairs.

Look for the conclusion in the
Buried Secrets miniseries
next month from Gail Barrett.

Wherever books and ebooks are sold.

Heart-racing romance, high-stakes suspense!

HRS27851

ROMANTIC suspense

COLTON CHRISTMAS RESCUE
by Beth Cornelison

Single mother and ranch veterinarian
Amanda Colton teams up with undercover agent
Slade Kent to uncover family secrets and find
the mastermind behind the crimes at the
Colton ranch in order to protect her daughter
from the people intent on kidnapping her.
Together, Amanda and Slade follow the loose
ends and new tips about the family's illicit past
as they hunt down the mastermind behind the
plot to destroy the Colton family. But to earn
Amanda's trust and love, he must risk his heart.

Look for the exciting conclusion in the
Coltons of Wyoming miniseries
next month from Beth Cornelison.
Only from Harlequin® Romantic Suspense!

Wherever books and ebooks are sold.

Heart-racing romance, high-stakes suspense!

www.Harlequin.com

HRS27850